CARDIAC GAP

A NOVEL

Bill Raskin

Cover design: Rachel Lawston at Lawston Design

Maps: Rachel Lawston at Lawston Design, with information from OpenStreetMap®, which is made available at www.openstreetmap.org under the Open Database License (ODbL).

Author Photograph: Fritz Partlow Design LLC

Formatting: Polgarus Studio

ISBN: 978-1-7329944-0-9 (Kindle)
ISBN: 978-1-7329944-1-6 (epub)
ISBN: 978-1-7329944-2-3 (print)
ISBN: 978-1-7329944-3-0 (large-print)

Part I

- 1 -

24 September 2035 – Former FedEx Shipping Center, Chicago O'Hare

Our democracy died in a shipping container. That's where Courtney Simons made his pitch in August 2029. Holding muted conversations in a rusting steel box as a thin rain tapped on metal. The open doors bringing in ambient light.

Yeah, no doubt, that day was the start of the great unravel.

I would know. I'm Mark Elliott, and I was there.

Now, I look around at the twelve of us, about to jump in and risk it all to reclaim our country. Back in the day, this fifty-by-fifty-foot room at the old FedEx facility would have been a sorting area for odd-sized shipments or high-value cargo. Which, funny enough, is basically what we are: high-value cargo.

Underneath fluorescent lights, our gear sits inspected and sorted. But everyone continues to double and triple check. Jessica Steel, the Alpha section leader, walks along the narrow industrial table set against one wall. The table holds our freefall parachutes. She's checking each rig to ensure the rip cord handles and locking pins are properly seated. The Bravo section leader is over in a far corner, inspecting his heavy weapons bundles that lie on a tarp.

Their faces are cool. Nothing in their demeanor betrays that when we board the C-17 cargo aircraft and infiltrate for the strike, the future of a nation rests on their shoulders. If our mission fails, the larger effort, to retake Washington, DC, will be futile.

As for me, the mission commander, I've mentally reviewed each of the contingencies ad nauseam. Here in our holding area, the most important thing I can do is project calm and confidence. I sit on the floor, legs stretched out, back propped against an assault pack. I'm looking down at the target area map, folded open like a book. But that's not where my head is.

For the past two weeks, ever since signing on to lead this mission, I keep coming back to the same thoughts. *Should* I have seen things sooner, before it all came to the surface in 2034? *Could* I have done anything more to alter the course of events? Or was it all inevitable, from that day in the shipping container to here? Each time, I run a different set of hypotheticals, but it always comes back to the same thing. Regardless of how we got here, all I can do now is double down on the task at hand. This strike must succeed.

- 2 -

Six and a half years earlier . . .
13 December 2028 – West African Airspace

"Sir." The Air Force crew chief grabs me by the shoulder to get my attention over the engine noise. "We've finally got Major General Saiz on the satellite net. The channel's not on the intercom back here. You need to go up to the console." He points to a spot about twenty feet up the fuselage of the cargo plane's open hold.

I move that way, trying not to trip over gear and people, as the MC-130 propeller transport plane bounces through turbulence. Our ad hoc team of nine Special Forces operators have assault kit and personal weapons consolidated aft, by the rear loading ramp of this special operations variant of the Air Force's workhorse cargo aircraft. That's where we'll position to rapidly exit upon landing. It's been a blurred rush since we received our warning order and pickup in Krakow, Poland. We're en route to rescue thirty-seven Americans who are fleeing for their lives from the US Embassy in Dakar, Senegal.

I get to the satcom console, unplug my headset from the body comms on my assault vest and plug the jack into the satellite voice feed. "Sir, it's Mark, you read me?"

"Loud and clear, Mark," Major General Saiz replies. "Glad we could finally patch through. The jamming has been terrible." Saiz leads Special Forces Command back at Camp Diamond, WV. We've been trying to reach him for the past five hours, ever since we crossed the Med.

"Sir, any idea who's doing the jamming?" I ask.

"Negative. Either the Russians or Chinese most likely. Someone who knows we're in trouble down in Senegal and wants to make it worse on us. Mark, I was offsite from headquarters when this spun up. Bring me up to speed."

"Roger that, Sir. Ulysses, Puppy and I, plus leadership from three A Teams, were in Krakow for initial coordination with the Polish Special Commandos. We're preparing to send our entire Special Forces Battalion there in early '29 as a strategic presence." Little green men, aka unmarked Russian units, have been making trouble inside Poland for the better part of the past year. The nine of us were meeting with Polish counterparts to sort out deployment after the new year for our Battalion task force of several hundred special operators.

I recently assumed command of 3rd Battalion, 8th Special Forces Group, stationed back at Camp Diamond. Two of my best friends also serve in the 3/8 command group and are here on the plane. Ulysses Harris serves as my Command Sergeant Major. Hugh "Puppy" Jackson is in the battalion ops section. We've grown up through Special Forces together, going back to the Qualification course.

Saiz replies, "I copy. You've just got nine operators including yourself. How are you set for equipment and comms?"

"Sir, we've got our personal weapons and assault kit. We've each got body comms plus one portable satcom radio for the team. Africa Command was able to chop two MC-130 aircraft for the mission.

The nine of us are on the primary bird. The trail bird is empty but will land with us for backup. Question, Sir. This is the first outside communications we've had since the jamming kicked in. Any word on Africa Command sending close air support or a quick reaction force, in case we get in trouble on the ground?"

"Negative to both, Mark. No extra support. You've got to love a shoestring operation."

"Roger that, Sir."

Unfortunately, shoestring operations are the norm these days. Ten years ago, this would have been a pushover. There were any number of American forces in a region to take on a mission like this. In Africa, for example, we had hundreds of special operators and a dozen military assistance units embedded with partner nations. Not anymore. The Second Great Depression, in '23, dealt a seismic and lasting blow to the US economy. With forty-million US workers laid off at last count, we lost any stomach to pay the bills for global presence. The '23 Austerity Act cut Department of Defense forces in half, and the '25 Prudence Act cut another third off that. Now we move band-aids from one crisis to another. So, instead of going in with fighter support and a full-up combat formation, it's nine random special operators in two unarmed transports.

"What's the situation in Senegal?" Saiz asks. "The news hasn't hit the media yet."

That's good. The less outside attention, the more likely our evacuees have made an un-noticed move to the pickup airfield. I give Saiz the rundown. "We don't know much detail. Boko Haram's making a play to take over the entire country. The national government's gendarmerie decided their backs were to the wall. Last week, they raided and captured Maktar Diallo. He was living openly, but Diallo has long been suspected as the Boko Haram franchise leader for Senegal. And he's got a real following. Rioting and violence broke out across the entire capital city, Dakar."

"How did our Embassy get in the cross hairs?"

"It wasn't at first," I reply, "but apparently, yesterday, the US Ambassador freelanced. He declared on social media that Diallo should receive the harshest possible sentence. Reports came in quickly that Boko Haram had mobilized more than two hundred armed militants to storm our Embassy and take hostages for trade. The Americans quietly departed the Embassy. Last heard, they were moving in a ground convoy to the airfield at Thies. That's an outlying town about forty miles from the Embassy. We land there in an hour to make the extraction."

"Copy that. Anything else, Mark?"

"No Sir. We'll get it done."

"I know you will. Let my aide know when you are on return to Camp Diamond. I want to be at the airfield to welcome home your team and thank them."

"Will do."

I plug my headset jack back into the body comms and give the crew chief a thumbs-up that our conversation is complete. Taking stock, I need this brief lull to address a personnel matter.

Ulysses has been sneaking peeks at that sonogram again, when he thinks Puppy and I aren't looking. Now he reaches across his body armor and tucks it into the left-sleeve pocket of his combat shirt. Can't blame the guy. Talk about a raw deal. Kathy didn't even tell him about the appointment. Then she spills in one conversation that he's going to be the father of twins. And, oh by the way, here are the divorce papers. That would screw with anyone's head.

But we're about to get busy. I motion for him to join me up by the console, where we can have a little privacy. He bends down, so we can talk over the noise. "Hey brother, I know you're hurting," I say. "But we really need you, need your head in the game. You good?"

I look over at the sleeve pocket.

He exhales hard. You can hear the pain. He nods a couple times, then dials those eyes and he's snapped in. "I'm good. Let's get to work."

I slap him on the back and we rejoin the others.

"Puppy, you get any word?" I ask, back in our scrum by the ramp. While I was speaking with Saiz over the satellite net, Puppy attempted comms with the Embassy security team. We need that info to put a ground plan together. The crew chief huddles with us in the cargo area, so he can ensure the aircraft positions for immediate takeoff after we land.

Puppy replies, "Roger, was able to reach the Gunny running their Marine detachment. He confirms a total US headcount of thirty-seven. That includes seven Marines, each armed with long guns and full kit. They've also got two RSOs" – aka State Department Regional Security Officers – "with long guns and kit. No one else is armed. The good news is they were on permanent drawdown. Their family members have already departed."

"Is the airfield at Thies still the plan?" I ask.

"Roger, Boss. It's a good call on the Gunny and RSO's part. We're light as it is, but it would be a hundred times riskier pulling them out of the capital airport at Dakar." Somewhere in the frantic minutes before takeoff, Puppy managed to print out satellite photos of the Thies airfield. The guy thinks of everything. He kneels, spreads them across some open space on the floor, and traces a finger through the situation as we know it.

"This is the main air strip. Just over six thousand feet long, oriented north-south. Gunny says they were followed out of Dakar, but he doesn't have the combat power to do anything about that. The Embassy convoy won't approach Thies airfield until right before our touchdown time, to avoid telegraphing our extraction plan."

Everyone nods. Good, the Gunny is thinking. I look around at our team. The three A Team commanders are all combat experienced Captains. I haven't worked with them, but they've got solid reps. The other three are Team Sergeants, handpicked by Ulysses and Puppy for our Poland coordination. Ken Bowerman is the youngest of the three. He won the Silver Star as an infantryman in Afghanistan about ten years ago. He went SF, Special Forces, shortly after that.

Puppy continues the situation brief. "The aircraft taxi apron is here, on the southern end of the airfield. Gunny will stage them at these abandoned Senegalese Army barracks just off the apron. He's been there before. Says there's a low cement wall around the three barracks buildings. They'll pull in there to take cover right before we land."

Now the crew chief steps in. "Master Sergeant Jackson and I looked it over," he says referring to Puppy. "I recommend we land at the southern end of the field, almost right on top of that apron. We'll wheel around with the rear ramp open, as close as we can get to those barracks. Your team and the Marines jam everyone on as fast as possible. Soon as you give a positive call that we're all accounted for, we hit the throttle and get out of there."

I look at Ulysses and Puppy, who each give a thumbs-up. It makes sense. Without any other security or eyes on, we may as well get in and out of there as fast as possible. "OK, chief, that's the plan. Anything else you need from us?"

"Negative," he replies. "The trail bird is empty but will still go in with us as a spare."

We review our key duties upon landing. Puppy will make personal contact with the Marine Gunny. Adrienne Clement is the senior Captain in our group. She and Ken Bowerman came up with a traffic control plan for the Embassy civilians. Ulysses and I will run overall command. Nothing to do now but touch down and execute.

Not long after that, the crew chief gives the first time hack, "Ten minutes!"

We line up two abreast, facing the rear ramp, ready to jump off and get to work as soon as the plane pulls onto that apron. Ulysses and I are the first two, ready to lead out. Puppy, Bowerman, and the rest of the team line up behind us. We hold onto webbing and stanchions, struggling to stay afoot as the pilots start their high G, ultra-steep combat landing profile.

The slam bounce of first touchdown almost sends us into the ceiling. I re-cinch my helmet strap without thinking. The plane settles and lurches violently as the pilots pump brakes to bleed off ground speed. Puppy gives the Gunny a commo check from our body comms, on our common frequency. Gunny replies. Good, the ground comms net is active.

The rear ramp opens to a late afternoon sun as we continue our high-speed taxi to the apron. It's a comfortable 70 degrees, but the dust is choking. We're still bracing to stay upright. Looking back off the ramp, you can tell when we transition onto the apron by the change from tarmac to cement. The planes wheel hard in their U turn and, sure enough, there are the Marines and RSOs pulling security behind the low cement wall. They've got the Embassy civilians crouched down low inside the barracks, just visible through an open doorway.

I feel a moment of relief. Then—

The explosion blows me off the ramp to a face plant on the apron. My bell is rung hard. Stars clear as Puppy lifts me roughly by the grab handle on my assault vest. Looking back, I see Bowerman and the crew chief sorting through a tangled pile of casualties in our bird. I'm dizzy for several more seconds.

"Mortar round hit center fuselage!" Ulysses barks to the gaggle that are still upright. "Our bird is down. Get everyone out and behind the wall for cover!" Flames already circle the belly of the MC-130.

We move behind the wall. The Gunny runs over to huddle with Puppy and me. He scowls. "We didn't have enough manpower to run a perimeter patrol. They popped three mortar rounds from the east side of the airfield. Probably twelve hundred meters out. They really know what they're doing to range your bird that quick."

Just then machine guns open up, from the same eastern side of the field as the mortars. Probably seven hundred meters away. We take cover. Tracers cut the air toward us and rounds impact loudly against the other side of the wall, just inches away.

"Gunny, you have any crew served weapons that can range them?" I ask over the noise.

"Negative," he replies. "We're small arms just like you."

Now the clincher hits. I'm about to give the order to load everyone on our spare bird. Then three dump trucks race in column from scrub brush bordering the west side of the airfield. They're just about five hundred feet up the airstrip from us. The trucks park in column, nose to tail, spread evenly across the width of the runway. The drivers scamper east to join their machine gun teams.

Our takeoff is blocked. A loaded MC-130 – i.e. our spare bird – needs way more than five hundred feet to get airborne. This is bad.

Bowerman skids in behind the wall, out of breath at first. Then he gives the casualty report. "We've got two dead: the copilot and Adrienne. Pilot and the rest of our folks from the primary bird are wounded bad. Boss, it's just you, me, Ulysses and Puppy still in fighting shape, plus the Embassy team."

Counting the Embassy shooters, that's a total of thirteen long guns, and no crew served weapons.

The enemy machine gun teams are disciplined, hitting us in alternating bursts. This keeps us pinned inside the barracks walls.

Surely, an assault element is moving on us from somewhere. Where? "There's their assault team." Puppy points to a spot over halfway between us and their machine guns. "Over a hundred of them on foot. Still out of range for our assault rifles. They're moving into the city. Gonna use buildings for cover, to close on us." We won't see them next until they occupy buildings just across the street. And then it's one hundred against thirteen in close combat. This is getting worse.

I put out the plan, "OK, Gunny give me three guys. Your three plus me and my three are going to launch now and ambush that column before it gets here. It's the best play we have. Hit hard and scatter them. Next, we'll make a flanking attack on the machine guns, knock them out and then move those trucks. So we can fly the hell out of here." At least the mortar rounds have stopped. They must have shot their wad on mortars, or else by now the other bird would be a smoldering wreck, too.

Puppy's not liking it. "Boss, that assault formation's moving well. Good tactical flow. I'm not sure seven of us on foot can scatter them too bad?"

"We don't have a choice!" I snarl. He's right, but we're down to all bad options. "Let's get going." Machine gun rounds continue to smack into the other side of the wall we're behind. The impacts kick up a small dust cloud, caking my mouth.

Ulysses shouts, "Wait!" He's looking in the opposite direction from the guns, due south several blocks into the city. "Hold them tight here, Mark. I can clear the center dump truck!"

What is he talking about? He can't run from here across the tarmac. Take twenty steps into the open and those machine guns will drop him. And running around the entire airfield under the cover of scrub brush will take too long. Ulysses knows this.

Before I can speak, he sprints off south, alone, into the city.

Shit.

I call out to the others. "All right, we're committed here now! Gunny and Puppy, lock down this perimeter. That assault will hit us in a few minutes, max." Here we go. Gunny and Puppy work together. They position most of our shooters on the side of the compound facing the city. It's just in time to engage as the Boko Haram assaulters take up positions across the street.

They're not rushing it either. The enemy commander knows his business. He's using a megaphone from a café on the corner, calling out commands in French. He methodically directs his men to positions in the buildings facing us, dispersing evenly on either side of the café. They start shooting and small arms fire snaps just overhead.

That's when I hear the motorcycle.

Looking back across the airfield, you can hear it racing along the west side, inside the scrub brush. It's Ulysses, riding like a madman. A line of dust kicks up to mark his progress. He pops out of the brush right by the dump trucks, from the same spot where they'd emerged originally. He drops the bike just short of the center truck, and climbs into its cab before the enemy realize what's going on.

Their machine guns immediately traverse and pump everything they have into that truck. The windshield spider webs with holes. Torn metal flies from the grill. Ulysses has already dropped below the dash, and I'm praying the engine block covers him. It must, because the engine fires up. You can just see his head peeking as he wheels that center truck around and back into the scrub brush, on the same western side from where he'd come by motorcycle.

The machine guns are silent now. They must have gone dry trying to stop Ulysses. But we've got other problems. The commander in the café has his assault line dialed. His megaphone commands echo along the street. He's got a hundred-plus small arms firing onto our courtyard. Rounds ricochet and kick up dirt. Gunny and Puppy keep putting shots into that café where their commander is holed up, but they can't get a good angle to take out the bastard. This is not his first rodeo.

I leave one Marine facing the airfield and put everyone else facing the enemy assault line across the street. "Get grenades ready if you have them!" I yell. "Slow your fire. Keep a full mag ready for when they bum rush." We're bracing, waiting for it.

And then, from around the corner, comes the Mad Max shot-to-hell dump truck, with Ulysses at the wheel and a demonic look on his face. The engine whines as he plows into the café at full speed. Glass and concrete fly. The impact takes out the enemy commander and at least ten of their assaulters.

Ulysses emerges from the smoking hole. He runs along one wing of the enemy's line of buildings. He's in their dead space, underneath windows, tossing grenades in every second or third opening. With their commander gone, and now several grenades popped off, they're freaked. Puppy and I grab two Marines and we assault onto their other wing to do the same. With the mayhem Ulysses inflicted, it's just enough. Their courage breaks and they fall back a couple blocks.

"All right, now's our chance!" I order over the comms net. "Gunny and Puppy, get the civilians out of the barracks. Organize teams to grab our casualties and get everyone on the spare bird!"

It's a total goat rope. But Ulysses' wild stunt bought a narrow margin for escape. He grabs four Marines, and the six of us cover the retreat onto our remaining MC-130. The Boko Haram gunslingers filter back into the nearest line of buildings. But by now we're all at the spare bird. The enemy can't range us well, with the low courtyard and a burning aircraft between them and us.

Puppy shouts that we've got a solid headcount.

Ulysses and I are the last two on the ramp. We give the crew chief all clear for takeoff. Everyone grabs hold as the pilots jam the throttle. The plane slices cleanly between the two remaining dump trucks still on the runway. The ramp is just closing as we lift off. I peer out until it seals, watching a couple Boko Haram firing harmlessly at us in frustration.

I turn around and survey the cargo hold. We're jammed so tight, especially with casualties laid out, there's little floor space. Ulysses moves all the way forward to the cockpit end of the cargo bay, to find a small patch. He's spent and slumps down against the bulkhead. All told, the man sprinted close to a mile under full kit.

Puppy and the crew chief organize treatment for the wounded. They also lay our two KIA back here near the ramp and cover them with camouflage ponchos. One of them is Adrienne Clement, one of our Captains from Camp Diamond. Like me, Puppy didn't know her before a few days ago. But you'd never know that from the pain on his face right now.

I thread my way to Ulysses, put my hand on his shoulder. He looks up as I tell him, "A long time ago I promised never to call you this again. But my friend, you really are, The Great Ulysses."

- 3 -

7 August 2029 – Camp Diamond, WV

Standing in formation for the last time, flanked by the Group's headcount of two thousand plus, it's tough to look at the viewing stands. The official guests flash looks of regret. But the family members, for whom today cuts to the bone, they've armored up with stoic faces and a proud bearing. A couple of the spouses have tears streaming, nothing more. Even the kids pick up the vibe. On-post schools and daycare let out for this. But up in the stands now, none of the little ones are wiggling or acting up. They know something serious is afoot.

Saiz will start his address in just a few minutes. Standing alone, in the command position for our battalion, I face about and troop the line one last time, walking just in front of the first rank. The late morning sun warms my neck, though clouds are rolling in. As expected, the formation looks perfect. Group headquarters had initially prescribed dress uniforms for today. But the A Teams all raised hell. They said we'd lived as field soldiers and that's how we'd go out. And they're right. The look of camouflage uniforms and our green berets are exactly how we want to leave the arena.

Welcome to the deactivation ceremony for 8th Special Forces

Group. You can't say it's a surprise. In the mid 2010s, the Army had 485,000 active duty soldiers and could sustain five active Special Forces Groups. Successive downsizing pared us to only two SF Groups by the 2020s. But now more cuts are here. With the Army about to drop below 185,000, it was clear there wasn't the juice to keep even two Special Forces Groups. Given that 8th Group is at the "flagpole," located with SF Command at Camp Diamond, everyone kept fingers crossed we'd be the lottery winner. But it was not to be.

So, 7th Group in Florida hangs on as the only remaining formation. The writing was on the wall as soon as they transferred the Poland mission over to 7th Group. Our coordination trip to Krakow, turned rescue mission in Senegal, ended up being our battalion's only deployment during my brief tenure in command.

And now for us 8th Groupers, it's out on the street. No partial pension, no severance. The kinder, gentler drawdowns passed a long time ago. With every third American adult desperate to find work, the country may thank us for our service, but that's not going to include any kind of gratuity.

The public address speakers fire up, and it's show time. I face back to the stands and align off Colonel Jensen, the Group Commander, who's in front of the battalions. I zone out.

About three minutes into Saiz' address from the lectern, I tune back in: "And so, today we give thanks for six decades of honorable service by the men and women of the 8th Special Forces Group. From the darkest hours in Tet, to the never-ending deployments of the 21st century, you undertook any mission. Whether in the desert heat of the Middle East, the hundred days of wind in Afghanistan, or the bone-chilling spring rains outside Brussels, you took care of your mates, and you never lost resolve."

You have to hand it to the old man. He's ramrod straight up at that lectern, keeping a poker face. It's got to be a knife in his side. Major General Diego Saiz is the most storied operator ever to serve in 8th Group. He raised most of us in the formation here today. Progressing through the ranks, he commanded a company, a battalion, and later the Group; all right here in the buildings around this parade field. He easily could have pawned the deactivation ceremony to a more senior Army general. We knew he'd never do that.

Saiz' speech ends. He turns the formation over to Colonel Jensen. We're released to Battalions, and I face my command for the last time, make my last statement on active duty. "Third Battalion, dismissed!"

And that's it.

Now I'm officially Mark Elliott: forty-one-year-old laid-off Army man.

I look around the parade grounds, knowing that years from now this scene will stick. The sky has clouded over, and a light drizzle falls.

Our sister battalions have dismissed also. Orderly formations give way to organic clusters of friends and loved ones. Several kids sprint out of the stands as soon as allowed. They make a beeline for dad, in most cases. In some cases it's a mom. Spouses are coming out of the stands and joining, too.

Linny is around here somewhere. What would I do without her?

We'll be OK. We can live cheap. Now my chest is constricted and I'm desperate to see her. Looking around, where is she?

"Hey there." She comes up from the blind spot over my right shoulder and gives a hug. I pull her close, wrap arms around her shoulders, smell her blond hair.

"Hey," I smile. "We need to invite Ulysses to dinner tonight. That OK?"

"Of course. Did Kathy even come out here?"

"Nope. They're fighting it out in court over visitation. She moved to Summersville. He's only even seen the twins a couple of times." I'm looking around for Ulysses right now.

There he is, about fifty yards away, talking to a couple of the more junior operators and their families.

I look back to Linny. "I'm going to link up with Ulysses and make the rounds, talk to our younger folks. The post is holding a job fair tomorrow. Most of the team guys and gals are saying they'll blow it off, knowing how junk the odds are. But it won't be any better doing cold calls wherever they move to. We're twisting arms to get max numbers of them to attend." Everyone's got a reason to blow off the job fair. The under-thirty crowd is just too pissed off and wants to blot out memory of this whole episode. The thirty somethings, or God forbid the forty somethings like me and our more senior leaders? Well, they figure what's the point?

Linny tilts her head up to give a peck on the cheek. "OK," she says, "I'll hit the store on the way home. Tell Ulysses dinner at seven. Invite Puppy too." She's the best. She knows better than I do that tomorrow will suck. If I'd been smart, we would have followed her career, and I'd have figured something to do. But I had to stay in and prove something to myself about being a commando. Well, it was more than that. But Linny, her only flaw was agreeing to give up on a topflight law degree and well-placed clerkship. She's found some decent work moving through Army towns, but nothing that will truly support us. Now here we are, entering middle age and starting over with almost nothing. And she'll never complain, not once.

I'm closing the distance to Ulysses. This takes a bit of time, pausing here or there where there's a chance to plug for the job fair, or console someone who's shell shocked.

"Boss!" It's Puppy. I had lost him in the crowd. He's striding over from thirty feet away.

20

"Hey," I say as we link up, "c'mon. Work with Ulysses and me to pump folks about the job fair. Then grab a six pack and head to our place. Linny's going to feed us our last meal in the ranks of the employed."

Hugh "Puppy" Jackson isn't the tallest or largest man you'd meet in a room full of operators. But afterward, that's how your mind would sort him. Despite the nickname, Puppy has presence. Some would call it edge, many others call it menace. He's the kind of guy you meet and decide you're really, really glad he's on our side.

"Hey, Mark, you need to come with me."

"What's up?" I ask, looking out again to survey the crowd. Most folks are migrating off the parade field toward their cars in the adjacent parking lot. No one wants to stick around, which is understandable. I'd like to say goodbye to at least a few more of the newer folks before they drive away. Now here's Puppy sounding like we've got a unit to run or something.

"There's someone you need to meet," he says.

"OK, great. But let's take ten minutes here first."

He's probably just offering some networking intro. There are a couple of executive-level headhunters in the viewing stands. But the reality is, odds with the headhunters will be even worse than at the job fair tomorrow. They'll want resumes from Colonel Jensen, and some of the other staff officers who've completed advanced degrees and grooming tours in the Pentagon. But me, I've spent my entire career down here on the line. Not one headhunter will care about numbers of line commands or combat tours. The flesh peddlers can wait just a little longer.

"No, Mark, I'm serious. You need to meet this person now." Puppy holds his look and adds, "I was directed to go get you."

I stop and cock my head, stare at him a second. "OK, Puppy, let's go meet your mystery contact."

The big guy leads out, with me at his side. He angles north and starts making his way between our base area buildings. They're beyond decrepit at this point: 1960s era, three-story, L-shaped, beige cinderblock monstrosities. We were the last Special Forces Group in line to get modernized space, due for the early 2020s. But that was when the bottom dropped out of the economy. The old billets had to suffice.

The misting clouds transition to a light rain. A smatter of raindrops splash across the grounds. We're about halfway through the courtyard between two buildings, and Puppy's not breaking stride. It's clear where we're headed.

"Hey man," I offer, "if we'll be standing outside, let's duck through the Battalion area and grab our Gore-Tex."

"Don't worry about it," he says, staring straight ahead and not slowing down.

His vocal cords are tight. Seeing Puppy nervous is not something I'm used to. It's definitely got my interest. That plus this double secret probation trip to the pad, it all adds up to suspicion.

"The Pad" is the nickname for our excess and contingency gear storage area. Located on the far side of our team and headquarter buildings, it's literally a square concrete pad, four hundred feet on a side. The pad holds a checkerboard pattern of twenty- and forty-foot shipping containers in a kaleidoscope of colors, along with the smaller ISU-90 containers in olive drab and tan. Stacked double high in some cases, this was supposed to be a temporary solution in the late 1990s, until our new construction came online.

But as the construction timeline slipped, this haphazard village of boxes took root. To increase storage capacity, every few years logisticians would push the existing containers closer together toward the center and add more around the periphery. They left just enough space to let forklifts maneuver between the rows. The rabbit warren of corridors and dead ends gives fits to new arrivals. It's a favorite way to torture a new team member who's getting on your nerves. Give them a description for a non-existent container in the center of the pad, then place bets on how long it takes before the badass operator comes back in defeat. Resellers have already put bids on the containers. They'll haul away the wares come dawn tomorrow.

But for now, the pad is apparently serving its highest purpose one last time. For generations of operators, the pad is where you'd meet offline to get business done. Got a guy on your team not working out? Don't want to fire him and ruin his record, but still need to make the change? Two Sergeants Major will meet at the pad and broker a move. Find an equipment accountability error that leaves you short for an upcoming inspection? Odds are, you'd find yourself at the pad, tucked out of the way and performing the necessary horse trading. All of which begs the question, why now?

"Dude," I say, "what's going on? There's no 8th Group business to conduct anymore." I ask this as Puppy's weaving us through quick left/right turns toward the center of the container field.

"Almost there," is his only reply.

We turn the last corner into a corridor. Forty-footers line each side of the aisle. The corridor dead ends at a red twenty-footer that is mottled with rust and has seen better days. Its loading doors are open. By the gray, overcast daylight, you can tell someone is inside. It's hard to make out who just yet. I walk closer.

And just about choke.

The man standing inside is Courtney Simons, one of the dozen most recognizable human beings on the planet. He's CEO of Enterprise Performance. Enterprise Performance, as in the largest conglomerate cloud service and computing hardware firm in existence. Simons is the third wealthiest person in the world.

And he's skulking inside a dilapidated container on the pad.

What the hell is going on here?

- 4 -

Courtney Bryce Simons, a Silicon Valley princeling. His mom directed the West Coast annex for Bell Labs during their last big heyday of innovation. Later, she and a cohort founded the first big dial-up internet outfit. Simons' dad established the quantum computing department at Stanford, and ran it for the next twenty years.

Courtney Simons didn't rest on family laurels, though. After the customary three semesters at MIT, Simons left and – famously – refused to take any of mom or pop's money for his next move. He founded Enterprise Performance, now often just known as "EP," at age twenty. He had the connections, he had the gumption, and he had his parents' brilliance. He also proved to have a twist of killer business instinct thrown in. The world has followed Courtney Simons' celebrity for well over two decades. And now, I'm ducking into a hideout in the pad to talk to him?

"Sir, I'm glad to see Colonel Jensen set you up in our finest accommodations," I say, while offering a handshake.

"It's Court. And Colonel Jensen doesn't know I'm here. I could care less where we meet. I'm here to talk business, and for now it needs to stay close hold. This location suits fine."

The direct manner fits his reputation. The appearance does not.

Someone has coached him how to walk in here looking like a contractor or off-duty operator. Simons stands about six feet tall with a fit build. He's wearing dark-brown field pants with a heavy-duty leather gun belt, a khaki-colored button shirt, and synthetic hiking boots.

Puppy's standing off to our side. He's part in shadow, but I can tell he's giving that 'you wouldn't have believed me until you saw for yourself' look.

Let's dive into this thing, whatever it is.

"Uh, Court, I don't think I'm in your business. In fact, as of about twenty minutes ago, I'm unemployed."

"Our businesses might be converging. What do you know about the United Arab Emirates?" he asks.

This gets my attention. "I probably know the same as you, just what's in the press. Russians moved in there two weeks ago. A successful *coup de main* it looks like, a surprise takeover. None of the intel feeds predicted it."

"That's correct. That matches the briefings I've received."

I'm curious. "So why, exactly, is a Silicon Valley executive taking briefings on Russian plans and intentions in the Middle East?"

"Mark, it's simple," he says. "Our national military capacity is dwindling. We can't compete with the Russians, Chinese and others the way we used to. But our national *interests* aren't going away."

"I agree with that. So why don't you and a gang of executives lobby Congress for more funding? Heck, we could reactivate 8th Group for relative peanuts."

He gives his first smile and laughs. "There's no stomach for that. You know that. And besides, what if we could? Get 8th Group reactivated that is. What would it change?"

I nod at this. Unfortunately, he has something of a point there.

He continues. "The political infighting, the gridlock. Look, if they immediately reversed *all* of the recent cuts, it wouldn't make a difference. Every overseas American deployment for the past decade has been paralyzed by political infighting. No one is playing to win any longer when they deploy our armed forces. It's politicians playing pawns for the best interests of their own election cycle.

"Take Belgium, for example. That was classic election year maneuvering, on both sides. The incumbent President sent over just enough US presence to get credit for responding, and to keep the Germans and French from denouncing our failure to act. But the President hedged. He knew if he sent too much, he'd get beat up for bleeding precious Treasury funds during our financial crisis. The other party used that opening for a political counter attack. They said we were failing to act tough enough on terror. Then, when the opposition took the White House in an upset, what happened? Nothing. The new administration hedged in the exact same way. Everyone was just looking for the right moment to declare success and leave. Anything to avoid another three-decade albatross like Afghanistan."

Everything he says makes sense. Heck, any second-tour special operator could give you the same rundown. As a nation, we're running in pure terror from the jobs crisis. But there's nowhere to run *to*. No one's got answers. So each side sharpens their arguments against the other, and tries to survive another election cycle. Meanwhile, we push out half-baked approaches to international strategy. His words sound too rehearsed, though. He's got his pitch down, whatever it is.

"OK, Court. All valid points. So, we don't reactivate 8th Group or any of the other units that were drawdown casualties. What then?"

"Enterprise Performance."

"Enterprise Performance *what*?"

"Enterprise Performance becomes the answer. I set up a spinoff company that hires on the right mix of recently downsized military professionals. But not *me*. *We*. You, and Master Sergeant Jackson here. And Command Sergeant Major Harris, Ulysses. I want the three of you to come on as my lead advisors. Together we'll build a force that can move, quickly, to dislodge the Emirates incursion. You're aware of the demands the Russians just put out? Do you realize the shockwaves that will send through the global economy?"

"Sir, Court, I'm fully aware, on both counts." I actually haven't dug into the details of the Russians' demand. We had non-stop admin work to meet our deactivation schedule. But it's something about the Russians, as new occupiers of the Emirates, wanting transit fees for all the oil that passes through the Persian Gulf.

Is Simons intimating that we'll simply hire on a bunch of random operators and change that?

I say, "Look, you're the best in the world at what you do. And I'm pretty good at what I do, or used to do. What you're implying here begs just a ton of hard questions. Any number of which could be show stoppers."

"Shoot."

"OK, first of all, why the three of us? Ulysses, Puppy and me?"

"You meet key criteria that I look for on any acquisition. You're good, you're available now, and frankly, you're cheap. Cheap doesn't drive the train, but it helps. How many nibbles do you think you and your folks will get at that job fair tomorrow? I'm talking about hiring *thousands* of ex-military. Right away. Even with offering higher salaries than your military pay, and I will, the cost-benefit to me of bringing over so many professionals at the top of their game can't be beat."

"That answers why you're seeking military. But why the three of us? Why not Colonel Jensen and his command team? Or leaders higher up the chain for that matter?"

He shakes his head no. "I'm not building to that scale. We'll need the people with most recent ground tactical experience to lead the combat operations. I know organizational dynamics. Who made the coordination trips to Poland? No one above Battalion level. I'm not trying to re-create the military. I'm trying to solve the problem in the Emirates. And your command team has spent more time studying Russia's M.O. this past year than anyone else. You only got pulled off the Poland mission what, three months ago? When they transitioned the mission to 7th Group?"

"Wow, you really do your homework."

"We're not the largest company in our field for nothing. And I bet you've been over to meet the 7th Group deployers since then? Passing on what you knew, and just plain wanting to follow what was happening?"

"Guilty," I say.

"What else? What other questions?" he asks.

"So far, you're just talking about ground pounders. But clearly, you've thought this through. Where are all the other enablers going to come from? We're talking 5th generation fighters, air transport, fire support. The works."

"Correct on all. I've made outreach to some others already. But ultimately this succeeds or fails based on actions on the ground. The ground team will be my lead advisors."

I make a mental note about the tone of his "correct on all" reply. *He's* grading *my* answers, even though we're talking about something in which he has zero first-hand experience. Whatever other conversations he's had, this dude isn't here to lobby. He's in charge. He's received backing from somewhere.

"What else?" Simons asks.

"What's your timeline? When are you looking for an answer from me? Because I have to tell you, I'm darn sure not giving one here.

And more than likely I'll be just coming back with more questions, before even thinking about a commitment."

"All fair. We have to move quick. But there's some time. A couple of days. Not a week. Here's my card, with a direct line for anything you need to ask me directly. My assistant, Paul, is on there too, along with his contact number."

He nods, and it's clear the conversation is over.

"Mr. Simons, it's been a pleasure to meet you," I say, wondering if he'll catch the hint of sarcasm. Puppy and I shake hands with him and walk out, back into the rain.

Once safely out of earshot I vent to Puppy. "Dude! What the hell was that?" We continue working our way out of the pad and head back toward the Group buildings.

"No idea," he says. "I got a text message to go over there. Caller ID was blocked, but it sounded legit. Something about needing to tighten up an inventory line before we close out the books for tomorrow's auction."

I'm listening closely to this, as Puppy continues.

"I get over there, and it's none other than the Vice Chairman of the Joint Chiefs of Staff, waiting to greet me. He said he was just there to vouch for the legitimacy of the meeting. But then I should go get you. And don't tell you in advance what it's about."

"The Vice Chairman? This gets crazier by the minute. He wasn't even in the stands. So, he snuck onto post too? Why didn't he stay until I got there?"

"That was Simons' doing. He asked the Vice to depart before you showed up. Said he wanted to lay out the arguments on their own merits. Didn't want you to think a four banger was trying to lean on us to say yes.

I ask Puppy, "Well, *are* you going to say yes?"

"Not without you and Ulysses, I would damn sure not. I've got all the same questions as you do. I'm gonna end up contracting somewhere, that I pretty well know. But what he's talking about is on a whole different scale. Not gonna sign on to that with just any old yahoos."

I nod in agreement.

"But with *you two* yahoos," he adds, "sure."

"Thanks for the vote of confidence, Puppy."

"Any time, Sir."

I remind him, "Don't forget about dinner. Seven p.m. We need to talk about this, but I need a bourbon first."

Puppy asks, "How's Ulysses?"

"Same. Just like you'd expect."

"Yeah. Hopefully he can get a good custody arrangement. I'll be there for dinner. Hey, you going to tell Linny about this just yet?"

"Of course. She's going to catch the look on my face about a half second after I walk in the door. May as well spill the beans and get it over with. Plus, I need to hear what she thinks."

Puppy stops walking, prompting me to do the same. He turns to look square at me. "Mark, what's your gut on this?"

"Not good," I say. "Beyond not good. I'm at ninety-five percent no already. But we need to talk tonight, and digest what this business with the Vice is all about."

He nods. Then he breaks off to grab his last box of gear from our office space.

- 5 -

I skirt the billeting area and head over to the east-side parking lot. Definitely not in the mood to talk with anyone else at this point. I just want to eat a good meal and start to make sense of this. The rain has let up. I look across the parking lot. It was full just thirty minutes ago, but sits almost entirely empty now. My car's at the far end, standing sentinel with a few other vehicles. Hopefully the post blotter report – a Provost Marshal summary of overnight arrests and incidents – won't be too severe in the morning. The local bars will be drowning a lot of sorrows tonight.

Walking toward the car, I scan the scene. Even the parking lot takes on a different appearance in light of our deactivation. This city block of asphalt took the pulse of 8th Group's ebb and flow of activity. A full lot before dawn on a freezing winter morning felt routine, comfortable. The lot would be pitch black, with just a little perimeter lighting, but the presence spoke to teams and support sections arriving for morning physical training, or PT. Alternately, eighty cars, clustered in one section of the lot at sunset, advertised a company of six A Teams was staying over for a night live fire or training op. And a weekend afternoon's smattering of dozens of cars across the entire lot – that generally meant a key leader alert for all unit elements, for some contingency crisis down range.

Most of the parking surface is crumbled, almost ground to gravel. Some spots have helter-skelter newer paving where the surface had given way to mud pools. Puddles form after the rain, in uneven spots left by the haphazard work. In other spots, extended cracks snake along and a foot of grass grows out. Over the years, I'd tuned out just how decrepit it really looks.

Nearing my car, I can see there's someone standing on the opposite side, by the driver side door. It's Major General Saiz, fresh from firing us all at the podium. His aide de camp is nowhere in sight. This means it's a personal talk. He probably wants to shake hands and say thanks, ask how the troops are doing. That's his style. Saiz was a Major, our company commander, when Ulysses, Puppy and I arrived for our first assignment in Group.

Diego Saiz embodies the old American success story, back when we viewed ourselves as a nation of immigrants. He grew up in Yavaros, Mexico, a fishing village on the mainland situated just across the Gulf of California from Baja. Sometime in the early 1980s, when Saiz would have been just four or five, his parents brought the family across the border into San Diego.

For the next thirty years, his mom cleaned houses in La Jolla. The only time I ever knew Saiz to cry was once on a deployment, maybe ten years back. He received notification that his mom had passed. He was a full colonel then, commanding all of 8th Group. If anyone in his charge had gotten that Red Cross message, he'd have put them on the next bird back to the States, no protest brooked. Go on emergency leave and honor your family, he would have said, it's worth five days out of theater.

But Saiz would never grant emergency leave for himself. We all pooled for flowers. A member of the stateside rear detachment flew out to represent at the funeral. On the day of the funeral back in the States, he didn't speak a word about it. He simply closed the doors to the plywood-walled dividers that formed a makeshift office in our forward operating base. His office had a small TV with cable feeds, and he must have thought he'd turned BBC News up loud enough to cover the sobs. We could hear him, though.

"Hey, Sir, thanks for being here today," I say, walking up to his side of the car. "It's a suck detail, but everyone appreciates that it was you up on the podium."

"Mark, you all looked good out there. Please pass word to the ranks how proud I was to see everyone standing tall."

"Will do, Sir. I'll see a lot of them at the job fair tomorrow."

"How's Linny?"

"Shoot, she's been the one carrying me the past few weeks. We took separate cars. I'm headed home now and will pass your regards. How are Jasmin and Victor?" He and Jasmin have been sweethearts since their childhood in San Diego.

"Jasmin's doing well. Victor, it's been tough. He's fallen in with the wrong crowd at school. We're trying to hold as strong a line as we can without pushing him away."

I nod. That's got to be eating him. He's been pulled in so many directions, the man's hardly ever at home.

"What will you and Linny do next?" Saiz asks.

"Not sure, probably go back to Maryland. I have no clue really. After all these months, waiting for the other shoe to drop on the downsizing, it actually feels good to have this behind us. We'll be OK."

Then he drops the bomb. He takes on a more serious tone and asks, "How'd the meeting go?"

I look at him for a second, not registering what he means. Then, "You *knew* about that?"

"Well, I *heard* something about it. I didn't know one hundred percent until just now. Mark, what were the take aways?"

"Sir, if you knew enough to be lying in wait at my car, you probably know the rest. But I sure as hell want to hear what you've got to say on this. Courtney Simons says he's switching markets. Spouting a crazy scheme to build a private military firm, on an entirely different scale. Says he's going to field a force that can push the Russians out of the Emirates. His pitch was to pull in me, Ulysses and Puppy as the primary advisors to stand up his ground force."

"And your thoughts?"

"My thoughts are, it's nonsense. With all the enablers it needs, how's he going to field a capability that *the entire US military* can't put together at present? Look, the guy's a genius. He's permanently transformed our economy, the global economy, got it. But being a genius in one area and having money to burn, that doesn't mean he knows what he's talking about here. Simons is crazy."

I was used to Saiz' poker face over the years. He'll take it all in, not betray a hint to his own thoughts. He looks at me a few more seconds.

Then he replies, "Mark, it might seem surreal. But don't confuse that with him being crazy. There are real forces in motion."

"Well, Sir, I'm glad to hear of your belief in his concept. So how about this. I'll escort you over there to his rusted-out corporate suites, and *you* can offer to build his army. Certainly, he'd much rather have a two star than my middling ass."

Saiz' eyes light up and he laughs.

"Mark, they won't let a general officer within a hundred miles of signing on to this Enterprise Performance effort. First of all, Simons himself wouldn't allow it. He'd be afraid that any G.O. he signed would start pulling levers in the old-boy network behind his back. That's the same reason it was you and not Alan Jensen, a Group Commander, in that conversation. Simons wouldn't even trust a full bird to be completely under his control. No, he might pull someone like me in later, if he's proven himself and then needs to scale up. But at first he'll only hire people of low enough rank he can squash if he needs to."

Saiz sees the expression on my face, so he adds, "No offense about the squashing part."

"None taken, Sir."

Saiz continues, "Plus the Joint Chiefs would *never* allow a general to join. Listen, you've got to understand what a precarious situation the military is in. No. The *whole* government. The Joint Staff is almost in anarchy right now. Half the service chiefs are holding on to a belief that we can get Congress to push through an emergency funding measure. Restore some of our critical capabilities. Or at least stop the hemorrhaging."

"But you don't agree with that, do you?" I ask.

"I agree with the sentiment, but I think that ship has sailed. This Enterprise Performance initiative kills me. You know me. It goes against everything we've ever sworn an oath to. But Simons has powerful friends in the administration. And he has at least *enough* friends on the Hill. So no, I don't agree with it. But I've come to believe that it's going to happen regardless of my opinion, or the opinion of the Joint Chiefs."

Then Saiz chuckles. "Of course, there are others in the Building," he says, referring to the nickname for the Pentagon. "They're looking at this as an opportunity. The Air Force can't afford a fraction of the F-35 fleet anymore. So, General Chaikin is talking up leasing whole squadrons over to Simons. I think he sees cooperating now as a way to get a good private industry job, later."

I'm starting to feel queasy. "So, what are we talking about then?"

"Mark, what I hope is that you, Ulysses and Puppy will accept Simons' offer. As bad as this is, it appears to be the direction our country is headed for now. With some good people on the inside, maybe we can at least build it the right way. And hopefully at some point we'll be able to rebuild more capabilities back into the uniformed military where they belong."

My frustration has hit threshold. "Sir, we are talking about *mercenaries*. This is going to make the current ecosystem of private military companies, which is already bad enough – this is going to make that look like nothing. We're talking about being able to invade countries with a force that has zero, absolutely zero, constitutional ties to the United States government. I know, of course, the administration will dress it up in nice-speak. And Simons will spin it the way he has every other thing he's disrupted. He'll say it's more efficient. It takes money that would have been wasted and instead puts it back into the economy. And he'll assure everyone that everything he does will be at the specific direction of the United States elected leadership. But it's not the same, and you and I both know that."

Saiz pauses for a long time before speaking. The thing about good senior leaders is, they know when to go light. The harder a G.O. leans on you, raises a voice, uses rank to club you into acting, the weaker their position becomes.

I thought about the tragedies of the past decade, among them remembering the two lives we'd spent in Senegal to evacuate the embassy, just because we didn't have the right forces to properly secure that airfield in the first place. And I realized why, over the past week leading up to the deactivation, I wasn't fearing the layoff as bad as I'd expected. Even with no career path and no prospects in this dead end economy, I was secretly relieved. I had given myself permission to step away from the madness and move on.

Saiz and I spoke for another twenty minutes, as the light changed from dusk to dark. We talked about old times and chuckled at crazy things that only deployments can generate. Like the time in Kunduz that we almost fired a junior support guy. Everyone's watches were disappearing. We found the cache of loot in the guy's footlocker, by his cot. He mounted a defense that no one believed until we remote-videoed his tent. Wild monkeys lived in the area, and one had gotten a fixation on watches. It had chosen the poor dude's sleeping area for a secret monkey stash.

This was all polite banter before parting ways.

Saiz and I both knew an unspoken agreement had been reached.

I would join Enterprise Performance.

- 6 -

9 August 2029 – Davidson, WV

Man, this guy moves fast. It's been two days since the deactivation ceremony, and Simons has already negotiated a fifteen-year lease for a third of Camp Diamond. Well, not *him*, of course. His team of lawyers and accountants do all the administrative grunt work. His fleet of lobbyists and fixers grease skids inside the DC beltway.

The man knows how to operate on a personal basis as well. I'm impressed with how well he's kept himself anonymous locally. Davidson, the municipality adjacent to Camp Diamond, is small town to the core. It grew up around Camp Diamond. A VIP never gets in and out of here without fanfare. If a congressman, or even a state senator, visits overnight for a post ceremony, you can bet the *Davidson Plain Dealer* will know the minute that person checks in at the local Best Western or La Quinta. The next morning there will be a front page, full profile article.

Simons' anonymity is especially surprising given the whole world knows his likeness. That speaks a lot to context, I suppose. Besides dressing the part of a contractor, he doesn't carry trappings that suggest importance. Here, in Davidson, Simons drives a subcompact rental with no entourage in tow. He'll wear a ball cap and sunglasses out on the street. With his demeanor and ability to blend, I'm not even sure that's necessary.

We've met Paul, his executive assistant, once, for less than five minutes. Simons calls him at least thirty times a day and delivers crisp, actionable instructions or research tasks. At least ten times each day, Paul calls back with equally brief answers or follow up. For a guy worth north of one hundred and fifty billion, Simons is a remarkably light traveler.

And he's clearly comfortable working in the shadows. I'm trying to figure out how much this bothers me. Simons is the ultimate disruptor. What's his angle?

By the terms of the Camp Diamond lease, we can't take control of facilities until tomorrow. At this breakneck pace, though, every minute counts. It means this morning we're holding a working breakfast at Hungry Hank's Biscuit Bistro. That's an ironic setting to plan the most seismic change to American national security posture of the last fifty years.

Hank's is an institution. Davidson's Main Street runs south from its small downtown and forms the western boundary of the post. All up and down Main Street you have the usual assortment of businesses that support an Army base: pawn shops, barber shops, strip clubs that city elders frown upon, and bars the same elders love for the alcohol tax. A few coffee joints dot the strip, although the Starbucks concession on post takes most of that business.

But Hank's is king of them all.

Hank Junior still runs the place, though he's way up in years. After World War II, Hank Senior returned home to Davidson and saw an opportunity. Congress had just changed Camp Diamond from provisional wartime status to a permanent post. Hank bought the vacant lot immediately across from the main entrance. Talk about minting money. The Biscuit Bistro runs 24/7. After all, troops have to eat. Whether grabbing something after morning PT, getting a quick lunch while ducking away from post for a haircut, or satisfying a young soldier's bar crawler munchies at 2 a.m., Hank's is there for you. I told Simons it's only right that he sample the wares of *Davidson's* most successful entrepreneur.

Driving from home, I park in the Bistro's lot just prior to our meeting. Shutting off the engine, the view through the windshield offers a sad reminder of Main Street's other eye-catching presence – panhandlers. On an average day, you'll see at least fifty of them along the three-mile drive from the main post entrance to downtown Davidson. Sometimes many more than that line the sidewalks and median. Even if it's raining or sleeting, you'll still get a dozen or more diehards.

Most are middle-aged men, but you can see any age, either gender. They generally keep themselves as clean and presentable as possible, to show they were part of the employed ranks until recently. These are casualties from the Second Great Depression. Pundits often call them victims of "The First Wave," when automation and AI took its first big bite. Interstate truckers and most commercial drivers became obsolete, almost overnight. Then virtually all jobs disappeared from the factories and distribution centers.

Davidson lies about fifty miles from Interstate 81. That artery fed the economies of nearby towns. Those towns offered affordable places for truckers to live. Over time, companies found them efficient locales for distribution centers. Modern manufacturing followed, since low cost of living kept the wages reasonable. Now, those business districts are ghost towns. The conglomerates need only a few hands to keep the machines running. The rest of the drivers and workers are castoffs. The castoffs make the trek to Camp Diamond because of the soldiers who, until yesterday, had solid paychecks and would help out when they could.

Sitting in the front seat of my car with the engine off, I see Simons pull into the lot and park nearest the street, farthest from my location by the Bistro entrance. He gets out and starts walking toward the restaurant. I'm just about to step out of my car to join him when a woman in her late twenties walks toward Simons.

Something makes me sit and watch how this plays out. She carries a toddler on one hip and holds the hand of a waist-high little blonde girl. She stops about ten feet away from Simons, the normal respect shown by First Wavers asking for help. Their words aren't audible from here, but I can transcribe it from body language. She's polite, making her case. He listens impassively, a subtle shake of the head and a couple words spoken. He walks straight past mom and kids, past my car, and into the Bistro. She walks away, composed for about ten steps. Then tears stream silently while she struggles to hold a dignified demeanor in front of the kids.

I jump out, walk to catch up with the woman, hand her forty bucks and wish her the best. Turning back towards the Bistro I slow my walk. This calls for a few seconds to cool down, thinking about the juxtaposition. The software running more than ninety percent of the automated industries in this country, the software that gutted this entire region's economy and put that woman on the street, that software belongs to Enterprise Performance. It's what earned the many billions of biscuits that Simons has in the bank.

I've just received a glimpse into Simons' sense of what he owes those who bear the price of his success.

Walking inside, I see that Ulysses and Puppy have already scored our usual booth and Simons has joined them. My normal spot is open and I grab a seat. For probably the thousandth time I make note of the dime-sized patch of missing veneer on the table's faux wood top. Given the vertigo of recent days, it's nice to hear Hank's familiar voice calling out orders from the counter. We're all dragging from a late night of mission analysis and research. But I get an immediate pickup from the waft of coffee, bacon egg biscuits, and hash browns.

Ulysses looks at me and announces, "You fly." It's the routine for the three of us, going back more than a decade. Today is Ulysses' turn to order for the group and pay, which he's letting me know he's already done. This must be Puppy's day for table cleanup duty. I get up, head to the counter, and grab our plastic tray heaped full with chow and beverage.

Between bites, we recap the salient points from our planning so far. Sipping coffee at the end, we preview the day's key tasks. We'll break huddle soon and each go work the phones.

"I'm comfortable with our progress to hire former 8th Groupers and other special operators," Ulysses says. "My main priority today will be tapping into folks over at the 11th Airborne."

Ulysses is spearheading the personnel review for our Enterprise

Performance force that will go into the Emirates. The other tenant unit on Camp Diamond, the 11th Airborne Division, also took a big hit yesterday. The nation's last airborne infantry unit, they are younger soldiers, more conventionally trained, but still a topnotch outfit. As part of the latest downsizing, the 11th Airborne just reflagged from a division to a brigade, and shed more than six thousand paratroopers. That's a lot of potential hires.

"Are you sure that's really necessary?" Simons asks. The guy's already proving to be a pain. Granted, the key to his ingenuity is playing devil's advocate. It's just a hassle to have to explain so much when we're racing through this buildup.

Ulysses holds his ground. "It's absolutely necessary. With the other assets you and Mark are pulling into the mix, you're going to need more manpower than just special operators. The special operations community simply isn't big enough to get all you need. Not to retake the Emirates. But we put together three super-sized battalions from the 11th Airborne, about twenty-five hundred paratroopers, and now you've got the reinforcements you'll want."

"That's almost half of what they cut yesterday. Will that many sign up?" Simons wonders.

Ulysses replies, "Have you *seen* all the people desperate for handouts around here? Of course they'll sign up."

Simons shows no reaction to the comment about desperate people.

Puppy speaks up. "Today I'm mainly focused on calls with think tank analysts who study Petrikov. We'll have a good briefing team built in time for our UAE planning sessions."

Dmitry Petrikov is the Russian commander in Dubai. He's their man for what Western analysts call New Generation Warfare.

Puppy adds, "Depending on progress with that, I'll start tracking down vendors for our comms and collection needs."

"What else?" Simons asks.

I jump in. "We need to know for sure that you've got access to the Camp Diamond facilities and training areas starting tomorrow. We're going full speed on this thing. You need us and our skeleton crew in there tomorrow, so that four days from now you can start hiring and filling out the maneuver formations. We're talking mission briefs in just over a week."

"It will be ready." Simons bristles a little. He doesn't like anyone questioning his ability to deliver. "My team closed all the paperwork yesterday. We'll have everything you need. We've locked in access to compounds N1 through N3, plus all the associated training areas and ranges."

"It's Cardiac Gap," Ulysses corrects.

"How's that?" Simons asks, cocking his head.

"It will help your street cred to know the local lingo. Call that series of compounds N1, N2 and *Cardiac Gap*. People rarely call it compound N3, unless in a formal briefing."

"And why is that?"

"Those are all old training compounds dating back to the fifties. They're actually older than that. In the nineteen-thirties, they were worker camps for the Civilian Conservation Corps. Compounds M1 through M4, and N1 through N3, those compounds were the original student barracks and training sites for the Special Forces Qualification course. When SF needed land and facilities to start out, those compounds offered a quick, turnkey solution. The Qualification course has since moved to more modern digs on the other side of post. Those old compounds now serve as simulated villages for training. Until Enterprise Performance leased the rights, that is.

"Anyway," Ulysses continues, "Compound N3 sits at the bottom of a crazy steep ridgeline. Back in the day, instructors at N3 would weed out sub-standard recruits by taking them on physical training runs up to a mountain pass that runs through the top of the ridgeline. Except in the eastern US, mountain passes get labeled as 'gaps.' Soon enough, the students called it 'Cardiac Gap.' Word of how bad it sucked made Compound N3 notorious. When SF recruits arrived at the reception center on main post, the ones who drew assignment to N3 were taunted for their death sentence to Cardiac Gap."

"Got it." Simons nods. Then he asks, "You guys ever run that ridge today?"

"Once in a while," Ulysses says, looking down at his coffee. He doesn't mention the personal history that the three of us have with the Gap.

We break up and exit to our cars. Ulysses' is parked next to mine. Walking across the small parking lot, it's just the two of us in earshot. He says, "You know, it's funny. I'll go back and run the more northern trails on that ridge, since those are the only ones that are still blazed. But in all the years stationed here, I haven't been back to the Gap itself since Puppy's big night."

"Me neither," I say.

- 8 -

Driving back onto Main Street, the talk about the Gap lingers for a bit. It brings up memories of the Qualification course. But farther back than that, it reminds me of personal origins, of my own path from suburban Maryland.

To be sure, a fuel on the path to Special Forces was the angst of the frustrated American athlete. Through elementary and middle school, my heart beat to the rhythm of every sport I could chase. Hockey and track mainly. But it was clear by high school that I'd never progress beyond varsity letterman. I could hold my own at left wing or at middle-distance running. But as much as I loved it, there was no path to Division One college or beyond.

And so, admittedly, a draw to being a special operator has been the reward of mastering the physicality. The creation myth paints operators as superhuman species, able to ascend heights where mere mortals would falter. Nothing could be further from the truth.

The fact is, you don't have to be the world's best athlete. You have to *want* it. You have to want it enough to put in the training, day in and day out. You need a decent but not huge amount of smarts, and good judgment. And you have to be a weird hybrid who is fully comfortable alone but wants to work as a team and make any team better. It also takes a big helping of stubbornness; you just plain refuse to quit.

That wasn't the start of the on-ramp, though, from life in the suburbs to the career I chose. The first push came courtesy of the Great Recession of 2008.

Looking back now on the late 1990s and the early-to-mid 2000s, it seemed like the apex of all things American. My formative memories in school were that we as a nation lived high on one plane of wealth, strength and security. Way down below was the rest of the world.

I never experienced want, ever. At Christmas, it was a given that the holiday season's must-have gift would appear under the tree. It wasn't a big ask. That's part of how Mom and Dad could demonstrate their status as providers in the chosen class.

There was no war for most of my childhood. Then we had the good war for about a year after 9/11. Then we opted for the other war, and the grownups all started arguing. The kids didn't talk about it. After all, you and your friends wouldn't go to the wars. We were busy hanging out after school at the Friendship Heights Chipotle, just off Wisconsin Ave, living in our bubble. The war was for other kids, over in Wheaton or Hagerstown. Or one of your cousins in Iowa.

Oh, you listened to parents *talk* about the wars a lot. There were friends' homes where you knew the parents were against the fighting. And then there were other homes where the parents were really, really for all the wars. But it never seemed to change anything. Except for things like, if there was an against-the-wars president in office, then the kids with against-the-wars parents had the best homes to hang out in. Because those kids' parents would be working crazy long hours as political appointees. Meaning no parents around. So that's where the crowd would gather to drink and smoke the occasional joint.

In 2007, I headed to college in the city. It was a free and easy existence. Just going along on the conveyor belt. I'd put in my time at Middlebrook Hall, where the Government Department held court, and get the Public Affairs degree. After that, I'd kill a couple of years at some think tank where a friend of Mom or Dad might get me an interview. Then it would be time to get serious.

You either got an MBA and went to a Top-5 consulting firm, or you went to GU or one of the Ivies for an MA in the correct flavored degree and started climbing the Federal rungs. Either way you aimed for a political appointment by your late thirties.

And twenty-five years later, you'd be your parents.

So all in all, college wasn't an unpleasant place to be. It was just a little sterile and boring during the day. At night you'd head with your crew to the bars on U Street or in Cleveland Park.

But the summer of '08, after freshman year, the bottom dropped out. I was crashing at home that summer and knocking out an internship.

Mom and Dad both lost their big jobs in the same week.

Six weeks later the house was gone along with the Lexus, the Mercedes, and my pride-and-joy used Beemer.

Two weeks after that, Dad got some crap job in Chicago, and off they went.

And on their way out the door, it was, like, "Hey, sorry, but no more tuition after this semester. Private college and all, we're tapped out." They offered a little more than that in terms of encouragement, but not much. It turned out funding my education was always part of a block check for them. It filled a certain category like the big jobs, the house in the right zip code, and the fancy cars. When that stuff went, so did tuition. I was completely upended, and for the first time, I needed to figure out a future.

On a scorching Thursday before Labor Day, I made a beeline across campus. Seven-year cicadas played their tune and crowded the footpath leading to the financial aid office.

After waiting in line, I spoke with the thirty-something woman in a summer dress and smudged glasses. She looked like she hadn't slept in a week.

"Can I help you?" she asked.

"Yes. My parents both lost their jobs and now they can't pay for college after this semester. And I'm six semesters plus a couple summer courses away from graduation."

"You want to know the status of your application for financial aid?"

"Um, no, I don't have any application. That's why I'm here. To apply."

She politely explained to me how *completely* the free-and-easy conveyor belt had stopped. The whole university, whole country, was swamped with students suddenly needing help. And the university was already maxed out with emergency applications. So, my timing was really bad. She politely suggested I come back at the end of the term, but it was just a gesture to get me out of the room.

I left the building and stepped onto the campus quad in a daze. Looking around at the matching façade buildings, I appreciated for the first time the richness of the atmosphere. Summer-term students walked by in shorts and t-shirts, chatting with backpacks slung. Coldplay piped from a dorm window. That world was over for me. I broke out in a cold sweat. It was time to get out of there and find some space to think. Without looking where I was going, I wheeled around to head back to the Metro.

And bounced off something like a tennis ball before landing on the ground. I'd shortly learn that this "something" was named Thomas Kim.

"Whoa! Where you headed so fast, partner?" the guy said cheerfully, pulling me to my feet with ease. He introduced himself by name.

I stared at him, trying to figure out how the collision knocked me over so easily but left him unruffled. Thomas was at least an inch shorter than me, and a good ten pounds lighter. But he was powerfully built. In his late thirties it looked like, he was in military dress uniform and wearing a beret that looked vaguely familiar. Don't ask me why, but between being in an unmoored mental state already, and then the disorientation of getting bowled over, I spilled my whole story to him.

He listened and seemed to really care. I told him about Mom and Dad and the layoffs, and the crappy Chicago job they'd decamped for. How I'd have to leave in December and had no idea what to do next.

Thomas had just come off a tour in Iraq. He was headed to the Tyler building to give a guest lecture for a summer course, but he had thirty minutes to kill. He grabbed me by the arm and started walking me toward the campus ROTC detachment.

And he changed my life.

I never ran across Thomas again. Heard from colleagues he retired out of 17th Group in 2014. But in a ten-minute walk across campus, he cheerfully and confidently prescribed the exact road map I should follow.

"We'll take you to the ROTC office, find a recruiter, and they'll sign you up."

"OK?" I said. By now we were walking under a tree canopy. Rays of sunlight stabbed through and glinted off indiscernible hardware on his summer dress uniform.

"Finish college," Thomas continued my walking tutorial.

"Yeah, I'd like to finish college."

"Request assignment in the 11th Airborne after graduation. It's the best place to learn. Request Infantry branch. Why bother to serve if you're not in the thick of it?"

"OK," I murmured, not really sure where this was going.

"As a lieutenant, listen to your NCOs, and try not to get you or your guys needlessly killed. You might have to get yourself killed on purpose, and that's allowed. But getting yourself killed needlessly is negligence, for which you'd be subject to court martial."

"But if I'm dead, how can they . . ."

"And this is IMPORTANT. When you make first lieutenant, they're going to start processing your orders to the Captains Career Course as an Infantry officer. And continuing as an Infantry officer, that's not bad at all. It's good stuff. But you've got other plans."

"What other plans, Thomas?"

"SPECIAL FORCES! What do you THINK we're talking about? Don't you recognize my beret?"

"How should I know what we're talking about? And *no*, I *don't* recognize your beret. I never even met an Army guy until one knocked me on my ass five minutes ago."

He grinned at me. "Alright, look. Look at me and remember what I'm telling you here. When you make First Lieutenant, track down a Special Forces recruiter. Got it?"

"Yeah, I got it."

"Say it, repeat it back."

"When I make First Lieutenant, track down a Special Forces recruiter."

"Questions?"

"What's a First Lieutenant?"

"Don't worry about that. Just remember it, and do it, and you'll thank me."

By now we were in front of the ROTC offices. Thomas walked me inside.

Four years later, on active duty, when I made first lieutenant of Infantry, I did exactly what he said. I declined my next Infantry assignment and tried out for Special Forces.

And I loved every part of it.

I loved that no one cared where you came from. No one was going to babysit you, chew you out, or cajole you to do anything. It was all on you. You had to want it. They just handed you the sixteen-week train-up program for the selection course. Said don't even bother to show up unless you'd done each and every workout.

And by week fourteen of the train-up for selection, you were out rucking alone early on a Saturday morning during off-duty time. You pushed past exhaustion, moving along a rutted dirt road in the post training area, with low hanging clouds and a forty-degree rain soaking you to the bone. Ruck straps digging in hard on your shoulders, but not slicing like week four, when you were still getting used to the load. Three rucks a week. Plus weights, running, swimming, and practicing foot maintenance. All of it building the chassis to properly carry kit.

Friends kept saying I was crazy to sign on for that kind of abuse. I wasn't sure myself why I was doing it. Except, it was the most distilled form of excellence I'd ever had the chance to pursue.

Next, it was off to the thirty-day tryout that would attrit most of the attendees. Only after passing this could you enter the twelve-month Qualification course, where you'd attempt to earn the green beret and Special Forces tab. On day nine or ten of the tryouts, I realized the sixteen-week train-up was just preamble. The only reason they had you do the train up was so, when they dropped a manhole cover on you at selection, it wouldn't kill you. Instead, it would just strip off the veneer. At selection they doubled the rucksack weight. It once again sliced my shoulders until they screamed. Callused feet turned to hamburger.

Anyone who wants to quit can quit. No questions asked and no harassment. Just walk up and tell any instructor, at any time, this isn't for you. Between days three and twelve, a ton of candidates did exactly that. About ten times a day, in misery, I wanted to quit in the worst way. My brain stem howled, *do something, anything, to stop the pain!* But you learned to shout down the brain, took the next step, and the next step, on hamburger feet. You tuned out the shoulders.

Because by then I had realized a paramount truth. I was surrounded by peers who'd all tuned it out as well. I'd never been around a group of people who showed this kind of dedication. They were hurting as bad as I was, but they kept going. These were people I could count on. They weren't going to walk out on you to Chicago. This was a place I could *belong*, and that meant something. Getting selected to attend the Qualification course was one of the most important moments of my life. And the Qualification course was where I'd meet Ulysses and Puppy.

There was only one catch, traversing from college to life as a career special operator.

The summer before senior year, Linny stole my heart.

From a slow academic start freshman year, I needed more classes to graduate on time. The first day of summer term I walked into Middlebrook Hall for an elective course – *Post World War II: Alliance and Stability*. Middlebrook has an airy lobby with free floating stairs that lead to the second and third floors.

I spied a young woman climbing the steps and invoked all powers of the universe for her to be in the same class as me. Sure enough, at the third level she stepped toward the interior hallway and disappeared. My heart rushed. It took every ounce of discipline to follow at a normal pace up the stairs. Taking a blind turn into my classroom, I was floored to not only see her seated in there, but there was also an open chair to her right.

I remember meeting Linny as if it were yesterday, like it was an hour ago. Her Midwest fair skin, blond hair and blue eyes captivated me. Her soothing voice and petite build belied a childhood working every nook and cranny of their family farm.

The farm upbringing showed in her work ethic. Whereas I entered college on cruise control, Linny worked tirelessly every step of the way. She was two years behind me, but had allotted herself just three years for a Bachelor's degree. Her plans called for law school immediately after. The rest of that summer and into fall of my senior year, we would spend every possible moment together.

As the holidays of my senior year approached, each day brought increased tightness to my chest. I knew the military path I'd aim for, and it pointed to a terrifying reckoning for our relationship. Linny had every opportunity in the world. But the career she wanted, that she could excel in, she'd never find in the small Army towns where I was likely to receive assignment.

The last day before winter break, we went on a walking date through the gardens of the Hillwood Estate, just off Connecticut Avenue. Bright, crisp winter air lit the bare branches and evergreens. We walked along chatting. The estate's tall hedges and perimeter stone wall muted the sounds of the surrounding city. I couldn't take it anymore.

"You know, come graduation, I'm off to active duty," I led off.

"I know," she said politely. Nothing else. How could I love her so much but feel so helpless to read her thoughts? She had a mysterious half smile that buckled my knees but left me clueless.

"Well, so, my first assignment will be a three-year tour in the Infantry."

"And after that?"

"Linny, look, we've talked some about my thoughts on the Army. But I have to make it clear. As soon as I'm eligible, I'm going to try out for a career in Special Forces. I don't know why, really. But the more I've studied it, and now had a chance to meet a few more operators during ROTC training, it's not even a decision really. It's just something I have to do."

"Why?"

We walked in silence, while I thought on this. "It's the men, really. I mean, I'm sure there are great people in plenty of other places and professions. But for me, the handful of operators I've had the chance to meet, there's something different about them. There's a sense of commitment, purpose. It feels like they're part of something bigger than themselves. I've seen enough just as a cadet to know the military is rife with bureaucracy and frustration, and politics and everything else. But if I don't at least try this, I'll wonder for the rest of my life, *what if?*"

She said nothing at first. Then, "Well, those sound like good reasons."

We walked in more silence, with me dying. Finally, I controlled my breathing enough to ask, "What do you think about that? I mean, what do you think about us? About us long term?"

"Well, I'm going straight to law school. I want to clerk right away after that. Which will, most likely, all be right here in the city."

"Uh huh."

"After that, I guess I'll need to find a flexible practice. Something I can take to different parts of the country."

"You know," I said, losing it, my voice quavering. "Some of those Army towns are really, really small. There's not a lot there."

"I know, I've been googling them."

"You have?"

"Yes."

My eyes welled up. "Why. Um, why have you been googling Army towns?"

She had a full smile now, beaming. "Because I figured someday that's where I'd move. To be with you."

I had tears streaming now, and didn't even care to hide them. "But why would you give up all the things you could do in a high-powered career, to follow me around?"

She looked straight in my eyes, still smiling. "It's not even a decision really. It's just something I have to do."

I lost it. I wrapped her in a hug and sobbed with happiness.

We wouldn't get engaged until she had finished undergrad. We married the next summer. But from that evening on, our lives together were set. Even during her early career when we lived apart, or when deployments took me to the most far-flung and wasted parts of the world, Linny and I were together in spirit. She's made me the luckiest man in the world.

- 9 -

Ulysses was already a household name by the time I met him in the Qualification course, held on Camp Diamond. He had just finished three years as an M1 tank gunner in the 2nd Armored Division. During this time, he'd been blogged about, trolled, memed hundreds of times, and burned in effigy once. Most of that occurred early in his enlistment, before he tried out for Special Forces. Word was, during basic training, the drill sergeants had to install extra security around his platoon barracks. Too many paparazzi were trying to come in and take the high payoff photo.

The first part of the Qualification course focuses on individual skills. Some of these are common skills, like weapons qual, advanced navigation, geopolitical studies to understand where the heck we're going to operate, or more importantly, *why*. Individual skills phase also is where you learn your specialty skills.

The beauty of an A Team is the blend of best-in-class fundamentals that are universal across the team, combined with a range of specialties spread among the individual operators. These specialties include weapons, communications/cyber, advanced medical, and demo/engineering. Officers and warrant officers receive training to take team command and deputy command.

The glue that holds every team together are two senior sergeants who have graduated up from the specialty skills. The second most senior serves as the intel sergeant. The most experienced and grizzled will be the team sergeant, aka *team daddy*. In the Qualification course, given that we were all trainees, the glue came instead from the instructor cadre.

Following individual phase, we formed into student teams for our field phase. This is where students take their shiny new individual skills and learn to make a whole that's even stronger than the sum of its parts. We grouped ten trainees to a team. Our two instructors, both seasoned combat veterans, filled slots number eleven and twelve on the team.

The core principle of the Qualification course is not to pump out automatons or hesitant newbies when we join our units. A new Special Forces operator is supposed to be a thinker, actor, and leader. A Green Beret functions extremely well on a team. But this team operates in the context of strategic missions where the team might split off individually or in pairs.

Each team member might advise a hundred or more indigenous military members in some remote war, with little comms and no backup. Any team member, even the newest, must be ready to size up the situation, make a plan, and act.

When we proceeded to team training missions, in field phase, the instructors didn't hover over us with clipboards and all-knowing looks on their faces. They functioned in and among us. They would lead and teach by example. A senior Captain served as team commander, and a genuine Master Sergeant became our team daddy. In this way, they'd instruct and evaluate while showing "what right looks like" in everything we did. Oh sure, out in our field training missions, they'd rotate putting one of us in charge of a given operation. This would test our chops at tactics and leadership. But the goal was, for the four months we'd spend with them, to learn by osmosis. If the instructors did everything right, hit every mark, then gradually so should we. And when we didn't, they'd hand us our ass.

Stephen Joll was the Captain. He was back from Afghanistan so recently that five times a day he had to pull some prescription goop out from the top flap on his ruck. He'd apply it to the weird scaly rash that covered the back of each hand. Watching that gave us training value too. It took the sexy sheen off the job and offered a welcome-to-the-life message. Alex Martel was the Master Sergeant. He had started as a young enlisted man with the Rangers in Mogadishu. In Special Forces, he'd served multiple combat tours throughout Afghanistan and the Middle East. Word was he'd been on that big op in '13. But he'd never tell you that. Stephen and Alex simply snapped in like the pros they were, treated each other as professionals, and set about building us into an A Team.

We prepped for field phase for a week, in our first taste of isolation planning. All our personal electronics were confiscated and locked away. We had only a limited news feed. This gave a taste of what it was like to be overseas, sequestered away in a remote base of operations. In this case, isolation came in the form of a fenced-off gravel compound that held two corrugated metal buildings. One served as the planning bay, and one served as our living quarters.

Ulysses and I met when they formed our field team and commenced isolation. At first, I shrugged off asking him about his story. It was none of my business. Besides, we were in close quarters with our instructors. Joll and Martel wanted to see us focused on developing mission skills, not blathering about our lives before the Army.

Two days after infil, on our first training mission, we had spread out in a patrol base for tactical rest and refit. Camp Diamond's wooded, tight ridgelines gave us students perfect terrain to practice the art of going to ground. It was just after dawn, following a night movement. We formed a small circular perimeter, fifty meters in diameter, down slope from a crest. Everyone lay prone on the ground, concealed among the oak trees and mountain laurel. By now we'd learned the protocol for patrol bases. The team sergeant assigns positions in pairs around the perimeter. One person pulls security while the other attends to maintenance, eats, or gets some sleep.

On that morning Ulysses and I paired off. He covered security, scanning through rifle sights in the early morning light while I was pulling off stinky socks and powdering my feet.

In my exhaustion and momentary boredom, curiosity topped good manners.

"So, you're *The Great Ulysses?*" I asked.

He set his jaw and didn't talk for a good minute. So far as I know, no one on our team had said that aloud to him.

"Look, dude, we're going to be on this student team for the next few months." He was still locked behind his rifle and scanning the sector, looking away from me. "You can either not say that again, or I can beat you unconscious. Your choice."

I considered my options.

He had at least sixty pounds on me. And we were two days into the most important grading period of the course. All the cost/benefit metrics were in agreement.

"OK, Ulysses," I said.

Other than team business, we didn't talk again for the next four weeks.

Coming off another night mission, we were back in a patrol base after dawn. It was dead of winter. Dead leaves and a half-inch dusting of snow crunched under our feet as we settled into the perimeter. Ulysses and I were paired up again.

We were all dead tired and freezing. By course design, the team was averaging four hours sleep per night. Our clothes accumulated grime and progressively lost their insulation. Several of the training missions had gone bad, and all of us were struggling to make grades on tactical evaluations. It would all shake out in the next few weeks. Either we'd keep it together, as individuals and as a team, and be deemed worthy to graduate. Or we'd succumb to the suck, feel sorry for ourselves and fail.

I pulled the first security watch, shivering in the prone while Ulysses sat behind me. He dug into his ruck for a ration.

"*The Great Ulysses*, what a bunch of bullshit," he muttered.

I continued scanning through rifle sights, covering my sector of the perimeter. "Sorry, man. I was just curious."

"You're good. You were just asking. Versus a gazillion people with no lives back then, wanting to beat up on some high school kid. And they've all got their agendas and don't even bother to get the full story. Case in point, what do you even remember of all that insanity?"

"Well, let's see." I thought for a moment. "You were the highest rated high school quarterback in the history of the sport. I remember the build-up to national signing day. The NFL was already researching waivers to let you sign pro before your sophomore year. But the colleges didn't care. They figured even one season would be a guaranteed championship run."

"Pretty good so far. Go on," he said between bites of his meal.

"Vanderbilt was making the big play to keep you in town. Eastside boy made good and all. But the commentators seemed to think that Florida or Alabama would win out."

"And?"

"And, well, signing day came and you no-showed. The whole sports world freaked. Florida's coach flew to Nashville and held a press conference downtown, asking you to come out of hiding. Then the haters and trolls started. A few weeks later someone figured out that you had inprocessed to basic training at Fort Benning. And, well, now here you are earning . . ."

A twig snapped seventy-five meters away.

I swung my rifle barrel to cover. It wouldn't be the first time that the role player enemy tried to jump us in a patrol base.

Instead, a deer looked up briefly then bounded away.

"And now here you are earning the big bucks," I continued, still scanning my outward sector. "From the smell of it, you're also eating MRE menu number 5: Chicken Chunks."

Ulysses chuckled. "All correct, right down to the chicken chunks. But what else do you remember? What about why? Why'd I do it?"

"I don't know."

"Of course not. No one ever bothers with that piece." He paused. "They think the story started on signing day, my senior year in high school. But it started four years before that. My mom and dad had bet everything on home flipping in the early 2000s. They lost it all in the '08 housing bust. In a month, we went from getting by just fine to living in a two-bedroom apartment. My parents struggled through bankruptcy court. I was in eighth grade and already in the national press. *Eighth grade,*" he emphasized, more to himself than to me. "Fourteen years old. And they were already sizing me up like a piece of meat on the menu. That's when the money came in."

"The what?"

"The money, dude. Some guy from Ocala showed up in the stairwell landing of our apartment one night. He was all smooth and helpful, wanting to make sure I could stay focused. Could he do anything to help?"

I stayed quiet, giving him some space.

"And I'm fourteen fucking years old and what do I know? Of course, I want to help my mom and dad. So I take it, the money, and take more money after that. It was well over six figures in all. We were desperate. It all went toward loan defaults. And then four years later, it's the night before signing day. My phone rings. It's a

Nashville area code with the last seven digits blocked out.

"I answer, and some middle-aged guy says how they know all about what I've been up to, taking Florida money. And I'd better sign to Vanderbilt, or it's going to get bad. And I'm a minor. So, it won't be on me. It will be my mom and dad going to jail." Ulysses got quiet and kept eating.

After a couple of minutes I asked, "So, what happened next?"

I could hear him putting the empty foil packets back into the MRE heavy plastic shell. He folded the shell to compress the air out and shoved it back into his ruck. Then he cinched the ruck tight.

"Just like you said," he replied matter-of-factly. "What happened next was, I signed up for the big bucks. And MRE menu number 5."

- 10 -

Hugh "Puppy" Jackson grew up on the streets of Providence, RI, in a situation that might tactfully be called a disaster. Mom did her best, but a combo of booze and occasional meth sunk its claws deep into her and refused to let go. By the time Hugh was fifteen, he had three younger siblings from two different stepfathers. Of course, also by fifteen, those upstanding men were no longer on the scene. Mom and the four kids bounced around. By his late teens Hugh was the family breadwinner, running drugs to the rich kids at Brown. He tucked into the nooks and alleys just off Thayer street, where he worked the hip row of coffee bars and eateries.

Like all things Hugh, he was a study in contrasts. When carrying product on the way to a drop or cash on the way back, Hugh would armor himself with an air of intimidation. He'd walk with a little bit of slouch that hinted readiness to roll an elbow strike or throat punch. His eyes were boarded up, all business. In the small of his back, beneath an untucked flannel shirt, sat a small frame nine mil and a five-inch fixed blade.

But if someone caught him close in a doorway, or got the drop and planted him on his back, that's when the right hand snuck in a flash down to an icepick shiv holstered on the inside of his left ankle. On those few occasions, the assailant ran away howling and holding a bloody, flapping wing of cheek.

For Hugh that was simply business. Life gave him a deck of cards, and he played it. But away from work, if you had the good fortune to meet him in amenable times and circumstances, you could recognize in him a friend for life. He had a heart and a soft side buried underneath. That heart was the real him.

Hence his nickname. One of the young siblings had trouble saying "Hugh." In little-speak it kept coming out as "Hush." This morphed in the family to "Hush Puppy," and eventually shortened to "Puppy." And that's what stuck. After all, in the logic universal to families, street hustle, or combat formations, what better name for the meanest, baddest dude around than "Puppy?"

I know nothing about Hugh's two younger brothers and his younger sister. The one and only time he ever showed Ulysses and me the picture of them, that said it all. In the picture, Hugh was sprawled on a rough weave, brown fabric couch. Both his feet were on the floor with him sitting in the middle. His wing span stretched end to end. At first you thought the picture was taken at a slight angle. Closer inspection showed it was just a front leg of the couch was missing and caused it to tilt. The rest of the brood nestled on either side of him.

The next oldest couldn't have been more than ten. He was trying to mimic big brother, seated on Hugh's right with his feet dangling off the edge of the cushions and his little arms spread out to either side. The other little boy was curled up on the opposite side, hugging Hugh with head tucked underneath a big strong arm. Sitting on Hugh's lap was the little princess of the family, a beautiful blond girl probably four years old. She wore a white t-shirt with hand-me-down fraying on the collar and a jelly stain on the left sleeve that matched the jelly smear on the side of her mouth. Her chin tucked up toward the camera in the model's pose of a natural ham.

You see Hugh's face in that picture. Beatific. Just happiness and love. He's got the signature glint in his eye, the one when he's letting his guard down and enjoying being with the people he cares about. For Hugh Jackson, there's nothing more he needs than that. He could have sat there forever.

But he didn't. Not long after the couch portrait, Hugh walked out of their latest flop pad one evening and was up on Thayer Street getting business done. Hugh's mom was several weeks into trying to make a go with man number next. The current dude turned out to be the worst of the lot; a wannabe dealer who couldn't even get that going. He avoided Hugh and would come around at night looking for what cash or pawn-able items he could scam. Hugh had tried for the longest time to get his mom to drop the guy. Finally, one night she'd had enough and apparently did just that. No one would ever know the full story. Hugh came home from work about an hour before dawn. He found mom and all three kids shot dead.

It wasn't until three or four years after we'd met that he showed Ulysses and me the photo of him and his siblings on the couch. Even then, he wouldn't take it out from a protective Ziploc bag. Later, after we'd known Hugh about eight years, he finally trusted us enough to open up the Ziploc and show the rest of the contents. From behind the picture, he pulled out a clipped and faded news article from the *Providence Journal*. Hardly anyone read paper copies even back in that day. Hugh had done some hunting to find the artifact.

The article was dated about a week after Hugh's family was murdered. It explained that police had identified the killer: a local man with prior record, including a history of domestic violence. When they found the man, he had a pistol on him that tested as the one used to murder the family. Powder traces on the man's hands proved he had fired the weapon. Other evidence tied him to the shooting on the night in question. The suspect himself never talked, never gave up any further information about that night. In fact, the police never even had a chance to make the arrest. Instead the man maintained silence, when they found him cold and slumped against the side of a dumpster, in an alley just off Thayer Street. An ice pick protruded out from behind the base of his skull. The police officially closed the case.

Five days later, two states away, Puppy Jackson enlisted in the Army.

- 11 -

Puppy joined our acquaintance in the Qualification course, two weeks prior to the end of our four-month field phase. Our student team was wired and on edge. Stephen Joll and Alex Martel, our instructor team leader and instructor team sergeant, had proved to be hard graders, though fair and consistent in their marks. The problem was, we had simply blown it on too many graded mission sets. For Stephen and Alex, their job was not to hold our hands and make themselves look good by passing us. Their job was to instruct, to mentor but hold to standards. It was on us to accomplish the rest.

They had demonstrated, to perfection, how to build a short-notice mission order while lying on our bellies in the January nighttime snow. We learned to work in pocket notebooks by red lens headlamp. Alex set the example to lie without flinching in a freezing L-shaped ambush position for three hours. Stephen brought in two hundred role-playing guerillas and demonstrated the ways of maneuvering an untrained horde onto an assault objective.

But watching and doing are two different things. As a team we had clicked late, after failing grades had already mounted. Now we were blade running – just one mistake away from failure.

It was against this backdrop that Puppy arrived. As usual, the weekly resupply helicopter brought in MREs, batteries, blank ammunition, and other routine supplies. To our surprise, Puppy stepped out of the bird. Student transfers at this point in the course were extremely rare and generally came from no good cause.

Great, we griped. Just what we need. Here was some screw up who was screwing up so bad they wouldn't even keep him on his own student team for the rest of field phase. And now, as if we didn't have enough problems, we would be forced to accommodate Mr. Screw up, too. The gouge was that he'd been kicked off his other team for fighting. That they even bothered to give him a second chance, on another team, was highly unusual. That we didn't clue in to this was a mark of our rookie-dom.

Only later would we find out that Puppy had caught his original team mates cheating. One of them had gotten crib notes on the mission profiles: where the opposing force would lay ambushes to attack the student team, etc. This allowed them to plan pitch-perfect assaults, avoid ambush traps, and make themselves look stellar for grades. They had approached Puppy to participate. Unfortunately, no one had given *them* the crib notes on Puppy. He may have broken laws in a past life, but like most converts he had adopted with zeal the code of his new world. Cheating to make grades meant you weren't really learning the assigned combat skills. It meant you hadn't built the tools to take forward to your first unit assignment. It meant you didn't deserve to be in the operational force.

Puppy said no thanks to participating in the cheating. The cheaters, realizing they were exposed, tried to threaten him. Two broken jaws and one dislocated shoulder resulted, none of which were Puppy's. The course leadership disbanded that team.

He joined us the first week of February. From his first mission on our team, Puppy erased any doubts or concerns that lingered in our minds. This was a go-to guy you could count on. But it was three nights later that we would learn what he was truly made of.

The Army Safety Center can give every detail regarding our student A Team training mission of 9 February 2017. The mission degenerated in the classic pattern of catastrophic mishaps. There was no single precursor. Instead, multiple small events conspired to reach critical mass. Had our team, the schoolhouse leadership, the support units – had any of these managed to break the chain of just one of those culminating events – then things might have ended differently. Instead, a good outcome stayed just out of reach. The Safety Center's full report delineates each of these factors in great detail. It attributes cause and effect, and records the accountability imposed on various members of the training cadre and chain of command.

What the report won't explain is a truism of the military and of life in general. Many times, our closest friends come from our worst days. This would be the day Ulysses and I became friends with Puppy Jackson.

As the surviving instructor, Alex Martel gave sworn testimony to the Safety Center investigators. His interview transcript provides a succinct account of that evening:

12 February 2017
Sworn testimony interview: Army Safety Center team to Instructor Team Sergeant Martel, pertaining to Training Mission 17-H-089, 09 February 2017

Army Safety Center: Please identify yourself for the record.
Instructor Team Sergeant: Master Sergeant Alex Martel
ASC: Please provide a brief background regarding the instructor team commander and yourself.
Martel: Captain Stephen Joll was the instructor team commander. He had two combat tours as an Infantry lieutenant, prior to joining

Special Forces branch. Most recently, he had completed a combat tour to Afghanistan in command of an A Team in Helmand province. I have seventeen years in service, fourteen of those in operational units. This includes eleven years on A Teams, four of those as team sergeant.

ASC: How many combat tours have you had during that time?

Martel: I'd have to go back and count. More than eight years cumulative time in combat zones.

ASC: How long had you and Captain Joll been assigned as instructors?

Martel: I had been there just over eighteen months. Captain Joll was nearing the one year mark.

ASC: Where were you in the course progression, and what was the mission on the night in question?

Martel: We had completed eighty-five percent of the team field phase missions. The team was continuing to operate from patrol bases, as part of their training and evaluation in austere environments. It had been an unusually cold winter, which was good. You want as hard as possible environmental conditions. This mission was short notice, driven by an intel tipper. It was a High-Value Target meeting. For those series of missions, we were operating to the east of the N-series compounds on Camp Diamond. According to the notional intel, the HVT meeting would occur in a specific building on the N3 compound. The meeting participants would have two SUVs parked outside.

ASC: Any other unique factors on this mission?

Martel: This mission profile was designed to test student resourcefulness in the face of extreme time/distance constraints. From the time of warning order, they would have four hours to move tactically over eleven kilometers through mountainous terrain. They would move the last half of that after nightfall, before the hit time. The time constraints meant it was not possible to carry full rucks, full kit, and possibly make the hit. The student leadership team came up with the generally desired response. They cached and concealed their rucks with most of their equipment at the patrol base. Twenty-five minutes after receiving the warning order, they departed in a combat light configuration.

ASC: What was the temperature at departure, and what cold weather equipment did the team carry?

Martel: The temperature had actually warmed up some. It was thirty-eight degrees Fahrenheit at departure. Each student and the instructors wore a Gore-Tex shell with a light insulating layer underneath. Each person had an additional layer stashed in their assault pack. One student carried an emergency sleeping bag, in a stripped down rucksack, in case of a cold weather casualty requiring treatment.

ASC: What other safety mitigators did you have in place?

Martel: We had several mitigators. The first was to confirm that the weather forecast was in parameters for a combat light mission profile. We checked about fifteen minutes before issuing the warning order. It was due to stay in the upper thirties with no precipitation called for. The sleeping bag was our in-team mitigator. We had three external safety mitigators in place. The first comprised the Camp Diamond emergency response helicopters stationed at main post. On the night in question, two UH-60s were on call for medevac. The second external mitigator consisted of ground response, from the HVT role players, in their pair of large SUVs. Red Creek Road ran through the central portion of our dismounted movement to compound N3. In the event of emergency, they would retrieve us along Red Creek Road and transport us either back to our patrol base or to main post. The final safety mitigator was an old hunting cabin, located in the last third of our movement corridor. The cabin was on the eastern slope of Cardiac Gap. We would pass through the Gap en route to N3 and we could shelter in the cabin if needed.

ASC: Describe what transpired as movement proceeded to the target.

Martel: The first half of movement was uneventful. Then the freak weather pattern came in. As I understand it, Camp Diamond and this portion of West Virginia was hit by an Alberta Clipper weather event, pushing down from the Great Lakes. It mixed with the warmer weather pattern that was already in the area.

ASC: And what happened?

Martel: We had an hour of driving rain. The temperature was approximately thirty-five degrees with gusts up to twenty-five miles per hour. Everyone was soaked to the bone, even with Gore-Tex. Then a rapid temperature drop started. The precipitation shifted to sleet and freezing rain. We kept pushing on to the target, as at this point there was no need to abort the mission. Pressing on also continued to move us closer to our safety mitigators, should we need them. Conditions continued to worsen. Footing became a problem. The slopes there are steep and alternate between wooded slope and rock formation. Ice built up from the freezing rain. We had about 1.5 kilometers to proceed until Red Creek Road. I anticipated we might have to abort at that point, due to the growing hypothermia risk. Red Creek Road would be the natural place to make the call, either to land the helicopters or load up in the SUVs.

ASC: What happened next?

Martel: This was when trainee Staunton slipped on a rocky patch going downslope. He sustained a compound fracture to his right tibia. We called an admin endex to the mission. The student medics applied a splint to Staunton. We then placed Staunton in the emergency sleeping bag for warmth. We rigged a poncho into an emergency litter and prepared him for transport.

ASC: What next?

Martel: We called for emergency medevac via the two UH-60 helicopters. It was dusk by now. Meanwhile we continued movement, carrying Staunton toward Red Creek Road. Main post was taking longer than normal to provide medevac confirmation. Fifteen minutes later, main post replied with word of a fuel contamination in the helicopters.

Both birds were down. Then the Alberta Clipper intensified. The clouds opened and the temperature dropped below ten degrees Fahrenheit. We were soaked to the bone from the earlier rain. Captain Joll and I knew this was potentially lethal. Wind gusts continued at over twenty-five miles per hour. In those conditions, we could not reliably build a fire for warmth.

ASC: What follow-up actions did you take?

Martel: We had just over a kilometer to Red Creek Road. We rotated carrying Staunton on the poncho litter. Captain Joll and I called the HVT role players to meet us for pickup on the road, in their SUVs.

ASC: And?

Martel: I think you already have reports of the main post weather conditions on file.

ASC: Please state for the record.

Martel: The whole post was immobilized with ice-covered roads. The HVT role players couldn't get to us. Main post tried sending Stryker wheeled vehicles also. But the approach roads up to the N series compounds were too steep given the ice conditions. By now it was full dark. For the record, the role players in the SUVs never stopped trying to reach us. They were digging up dirt with their entrenching tools and applying it for traction under their tires. But it was just too slow. They weren't even making a kilometer an hour.

ASC: You reached the road by the time you determined that ground evacuation by SUV was also not feasible?

Martel: Yes, at this point we're on Red Creek Road. We were all spent from carrying Staunton that far. But only one play was left. We had to climb the twelve-hundred feet up to the cabin at Cardiac Gap. The approach up that eastern slope to the Gap is extremely steep, and primarily rocky terrain. By now, there was a three-quarter-inch sheet of ice on every surface. It was the tipping point.

ASC: Please describe the movement up to the cabin. Including, to the best of your knowledge, where the fatalities occurred.

Martel: We started up the slope, carrying trainee Staunton. For two hundred feet we could navigate the slope with his litter, just barely. Two or three students would step up a few rocks, and the rest of us would push the litter. That took ninety minutes. We'd slip back down at least every third try. It was hurting Staunton terribly. He'd scream out. Then we hit the steeper part of the slope. That litter simply wasn't going any farther. We were spent. Everyone was shaking violently. The winds continued steady at twenty miles per hour with gusts over thirty.

ASC: So you proceeded to the cabin?

Martel: Yes, no. We need to give context. That's when Puppy, I mean trainee Jackson, that's when he performed one of the most incredible actions I've witnessed in seventeen years as an operator.

ASC: Under your and Captain Joll's orders?

Martel: No. I have to be very clear here. Joll and I were working the situation, yes. But we were all barely conscious at that point. Trainee Jackson, of his own initiative, removed trainee Staunton from the litter and strapped Staunton onto his back. He then proceeded to carry Staunton the remaining nine hundred feet of the scramble climb to the cabin. Jackson got the cabin opened and, from what I could see from down slope, it only took him a couple of minutes to get a fire going and a lantern hung to vector in the rest of the team.

Martel (cont): At this point, the rest of the team was barely making a hundred feet every twenty minutes up the slope. Guys in twos and threes were trying to help each other. But now others were starting to succumb to hypothermia. After hauling trainee Staunton, I don't know at all how trainee Jackson found the stamina to return back down the slope to us. He kept making laps until we were all accounted for in the cabin. Joll and I were helping trainee Jones. Every time Jackson came back down, we directed him to whichever student was hurting the worst. Jackson would grab or sling that student and head up the mountain. I can't remember when I lost consciousness. The other students were adamant that Jackson personally saved at least three teammates that night. Trainee Jones and Captain Joll were too far gone and succumbed to hypothermia by the time Jackson got them inside. Staunton survived. His leg is expected to fully heal, though slowly. Once the pins are out and rehab is complete, Staunton states he will apply to re-enter the next available Qualification course.

ASC: Thank you for your comments. Is there anything else you would care to add?

Martel: Yes. Jackson's teammates have unanimously recommended him for course honor grad. That's a no brainer. I will also submit him for the Soldier's Medal, the highest peacetime award for valor. I'd ask that this transcript be provided to the command, to serve as supporting documentation for the award nomination.

ASC: Thank you. For the record, yes, we will submit this transcript in support of that nomination.

- 12 -

19 August 2029 – Compound N3, Camp Diamond, WV

Puppy and I stand at the center of the compound. We each savor a second cup of coffee before the crush of morning work begins. I enjoy the old compound digs and their simple functionality. The buildings have rough cut, unpainted wood shingles and siding. Inside, they have simple appointments with linoleum floors and bare-wood furniture. The sleeping quarters house thin-mattress wooden bunks. Each of the M and N series compounds follows a common template. Large one-story buildings at center provide common facilities for the mess, ops center, washrooms, and logistics. Around them spread two concentric rings of sleeping cabins, each housing ten to thirty individuals.

This place was deserted a week ago. Today it's crawling with more than four hundred former special operators. We'll work and billet here until deployment. The other leased compounds are also filling up. Ulysses continues to supervise the personnel hires. As operators arrive, he assigns them into teams of twelve.

Looking around, several teams are returning from extended morning workouts. They're soaked through with sweat. One team in full kit carries a field stretcher with one of their mates on board, a simulated casualty. Another team, in running garb, drags back home. They look exhausted, sporting scraped knees and blank stares. From their condition, I'd say an old-school team sergeant has just run them up the Gap.

Puppy sees that team and then looks up to the Gap itself. "It doesn't seem like it's been twelve years," he says.

I feel the humid air and look along the ridgeline to see green leaves on the oak trees. "Twelve years and two seasons."

He chuckles. "You know, we'd all be dead if that training mission happened today. They tore down the old hunting cabin four years ago. We'd have all frozen to death."

"You ever hear from Alex Martel?"

"Not lately. Crossed paths with him a couple times on deployment. I heard he retired out to Wyoming."

My thoughts shift to the task at hand. I'm gradually coming to accept that this mission will happen. A private army from Enterprise Performance is going to attack the Russians in the Emirates, with intent to evict them.

For sure, Simon's lobbying team has built a tailwind of public support. He's packaged the right pundits and elected officials. They carry a unified message: removing the Russian choke hold is critical to global economic stability. Ideally, the talking heads all caveat, diplomacy will resolve the crisis. But if not, we must act by force. And given our American military atrophy and political gridlock, this country needs a better, faster, cheaper way to get the job done.

Yesterday I paid a visit to Major General Saiz at his office. I needed to hear, one last time, that the Joint Chiefs and senior Army leadership saw this mercenary task force as inevitable. We met in his wood-paneled executive suite, where the walls spoke to why he served. No ego fluff hung there, nor any of the perfunctory VIP photos and awards that he often received. Instead, you see pictures of him with family, and photos of a younger Saiz in the ranks with team mates.

In all, our meeting lasted less than ten minutes. Neither of us had time to waste.

"Sir, I'll follow through," I said to Saiz. "But it's disturbing, unprecedented. Are you and the senior military absolutely sure there's no backing away from this?"

We sat in matching armchairs, in one corner of the office. For a reply, he didn't speak. He simply picked up a remote to the flat panel TV on the wall. In quick succession, he flipped through cable news interviews that included a current Senator from one party, a recent White House Chief of Staff from the other party, and one of the more popular national pundits:

". . . If this administration had the guts to enact the reforms we'd asked for, then we wouldn't be in this situation . . ."

". . . Charlene, what you have to understand is, our party could have fixed most of these problems years ago. But the gridlock in Congress prevented any meaningful action . . ."

". . . look, it's too late to argue about how or why we got here. The reality is, Simons' proposal for an Enterprise Performance private military solution is the most viable option we have. And frankly, it's about time to give the private sector a crack at it. There are surely efficiencies to be gained . . ."

Saiz pulled over his laptop and set it open on the small coffee table in front of us. He scrolled through social media feeds that ranged from mildly supportive to rabid endorsement of Simons. He looked at me and with a resigned but weary tone said, "Mark, this horse has left the barn."

So that's it. If the elected leadership comes to its senses and calls this off, or if diplomatic engagement rises to the occasion and negotiates a peaceful outcome, that will be someone else's job. My job is to take this mad experiment and make it succeed.

Now Ulysses walks over from the Ops Center to where Puppy and I are standing. "Hey, gents, time to get started."

"Roger that," Puppy says. He slings coffee dregs into the grass. "Let's officially kick off this freak show." He walks inside with me not far behind.

We enter the long, low-slung ops center. It's alive with mission planning. Puppy organized the work space. He's left most of the building configured for free-flow collaboration. Planners cluster four or five to a table. Each planning team works specific subcomponents to our deployment. Large flat-panel screens on one wall tally the status of our buildup or other universally required information. One screen carries a muted multi-channel feed, with cable news in the main panel and smaller scrolls of social media, so we can catch any flash updates from the Emirates.

Past this planning area we walk into a partitioned-off briefing room. It can hold six full teams and it's already at capacity. Simons is seated in the first row of bench seats with one of the teams. That's good.

Ulysses and Puppy were adamant to Simons about the need to establish a personal connection within any operational unit growing as fast as ours. Fortunately, from Simons' time building flat, dynamic e-commerce companies, he understood this. Even though we'll disperse widely before it's all done, every newly formed team spends its first week here at Cardiac Gap. Simons will have time to meet them all.

Bringing each team through here also gives Ulysses and me time to make sure they form to our liking. We can impart expected standards. This indoc period gives us time to personally brief each team on the information we have to date. We can frame a common understanding of the problem set. And they can gain confidence in the rigor of the mission planning.

We rotate individually among the teams during that week they spend here. From the looks of it, Simons partook in early morning combatives with the team he's shadowing today. They surely went easy on him. But he's got a red crease over one eye. Inside this compound, that buys more cred than anything he brings from Silicon Valley.

I step up to the front of the room, where the display screens are dark at the moment. It's good to look out and see familiar faces. Everyone's in matching field camo – a good sign that our logistics are keeping pace. It's also a simple but important visual cue to the operators that this is a real organization that has its act together. A mismatch of everyone wearing whatever cammies they'd brought would send the wrong message at this stage.

Time for me to kick off. "Hey folks, it's good to see the teams forming up. We have a lot of familiar faces in this bunch, and not just from 8th Special Forces Group. It's good to see former SEALS, Marine Raiders, Rangers. A lot of us have worked together on joint task forces in the past, and it will be exactly the same here. Given the speed of the buildup, we're pulled in a lot of directions. Right now, we'll cover some key information and then cut you loose to continue getting work done."

I gesture to Simons, who stands up in the front row and turns to face the group. He's silent for several seconds before speaking: his sometimes halting style that takes some getting used to. "I've met three of the teams in here. The other three, we'll spend time together before you proceed to your assigned compound. Hopefully without too many more souvenirs." He points to his combatives welt. This gets a few laughs, all in approval.

He continues. "We're building something new here. How to build it, how to do what you do, I can't speak to any of that. But one thing I am good at is disrupting the old order when it no longer works. And for whatever reason, we've arrived at a place where, as a nation, it seems like too many times we haven't been able to make things work the right way. Enterprise Performance makes things work, in anything we've done. And we have deep pockets. What we don't have financially, we can leverage. I'm confident that this endeavor will work, and I'll stake everything I've got on it. If this is what it takes to push the Russians out of the Emirates, then this is what we're going to do." He looks at me and nods, then retakes his seat.

"All right," I pick up, "we're at 19 August today. Presuming diplomatic efforts fail, Enterprise Performance will strike Russian positions in the Emirates and regain access to Persian Gulf sea lanes by October first. That's six weeks to build, plan and execute against a seasoned force. That's the tough news."

I look around. The faces are serious. "The good news is, we have things in our favor. The Russians have gotten used to their *fait accompli* model. For twenty years, no one has called their bluff when they took hold of a new chunk of territory. It will add to the shock value when we do call that bluff. Also, we're going to put some twists in the ops plan that should give them fits. That's under wraps for now. Today, we'll cover the enemy situation and intel." I grab a seat off to the side.

Puppy stands up to open the intel brief. "The first thing is to introduce Dr. Laura Evan." He motions to the back of the room, and she joins him. She can't stand more than five feet tall. "Dr. Evan is on faculty at Georgetown. Around 8th Group, she's been a valued consultant for her expertise on the Russian military, especially regarding their intervention strategy of the past few decades. She's also the most knowledgeable US scholar on Major General Petrikov, the Russian commander for this Emirates incursion. She just arrived, and you're lucky to be the first cohort of teams to receive her brief. Dr. Evan, over to you."

"Thanks, Hugh. I know your time is compressed. We'll stick to the essentials. The first is to gain a little understanding of Petrikov, both his history and how he operates. Mr. Simons, have you ever studied him?" She looks over to him.

"Court," he corrects.

"Very well, Court, do you know much about Petrikov?"

"Not much. Yes, please start with the very basics."

"Very well. Petrikov is a Major General in the Russian Army. But his rank is misleading. With his connections and battlefield success, he has the same throw weight as any other full Army General in the Russian System. If and when Putin ever steps down, many consider Petrikov a legitimate contender for succession."

Ulysses asks, "Does Putin consider him a rival?"

"Great question. You'd think so. But no. We think that comes from a symbiotic arrangement. Petrikov stays out on campaign. For now, he appears content in his autonomy as Putin's favorite fixer out in the field."

She stops and thinks silently for a moment, half smiles at a connection she's just made. "Actually, you know, Petrikov now has a fair amount in common with this Enterprise Performance effort."

That catches Simons attention. "How so?" he asks.

"Well, Petrikov started out as a purely military leader. But over the years he morphed a large portion of his Battalion Tactical Groups over to private contractor models. It's provided him more flexibility and deniability in their employment. Some speculate he's also got an ownership stake in the companies that hold the contracts."

Simons nods, but his face gives no window into his thoughts.

Dr. Evan continues.

"Petrikov started as a young Airborne officer. At some point, he transferred into Spetsnaz and then rose through the ranks of their Special Operations Forces. He gained notoriety during an early career event at Katyr Yurt, during the Chechen campaign. Does anyone know that story?"

About a third of those present nod their heads. The others perk up to hear details.

"He was a young lieutenant. Katyr Yurt was a remote village in his operational sector. One morning Petrikov led a convoy of armored vehicles escorting aid supplies to the village. The population there had dwindled from several thousand down to just a few hundred. The Russians considered it a strategic location, so the Army had orders to continue humanitarian aid.

"The soldiers hated it because of the risks involved. Strong rebel units operated in the area. On the morning in question, Petrikov's convoy was maybe a kilometer from the edge of the town, Katyr Yurt, when a young girl ran in front of the lead armored vehicle. The vehicle commander yelled at the driver not to stop. They were in an obvious kill zone and the Russian units held no concern for the life of a bystander. But the vehicle driver froze.

"Petrikov lost half his vehicles and men to well-placed RPG fire. The Russian vehicles had heavy weapons and eventually gained fire superiority. They drove the rebels back into the town. But now the rebels spread throughout the entire village. Petrikov only had a platoon left, not enough men to clear house to house. He was furious at the losses he'd taken. Plus, he knew that the residents were sympathetic and harboring the rebels.

"Petrikov ordered his tanks to shell any buildings that appeared to hold occupants. Civilians took some casualties, but most hunkered down. The Russians were beside themselves to make the rebels pay. After an hour, Petrikov addressed the town by loudspeaker from his vehicle. He announced that an air strike was inbound. The village had a school with the buses still parked out front. Petrikov gave the villagers twenty minutes for all non-combatants to board the buses and evacuate. They could tell he meant business. The civilians rushed onto the buses and departed. The convoy made it about four kilometers out of the Katyr Yurt when the air strike hit.

"Petrikov had received four fast movers, fighters, for the air strike. He directed them all onto the civilian bus convoy. The planes dropped fuel air explosives. No one on those buses survived."

The lecture hall grows quiet. This is a seasoned crew. But you can tell by watching who hasn't heard this story before.

Dr. Evan continues. "That's Petrikov math. With four aircraft, he couldn't take out rebels spread throughout a large village. But he could make sure the rebels knew who he was, and this was his message to them: Find other Russian units to attack. And it worked. Petrikov patrolled that sector for the rest of their rotation in Chechnya. The rebels never fired another shot at his formation."

At this point, Ken Bowerman walks up to the front of the room and joins Dr. Evan. I haven't seen Ken much since the Senegal rescue mission. Bowerman was one of our best team sergeants in the old battalion. Ulysses pulled him in to help plan the overall operation.

Dr. Evan greets him. "Thanks for joining, Ken." Then to the teams she explains, "Since we're tight for time, I asked Ken to keep us focused on information most helpful for the incoming operators."

"Thanks, Dr. Evan," he replies. "Could you hit the milestones of Petrikov's career in the years since?"

"Very well," she says. "We know Petrikov held a mid-level command during the 2008 Georgia intervention. He rose through the ranks in the Ukraine, and by the time of their Syrian operation he became the chief Russian strategist for what they call New Generation Warfare."

"And just to get us on the same page, Dr. Evan, how would you define New Generation Warfare?" Smart move on Bowerman's part. The person in the audience who probably knows the least on this is

Simons, and he'll need to understand it.

"Sure thing, Ken. New generation warfare takes a more nuanced, targeted, and indirect approach to military aims than the old Soviet models. Their World War Two and Cold War formations relied on mass. They would overwhelm opponents with large conventional formations, heavy with tanks and artillery. That strategy sought to bludgeon their enemy with brute force."

"What caused them to change?" Bowerman asks.

"Great question. Part of it was monetary. The massive scale of their old military buildup bankrupted the Soviets. Part of it was tactical effectiveness. In the Georgia incursion of '08, the Russians tried to rely on their old model, leading with armored columns manned by draftees. They took heavy losses. This led them to develop smaller, better trained formations. The third factor for change was geopolitical. The overt Georgian incursion incited huge political backlash from Europe and the US, which is little surprise."

"So, the Ukraine operation and since have been this New Generation Warfare?"

"Exactly. In the Ukraine, for example, hundreds of undeclared combatants flooded across the border. These were the so called 'little green men.' They fought as Battalion Tactical Groups of several hundred soldiers, augmented with larger paramilitary forces. In the Ukraine these were generally ethnic Russians, sympathetic to the cause. In Syria and later they have co-opted support from whomever they can."

"What can you tell us about numbers of soldiers involved?"

"That's an interesting point," Dr. Evan replies. "They've refined their approach. Their formations continue to become smaller. In the Ukraine, we know they deployed several tens of thousands. By Syria, they limited their numbers to around ten thousand in total. And now – this is interesting – we estimate they took the Emirates with roughly twenty-five hundred ground troops. This includes a mix of special operators, armored vehicle crews, and missile battery crew for their anti-air and anti-ship systems."

"Thanks, Dr. Evan, that's a good segue to review the Emirates specifically."

"Absolutely. Their move on the United Arab Emirates, or UAE, shows the Russians' most sophisticated incursion yet. On the 22nd of July, large-scale cyberattacks hit the entire country. This also took down the electric grid. The combination had immediate effects on the Emirates' Federal Defense Force. It also crippled their government leadership's ability to respond. Emirati communications went down and, for the most part, never recovered."

Dr. Evan continues, "The treachery of Russian strategy became apparent over the next several days. Like most modern Middle Eastern countries, the Emirates had developed complete dependence on air conditioning for their commercial and residential architecture. Even more critically, they depend on ocean desalination for fresh water. Neither of these functions without electricity. News feeds show it best."

She points a remote toward one of the screens, and pulls up a newscast recorded on July 29th. That's just over two weeks ago.

A British-accented voice narrates, *"This is Brent Tighman with World News Network. It has been five days since cyberattacks and power outages first wracked the Emirates. With daily highs topping forty-five degrees Celsius, or one hundred thirteen degrees Fahrenheit, the situation has quickly gone from unbearable to lethal. Desalinization plants remain offline. The UAE can meet less than ten percent of daily freshwater needs from its legacy-sourced well water. Without electricity, however, even well water becomes inaccessible. Lack of air conditioning has compounded problems, turning the skyscrapers of Abu Dhabi and Dubai into near-ovens. Water riots commenced late on the 22nd and have quickly grown."*

Date stamped footage shows rioting crowds that appear to be in the hundreds on the 22nd, and in the thousands on the 23rd. By the 24th, the crowds are somewhat smaller, and the first bodies on the street are visible. By the 25th, the entrances to skyscrapers are flanked with several dozen bodies stacked two- and three-deep.

"The young, the old and the infirm began succumbing on the second day. The problem has cascaded since then. By the third day, heat related deaths reached epidemic proportion."

The scene cuts to Dubai International Airport, with long snaking lines of people. The next scene shows two jetliners burning on the tarmac.

"Upper class Emiratis and Western expats clamored to leave the country on outbound flights. At the same time, international aid groups began emergency shipments of water and humanitarian supplies. Then, on July 24th, the Emirati Liberation Committee, or ELC, a previously unknown terrorist group, began bombings at airports and sea cargo facilities in the country. With the Emirati defense forces already hobbled, the ability to maintain order has crumbled."

Another scene shows a burning cargo ship in the Zayed port facility in Abu Dhabi.

"The ELC claims responsibility for the cyberattacks in the Emirates. The next day, on the 25th, the ELC claimed responsibility for bombings in Damascus, Baghdad, and on the main Russian military base in Syria. The ELC declared their sovereignty over the Emirates. UAE Prime Minister Al Nahyan vowed to quell the mysterious terrorist group. But by the 26th, with Emirati oil and gas exports cut off for almost a week, and with a new ELC-attributed bombing in Cairo, world patience has grown thin. Two days ago, the 27th, Vladimir Putin declared that Russia will intervene for the sake of regional stability."

The video feed cuts to aerial imagery of Abu Dhabi. Reports state that the Russians pummeled the capital with cruise missiles to "pacify the ELC" before their ground forces deployed to the country. A panoramic of the Abu Dhabi skyline shows pillars of smoke climbing toward the sky. Several skyscrapers are on fire, and at least one has toppled. The camera zooms in to show the Al Akhdar Presidential Palace is nothing but smoking rubble. Bodies float in one of the large reflecting pools on the palace grounds.

The final clip, from July 28th, shows Russian special operators disembarking from large transport planes at the major airports and from helicopters that flew directly into Dubai and Abu Dhabi. A concluding scene shows food supplies at the airports and a still photo of Dubai's major desalinization plant. The narration concludes:

"Yesterday seemed to bring a turning point. Russian forces claimed to have neutralized ELC opposition. Major General Petrikov, the commander for Russian stabilization operations, has declared his number one priority is protection of the populace and restoration of life-support functions. International aid flights have resumed with Russian forces safeguarding distribution in the country. Our sources report that power was over eighty percent restored by yesterday evening. As of this morning, we understand that more than three quarters of the country's desalinization capacity is back in service."

The clip finishes and one of the newly arrived team leaders poses the obvious question. "So, just to be clear, no one here thinks the ELC was anything more than a strawman excuse for the Russians to enter the country?"

"That's the consensus of the Western intelligence community," Dr. Evan replies. "There has been no previous reporting on this group. It's consistent with Petrikov's approach in past campaigns. They want to contrive a political fig leaf to justify their incursion. Even if it's not believed, it causes enough hesitation that by the time the international community can agree to a collective response, it's too late. The Russians have consolidated their gains."

Ken Bowerman asks, "Dr. Evan, from the footage it looks like they hit Abu Dhabi harder than Dubai. Can you comment on what you know of their tactical and strategic aims?"

"Certainly, and Ken you're correct. They hit Abu Dhabi hard with surface-to-surface missiles and SU-57 fifth-generation fighters, all based in Syria. In short, the Russians consider Abu Dhabi expendable. As the national capital, they hit Abu Dhabi hard to render the Emirati leadership unwilling to resist. Dubai is the Russian center of gravity for their follow on efforts. It's the closest major city to the Strait of Hormuz. The strait is the choke point from the Persian Gulf into the Gulf of Oman and then the Arabian Sea." Dr. Evan scrolls one screen to a map of the region.

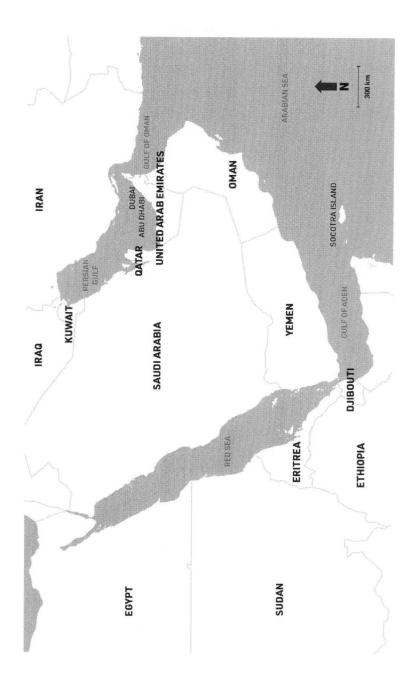

Looking up at the screen, she continues, "In the days after Russian troops arrived by air, they consolidated their gains with heavier firepower. We've counted one hundred fifty of their new Armata armored fighting vehicles on the ground. The T-14 is the tank variant, with a one hundred twenty-five-millimeter main gun. The T-15 variant has a thirty-millimeter auto cannon and can transport nine assault troops in the back. Both versions also carry Kornet anti-tank missiles. In and around Dubai they've placed batteries of S-400 anti-aircraft missiles, the long-range versions that can reach out four hundred kilometers.

"To control Persian Gulf shipping, they've seeded the land approaches to the strait with K-300 anti-ship missiles. Those missiles can range over three hundred and fifty kilometers. The strait at its narrowest is less than sixty kilometers. The bottom line is, they can shut down shipping any time they want. Twenty percent of world oil production flows through the strait. The Russians say they need to stay in the Emirates to assure the continuous and free flow of oil. To 'subsidize' the cost of their protection, they are demanding first rights to all oil that flows through, at sub-market prices. And for the oil that does pass through for international distribution, they're demanding transit taxes. This has Western Europe, the US, and Japan all in an uproar."

Ulysses gestures to wrap things up. "Thanks, Dr. Evan. We have to get this crew outside right now. It will take a few tricks up our sleeve to get the drop on Petrikov. We've got a chance to see one of those right now. You're welcome to join us."

Everyone follows Ulysses outside. We walk past the outer ring of cabins to an open area. For a minute or two, there's dead silence. Team members look around.

A faint whirring registers in the distance. As it grows louder, you can distinguish by sound a pair of prop aircraft approaching at high speed from the North. They're coming in low, not visible yet over the ridgelines. One of the new arrivals smiles and says to a buddy, "Tiltrotors."

More faces light up. In the early 2000s, the US military fielded a few hundred V-22 Ospreys, the first generation tiltrotor aircraft. The size of a commuter plane, they take off like helicopters, then arc the rotors to the front and gain forward flight. But the V-22s were first generation and had extensive teething problems. Expensive to maintain, the military inventory dropped below fifty airframes by the mid 2020s. Not nearly enough to make a difference for our needs.

Ulysses gives the answer, right as the two birds pop over a ridge at over two hundred and fifty knots, maybe a mile out. "It's the V-280. DOD couldn't afford them when they came online several years back. But Enterprise Performance can afford them."

From about two thousand feet in the air, they swoop down directly toward us. Twin props whir at the outboard of each wing. Painted dark green, they're smaller and sleeker than a V-22, but they can still transport fourteen combat troops in the back. At the last minute, while headed straight for us, each 280 pitches nose up and arcs their rotors into hover mode with the blades overhead. Carrying forward momentum, they settle into a perfect landing right in front of us. Downwash air blows dead grass and hot dust into our faces, but most everyone has a grin. This is more evidence that we're playing to win.

The engines shut down, and crew chiefs open the large sliding doors on either side. "Alright," Ulysses says loudly over the noise, "you're the first teams to train on them. You've got forty-eight hours. Take them out, day, night, every mission profile and infil/exfil scenario you can think of. Get the air crews' input, too. Exactly four days from now, provide written SOPs that we can disseminate to the rest of our force. You're now our air mobility experts for the V-280."

The teams step forward, meeting the crews and crawling through the airframes like kids at Christmas.

- 13 -

19 September 2029 – Atlantic Ocean, 100 NM East of
Charleston, SC

What a way to go to war. We're packed in the *Sandefjord,* a civilian
leased ro-ro, or roll-on/roll-off cargo ship. It will get the job done,
though. Launched in the early 2020s, the Mark VI class of ships are
the pride and joy of the Norwegian Karlsen Group. At three hundred
twenty meters, *Sandefjord* and her three siblings are the largest ro-ros
ever to sail. This feels like being in a shopping mall that's traveling
across the ocean.

We need every inch of her seven decks. I'm standing on the
bottom deck right now, filled with V-280s. Each deck runs the length
of the ship with almost no obstructions. This makes a good modular
setup for our needs. The second deck holds the balance of the 280s,
with leftover space that serves as our ops center. Third and fourth
decks remain open, for physical training and rehearsals. That leaves
the upper decks for modular living quarters, installed for our transit.

Four hours into this leg of the journey, everyone's got their
personal gear stowed and we're ready to get to work. I head to the
second deck ops center, where we've got our command element and
fifty key leaders assembled. This planning group is facing two large

mission screens, with Ulysses and Puppy up front. Simons is seated off to one side. Half the group is sitting. The others don't bother. We've got a lot to do, and they know this will be quick.

We're running a flat task organization for the Emirates op. The teams cluster in threes. A senior team leader in each cluster has primary responsibility for planning and training. The other two team leaders report to that senior until we infil for the mission. Every team is interchangeable, but this structure lets us spiral out updates and mission mods quickly.

"OK," I say, "this is an initial info dump, so you can shape the ops context for your teams. We'll refine with daily reviews during our time in transit." Our four weeks at Camp Diamond allowed the teams to train up proficiently. One drill included fluid combinations for multi-team tactics to eliminate an enemy strongpoint, then break back to separate teams after defeating the threat. This keeps our formation unpredictable to the enemy. It also makes it harder to take out multiple teams at once.

For today's brief, I need to review how we'll parse the enemy's strength, turning the Russians' tactical array in the Emirates into a weakness we can exploit. "You'll recall, from Dr. Evan's intel brief, that Petrikov took a force of twenty-five hundred Russians into country. That's the gross. Let's look at what we'll have to fight by component. Take out the logisticians, and battery crews for their S-400 anti-aircraft missiles and K-300 anti-ship missiles. That effectively cuts a thousand from their ground combat headcount. They have one hundred fifty Armatas, either tank or infantry variant. Each Armata takes a crew of three. That takes it down to a thousand special operators they'll have on the ground. And yes, that's a powerful combination of Armatas plus special operators."

I click open the same area map Dr. Evan had used and gesture with a laser pointer.

"But look at the problems they bought. They need to cover almost two hundred linear miles with that force. Their force is spread between Abu Dhabi to the southwest, Dubai in the center, and then their K-300 ship batteries pushed dozens of miles to the northeast where they cover the shipping lanes."

I circle Dubai, in the center. "We'll mass here. Dubai is our center of gravity. We expect they'll have one hundred Armatas and six hundred special operators holding Dubai itself. We can best a force of that size. And taking Dubai pays off big. That's where Petrikov has placed his command center. It's also where the Russians run their logistics support. We take out their Dubai footprint and the rest dies on the vine. Also, their S-400 anti-air missiles are in Dubai. We take those out and then our reinforcements from the former 11th Airborne can jump in to support. Now, Ulysses will break out the full force we're bringing to bear on the Russians."

Ulysses clicks to the second slide with our final task organization. "Let's start with air superiority. Latest intel states the Russians have twelve SU-57 fighters in Syria. That plus the S-400s will make for highly contested air space. Against this, Enterprise Performance will field forty-eight F-35 Joint Strike Fighters, staging from Kuwait. Their call sign is Lightning Flight. Technically, the airframes are leased to EP with the pilots and support crew on leave from the Air Force for the duration of their contract."

The lease and contract status generates side-long glances throughout the room. No one said this arrangement was pretty.

Ulysses continues. "Part of Lightning Flight will fly air cover against the SU-57s in Syria. Lighting's remaining F-35s fly interdiction against the S-400s. That's really the key. Take out the S-400s. Then we can keep using the F-35s to pummel the Russian Armatas, and to provide close air support when the paratroopers jump in to reinforce us."

"Where are the S-400 batteries located?" one of the team leaders asks.

"Great question. They move periodically," Ulysses replies. "We'll track them until H Hour and adjust the interdiction plan as needed. OK, now, more info on the airborne reinforcements. Thanks to the 11th Airborne deactivating two of its brigades, we have twenty-five hundred paratroopers on contract and ready to jump. They'll operate as Task Force Zeus, and jump from forty-eight Air Force C-130Js, once we give them all clear that the S-400s are out of action. And yes, it's the same arrangement for the Zeus C-130s, temporary lease and contract."

Folks are getting the drift. Courtney Simons negotiated the use of prime Air Force equipment and crew for a total of two month's rent. He's getting several billion dollars' value in airframes and career training costs. I have it on good authority that the lease costs him less than ninety mil.

"Now for our main assault force." Ulysses points to our task organization diagram. "We have one hundred fifty V-280s, call sign TF Valor. Twenty-one hundred of us will infil this way. Mark, Puppy and I will be in the command element in the first bird. The other hundred and forty-nine airframes each carry a team."

A hand goes up in the back. "Where did the V-280s come from?" she asks.

Ulysses hesitates slightly, long enough that Simons speaks up. "Four years ago, Enterprise Performance bought them direct from the assembly line. We got them for a steal after DOD couldn't follow through on their purchase. We subcontracted them to regional transport companies in South America. When the Emirates mission hit, we pulled them back for refit to military spec."

I'm sure several have the same question as me. Simons bought the 280s four years ago – coincidence?

Puppy steps forward. "OK, if you paid attention back at Camp Diamond, you saw that not all the teams came with us onto the boat. While we infil by air in TF Valor, the other teams will conduct a ground infil as part of TF Mauler. Here's their ride." He points behind the group. No one had paid much attention, but to get to our briefing area, we had walked past two large pieces of equipment, each tarped.

Puppy walks over and removes both tarps to reveal Israeli Merkava tracked fighting vehicles. That generates some priceless looks, even some hoots. Each Merkava weighs sixty-five tons, built squat at twelve feet wide and about six feet tall to the top of the hull. Wedge-shaped turrets take the overall height to nine feet. Desert tan paint decks out both vehicles.

Puppy explains, "Courtesy of US diplomatic engagement, the Israelis are leasing us two hundred copies of their top-end armor. They'll operate as TF Mauler. A hundred of them are the tank variant, with one hundred twenty-millimeter main guns. The other hundred are the Namer infantry variant. The Namer has a thirty-millimeter auto cannon and can carry up to nine troops in the back. Both variants also fire Spike anti-tank missiles.

"We'll send fifty teams in with TF Mauler, in the backs of the Namer variants. Of course, the vehicles need crews, too. Fortunately, the recently deactivated 2nd Armored Division gave us plenty to choose from. We picked the best crews and sent them to the Negev for two weeks of familiarization training on the Merkava. We brought these two vehicles in with the *Sandefjord*, when it came to pick us up. We'll move them up to the training deck. Get your folks familiar with them. Things will be fluid once the fight starts. We expect every team in the force to be prepared to cross load and fight from a Merkava."

This takes everyone a moment to digest. It's not every day you're part of an American mercenary invasion that's also operating leased Israeli tanks.

With task organization covered, now it's over to me for the maneuver plan. I use the laser pointer to go back to the area map on screen. "All right, we appreciate everyone's patience with not getting the compartmented plans until now. The element of surprise is key. That's why we couldn't get into this level of detail until being sequestered here in the *Sandefjord*. The whole world is watching our Lightning Flight F-35 fighters and TF Zeus airborne formations as they stage in Kuwait. We can't hide everything, so Lightning and Zeus become the shiny objects that hold the Russians' attention. They'll expect an assault from Kuwait to their north. For the opening move, though, we'll stage TFs Mauler and Valor to hit from behind, from the south."

I point to Sohar, Oman, located on the Gulf of Oman just forty miles southeast of Dubai. "With the Russian grip on Persian Gulf oil, every country in the region is scrambling to build alternate capacity. Sohar is a major Omani production center. We already have the Merkavas en route to Sohar, in and among heavy drilling and refinery equipment going in. The Omanis are in on it, of course. They have good incentive to cooperate. The whole region is terrified of Russian expansion. TF Mauler's armored crewmen and special operators will blend with the expat labor that's surging into the area. They'll stage in a series of warehouses on the outskirts of town."

A different team leader asks, "That's good for the folks going in with Mauler. How about us, going in with TF Valor? The whole world knows we're going to offload in Brindisi, Italy. Won't they just track us from there?"

"Great question," I answer. "And in fact, the Russians have placed a couple of trawlers at the Gibraltar Strait. They'll track the ship even before we get to Italy. That's why we'll perform evasive maneuvers."

This gets several looks. I explain, "Our ship, the *Sandefjord*, has an identical sister ship, the *Vierland*. Thirty-six hours ago, the *Vierland* sailed from Norfolk with a load of used cars, bound for South Africa and resale on the continent. Later tonight, their two courses will intersect. Under cover of darkness, the crews will swap ship names on each hull. They'll also swap transponder codes. The *Vierland* then turns to sail for Italy, looking as if they are us. They'll arrive on October 2nd. The Russians will be waiting to watch that offload. But by then we will have taken Dubai.

"Tonight, after we swap names with *Vierland*, we sail her original course at max speed south and around the Cape of Good Hope. We've modified this ship to launch our V-280s direct from the open ocean, both up top and from the rear loading ramp. By September 30th, we'll round the Cape and launch TF Valor for an over-water flight to Socotra Island. Socotra sits in the Arabian Sea, six hundred miles south of Dubai. We'll forward refuel there, and then commence assault infil from Socotra to Dubai the following night. Lightning Flight F-35s will start pre-flight in Kuwait at H minus 2 hours, and launch at H minus 0:30. TF Mauler will start their armored drive from Oman at H minus 1:30. We project H Hour for synchronized attack on Russian positions at 2000 hours on October 1st."

Faces are looking pretty serious. It gets this way when you come up close and personal with the plan you're staking your life on. This operation had seemed distant. Now it's real. We'll use our next eleven days in transit to drill deeper in the plan with each of our teams. For now, the plan should at least give them appreciation that we're not going to rush the Russians' front door and hope for the best. We've got a good chance to start the fight at a time and means of our choosing.

Next, the part I'm dreading.

It's time for Simons' announcement. Ulysses, Puppy and I have been arguing against this for the past few days, but he won't listen. He stands up to face the group. The operators are listening keenly.

"I've always rolled up sleeves at any endeavor that Enterprise Performance has undertaken. Against the counsel of several of you here, counsel which I greatly respect, I will be right alongside you on this attack. I'll be flying in with TF Valor, in the command bird. Thank you for all you're doing to prepare this effort."

That's that. I hope we don't get him killed. Most of the audience take his announcement in stride. Some look amused, a couple register disagreement.

Ulysses brings the meeting to a close. The group breaks up, and the team leaders head off to brief their subordinates.

Puppy has been in the back of the room for the last part of the briefing, leaning against one of the Merkavas. He's doodling something on a scratch pad. The rest of the room has emptied out and it's just the two of us left.

He walks up to where I'm standing in the front of the briefing room, and shows me some numbers on the pad. "I've done a little back-of-the-envelope math. Back at Camp Diamond, I saw some of the EP invoices. Looking at how much US government assistance Simons is getting, either free or for way less than cost, you have any idea how much cash Enterprise Performance stands to gain from this invasion?" He points to the net profit at the bottom of the page. It's staggering.

I look at Puppy, unable to think of anything to say.

- 14 -

01 October 2029, H minus 1:18 – Gulf of Oman Airspace

"Warning, Pull Up! Warning, Pull Up!"

The sterile voice blares in our headsets prompted by the V-280 terrain avoidance radar.

The pilots push 300 knots through the evening dusk, maybe forty feet off the wave tops. Occasionally a rogue wave pops up to nearly our height, slaps loud spray on the windscreen, and sets off more computerized alerts. But it beats the alternative. We go any higher and an S-400 could find us. Even down this low, there are no guarantees. Our wingman aircraft flies one hundred meters to our right and just aft. Task Force Valor spreads across several dozen square miles of ocean, all barreling toward the coast.

Right on schedule, we flew TF Valor to Socotra Island for overnight refuel. The Saudis got nervous about us doing a direct overflight approach, from Socotra to Dubai. So instead we launched northeast over ocean, past the tip of Oman. With a northwest swing up the Gulf of Oman, we have a direct bead for Dubai. It pretty much aligns us with TF Mauler's ground approach as well.

Inside our V-280, I'm in the left front assault seat, in the row of three just behind the pilots. Court, as we've more and more taken to calling Simons, is in the center seat. Puppy sits to his right. Ulysses and Ken Bowerman are behind us in the next row. We've got a full assault load, with nine other operators filling out the aircraft. Our five-point harnesses have us cinched tight, and we're feeling every hard buffet as the bird jinks up and down. I've filled two barf bags, and now the dry heaves set in. Despite the wild ride, the harnesses keep us locked in and focused on status screens that are mounted in front of us on the backs of the pilot and copilot seats.

There's an old saw in the military that no plan survives first contact. This is true, proven over thousands of years. In our case, I wish the plan could have survived that far. We didn't even make H Hour before planning factors disintegrated. Someone spotted TF Mauler moving from its staging area in Sohar, Oman, when Mauler commenced its twenty-mile ground movement to the UAE border.

That was always the weak link. The Omanis guaranteed a cordon around the refinery warehouses, where the Merkavas had been hidden for the past two weeks. Their military kept civilians away. Fifteen minutes ago Mauler rolled out into the open desert, to start their march to Dubai.

And when the sixty-five ton Merkavas exited the warehouses, the sight was more than one overly enthusiastic Omani private could keep to himself. He uploaded a photo to his social media page. Now, all has gone to hell on the synchronization.

Ten minutes ago, the Russians launched protests from the Kremlin, fed to all major news outlets.

Nine minutes ago, every satellite feed on our aircraft filled with static. It's Russian jamming. This comes as no surprise. Gone are the days of ubiquitous communications. American combat formations lived a spoiled life for too long. From the early 2000s onwards, our military went to war with a "God's eye view" of the battlefield. Just like using one of the early generation ride hailing apps, we could pull up a screen to show the real-time location of every friendly vehicle and aircraft, and all known enemy positions. It allowed us to maneuver large, dispersed formations with unprecedented precision.

Now, the Russians block every part of the satellite spectrum they expect us to use. We're doing the same to them. That is, we've leased some US government systems to jam the Russians for us.

Without satellite comms, we're back almost to the same picture that Civil War generals had when maneuvering forces on the approach to Gettysburg or Richmond. We get a random and disjointed set of updates. We use mesh networked, laser line-of-sight communications. Laser comms are good to defeat jamming, but they only travel point-to-point from one vehicle or aircraft to another. Consequently, we can't receive a cohesive picture of what's happening across the force.

Instead, the mesh network acts as a series of electronic couriers. The laser comms pod on each vehicle, aircraft, or dismounted radio set automatically looks for any other sister pod in the force. When they ID each other, each pod simultaneously bursts updates to the other. The status and location of a vehicle or dismounted assault element at the far reaches of the force will bounce randomly from pod to pod. Ultimately it will end up hitting our aircraft pod, showing up as a position update on our status screen.

Only there's no way to determine the latency of each update. One icon might show a position or status that's over an hour old. The icon next to it could show a status that's less than a minute old.

This means you can't trust what you see on the screen. Instead, you have to absorb that visual data, factor in what you're hearing on verbal updates that also bounce in by laser, apply your military assessment of how the overall fight is going, and then use gut instinct to fill in the rest of the unknowns. It drives all of us digital natives crazy. We came up through the ranks able to see the entire battlefield in one clean, crisp, all-knowing feed. Most of us suck at these new rules for spatial awareness.

Fortunately for us, it turns out that a great way to prepare for this infomatics schizophrenia is to cut your teeth as a drug dealer in Providence, RI. Puppy can sort through the data chaos better than anyone we've ever met. Apparently, he used similar skills back home, where he filtered conflicting and unreliable information to navigate a precarious mental map of suppliers, customers, rivals and cops.

"What's the hnnnnnnnh . . ." Court tries to ask Puppy a question, but the 280 just dropped hard, and the harness takes his air away.

He takes a few breaths to reset.

"Puppy, what's the attack look like now?"

Puppy's immersed the screens to our front. He gives the update. "From the looks of it, our TF Mauler did the right thing. When they realized their Merkavas were compromised, they adjusted immediately to an echelon attack formation and ramped up to max speed. They're hitting the border about now. Looks like Petrikov pushed out twenty Armatas as a screen line to oppose them. That's not enough to stop Mauler. The Russians will play a delaying fight with that screen. They'll knock off as many Merkavas as they can and use that contact to determine TF Mauler's objective. Lightning Flight, the F-35s, they also launched from Kuwait immediately after the Mauler compromise. They've crossed over Bahrain and are just starting to engage the S-400 batteries."

"Missile Alert! Missile Alert!"

The worst computer warning of all.

"S-400. Ten seconds out!" the pilot adds in a short, clipped tone.

We drop down another ten feet. Sea spray whips hard across the windscreen. We hear loud pops in back as the pilots fire chaff and flares for decoy.

Our wingman aircraft calls out by laser comms, "We're hit!"

Looking to the right, the scene plays in slow motion. The missile warhead explodes just off that 280's left wing. The aircraft wobbles but stays on track for a few seconds. Then it corkscrews down. The left wing's engine hits the water first, and the V-280 cartwheels twice before disintegrating.

Our intercom's silent. Four 280s trail the main TF Valor formation, ready to serve as search and rescue. Our pilot will have automatically hit a distress call beacon for our wingman. But from the looks of it, there won't be anyone to save.

"Stand by," the copilot says over intercom, as he and the pilot gesture amongst themselves.

"What's that?" Court asks.

I inform him, "The S-400 that splashed our wingman, it punched some shrapnel into us too."

"Really?" he says. "I didn't feel a thing."

"That's because we're all jacked on adrenaline," Puppy explains, pointing out his window. "You can see some of the fragment holes in the right wing." Jagged contours outline where the shrapnel embedded in the wing. Composite carbon flails wildly in the slipstream. It makes a racket we can hear despite our headsets.

The pilot reads instruments, then gives the news. "All right, we're flyable. Not gonna trust the tiltrotor mechanism for a hovered landing though. We'll have to use a rolling approach when it's time to set down."

To Court's credit, he seems to take this in stride. The pilot just told us we'll resort to a controlled crash. The tiltrotors are the size of small helicopter blades. If you land with them in the horizontal, forward-flight configuration, they chew up and break apart. Hopefully the rest of the aircraft holds in one piece. For now, we have bigger fish to fry.

"Puppy," I ask, "you have any sense of how the air fight is going? Those S-400s should start paying more attention to the F-35s in Lighting Flight, the closer they come in from Bahrain."

"Yeah, just looking at that," he replies. "The good news for us is, yes, the S-400s are starting to pay more attention to Lightning Flight. I think we lost four 280s on the salvo that just hit. But we probably won't catch any more missiles heading our way for now."

Puppy's leaning forward and squinting hard at the screen in front of him. He's also listening to Lighting Flight voice calls that have bounced over to us. He adds, "The bad news is, I don't think Lightning is going to sufficiently degrade those S-400s. The Russians are using their SU-57 fighters differently than we expected. We thought they'd come out and fight our F-35s head to head. We wanted that, and we could have downed them. But instead, the SU-57s are hanging back and using their radars as network relays for the S-400 missiles. The 57s are hanging back toward Syria, behind the F-35s, so they get a better radar picture looking at the F-35s' ass end. They're guiding the S-400s into our fighters. Lightning Flight has lost at least four aircraft already. They're having to divert more planes than expected to try and drive the SU-57s away."

"How about TF Mauler?" I ask.

"Mauler's heavy into the fight now. They're approaching Dubai in an attack formation of three wedges. Two up, one back. They're pushing back the Armatas, but also taking losses. They won't make it as far into the city on their own as we'd planned."

Puppy spreads his Dubai hard copy map between him and Court. We study it.

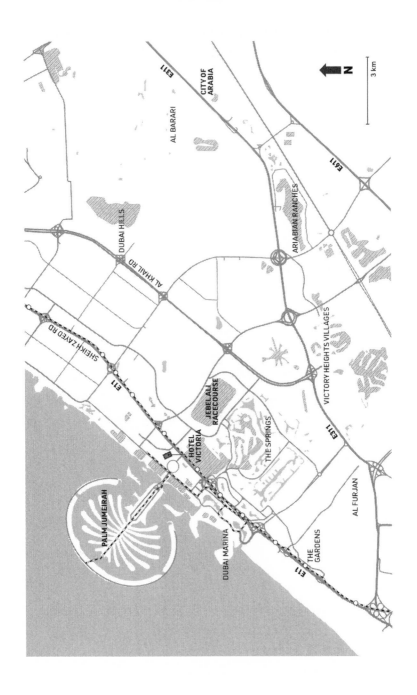

We're now about thirty minutes out from feet dry, the point where we cross overland into Dubai airspace. It's time to call our key move: where to commit TF Valor and the two thousand special operators we'll bring to the fight.

I feel a pang at realizing Valor has taken more than sixty KIA already, from the initial S-400 hits. Then it's time to push out those thoughts and get back in the fight.

I recap Puppy's last info. "OK, copy that Mauler isn't advancing into Dubai as fast as we'd needed. How about the Russian Armatas in the city? Are more of them coming out to engage TF Mauler?"

"Yes," Puppy replies. "It looks like Petrikov has pushed all his Dubai-based Armatas out to engage TF Mauler. That's what's slowing Mauler down. The main arc of the fight is out just beyond the E611 ring road."

"Next question. Understood that Lightning Flight is getting pulled in too many directions to destroy a critical mass of the S-400s. But how about their electronic warfare jamming? Are they having good effects?" Part of the F-35's high price tag is that they were built with electronic warfare capabilities organic to the platform. They perform well as jammers against enemy radar.

"Yeah," Puppy says. "Their jamming against the S-400s appears to be working well. It's probably the only reason we're still alive. But they can't keep it up indefinitely. Those SU-57s really have Lightning Flight in a bind. Our F-35s are still taking losses. They can jam the S-400s another hour, maybe a little longer. Then they're going to have to disengage and go deal with those SU-57s."

"Puppy, do we know where their S-400s are concentrated?"

"They've put a critical mass of their batteries centered around Palm Jumeirah, on the island itself and along the mainland beaches. The missiles orient northwest out into the Persian Gulf. Our overt staging in Kuwait did its work as far as that goes."

"OK, last question." A picture is starting to form in my head. "The S-400s are oriented northwest. Our current line of approach is opposite that, from the southeast coming off the Gulf of Oman. If we fly a line direct into the city for air assault landing, we can get there while the F-35s are still on station and jamming the S-400s. Will that sufficiently mask our approach on their radar?"

Puppy thinks for several seconds. "Yeah. Especially since the spine of Dubai's downtown is between those batteries and our line of approach. The skyscrapers will heavily degrade the ability for their S-400s to look our way. It was SU-57 redirects on radar that sent missiles our way the first time, but as we get closer the skyscrapers will help block that."

I look back at Ulysses and Ken Bowerman over my shoulder, asking them over the intercom, "What do you think?"

They both nod. Ulysses sums it up. "Petrikov's committed all his Armata armor ten or fifteen kilometers south of the city, engaging Mauler. That means instead of us *following* Mauler's lead into the city, we leapfrog them?"

"Exactly." But now I need their thoughts on the next piece. "Where do we allocate the Task Force Valor teams for air assault?"

Bowerman leans forward. With a Nomex-gloved hand he points on the map. "Here. You put a third of the teams down along the Sheikh Zayed Road, but block out four kilometers around the Jumeirah as a no-landing zone. It will be too hot there. Put the other two thirds down along Al Khail Road. Key task for all teams is movement to contact from their infil point to Palm Jumeirah. Teams mutually support, combine combat power where needed, and develop the situation. After team insertions, the V-280s all exfil back to Oman before we lose the jamming."

"Sounds good to me," I say. Ulysses nods in agreement. I look over at Court, who's taking it all in. "Boss, this is the plan we're going with."

He nods his consent.

This flexible plan for ground assault in the city comes courtesy of principles Ulysses and Ken insisted on. Years of communications luxury had made the US military far too addicted to set-piece orders that attempted to control the movement of each sub-element. Instead, Ulysses and Ken presented the Normandy airborne drops from World War Two as a case study. That operation succeeded precisely because, in the chaos of dropping several thousand paratroopers into darkness, each warrior understood the assault objectives, and each had the initiative to adjust the tactical fight on the ground. Our teams will operate in the same way. Once they land in the city, they have broad autonomy on how they maneuver and destroy the S-400s.

Looking outside the bird, I realize it's last light out. We'll need night vision goggles or red lens lights in another five minutes. I give Puppy the thumbs up to disseminate this update to the rest of the force. He makes the calls.

It's fifteen minutes to feet dry. Another ten minutes after that until we hit Dubai's outer limits. Best case, with all the jamming going on, it will take fifteen minutes for this update to relay to all the V-280s in TF Valor. This means a good thirty or more of the 280s won't get the word in time. They'll dump their teams behind TF Mauler's line of advance per the original plan. So maybe we'll get a hundred aircraft and fourteen hundred special operators actually landing for assault inside the city. That's OK. With Petrikov's Armatas drawn to the outskirts, past the ring road, we'll have enough relative combat power.

For the first time in what seems like forever, I'm actually feeling good about our situation.

Then Puppy bursts the bubble. "Hey, Mark," he says, "don't forget we're flying on a broken wing here. Can't hover for landing. We're going to have to figure out how to get down to the ground."

- 15 -

01 October 2029, H plus 0:10 – Five minutes until Feet Dry

Time's up. We used a couple minutes to each study the map, what we know about the ground situation, and come up with ideas. Now we have to commit. Once we hit land, the pilots need to dial the flight profile for our bird's projected landing zone.

"All right," I speak up. "The open desert will be the best place to make a running landing. We can come in behind TF Mauler's line of advance, and put down with their command element." That will be a cluster of four Merkavas, rigged with extra communications for their command team. We had a similar comms package, rigged on two ATVs, but they were in our wingman's bird. The one that burned in from the S-400. Now we'll just have a less capable backpack set that Puppy will carry. "From the Mauler comms suite, we can best monitor the fight and figure out how to maneuver Mauler's armor into the city."

Puppy, Ulysses, and Ken all nod agreement. They're likely thinking of the same unspoken advantage: Landing behind Mauler means we don't take Court on the leading edge assault into the city.

"Negative," Simons replies immediately. "I'm not going to hang back behind our armor while the rest of TF Valor goes into the thick of it."

Sweet Jesus. I choose my words carefully. "Look, Court, that's admirable. Really. But there are about a dozen good reasons for us to land outside the city and plug in with TF Mauler. Your personal sense of obligation should not override that."

"If I wasn't in this aircraft, where would you land?"

"Well, you *are* in this aircraft. And the base plan with bringing you along was to land with TF Mauler."

He parries. "But *now* the situation has changed. It's changed so drastically that you are compelled to leapfrog TF Valor ahead of our armor and land directly inside the city. And that's because it's the best chance to take out the S-400s. That's the critical point on the ground. That's where I'm going."

Well, he bought and paid for this invasion. The other fellas are looking at me for an answer. "OK, I get it. We land with TF Valor in the city. Puppy, what's the word?"

Puppy has been talking on a separate intercom channel to the copilot and crew chief. He gives us the rundown on options to perform a running landing in the city. "We can't land on the Sheikh Zayed or Al Khail roads. All our other birds are using those. With the latency of the comms, we're liable to plow into a V-280 that's hovering to insert a team. Most of the rest of city is built up too much. To get to the nearest open desert, we'd have to land darn near at the E-611 ring road."

"Where their Armatas might see us come in," Ulysses comments.

"Exactly. An Armata catches us in open desert and we're toast. Plus, we'd be isolated from both TF Mauler *and* the rest of TF Valor. We'd be irrelevant to influence anything at that point. So, check this out. Here's the least worst option."

Puppy points on the paper map to the Jebel Ali Racecourse. A local track for thoroughbred horses. We stare at it for a few moments.

Ulysses leans forward from the second row, to look closer and give his thoughts. "OK, if that's the best we've got, so be it. We just need to keep in mind it's threading the needle. We'll be just about three kilometers from center mass of their S-400 batteries. They'll have local security on those missiles. We need to put down as far to the western end of the straightaway as we can."

On a tablet Ulysses had preloaded, he pulls up overhead imagery and shows it to us. "There's strip malls and residential houses just about three hundred meters north of the track. After landing, we can head up to those stores or houses to hole up. Our assault teams will be crawling all through that area. We need to stay out of their way and get our bearings on how the overall fight progresses. Then we can call out adjustments to the overall plan."

"That sounds good to me," I say. "Anyone got objections?" No one has any, though I catch Court's irritated look. He's none too pleased at my pushback about him landing in the city.

"Feet dry," the pilot calls on intercom. Puppy goes back to their private channel and advises the final infil plan. The pilot nods, and now he and the co-pilot confer on their approach profile.

After crossing straight over the desert for several minutes, our night vision picks up TF Mauler's fight with the Armatas. You can see the large flash and streak of tank main gun rounds trading back and forth. This mixes with cascades of automatic fire from the thirty-millimeter auto cannon that both sides' infantry variants use. An anti-tank missile pops up on final attack profile, then strikes home in a spectacular explosion that lights up the night sky and briefly washes out my night-vision lenses. I can't tell if it's one of our Spike missiles that took out an Armata, or one of their Kornets that hit a Merkava.

The pilot's seen enough. He banks hard right, pressing us down into our seats. This wheels us north, around the armor-on-armor fight.

A few minutes later, the pilot must feel that we're clear of that danger area. He starts a wide bank back to the left. He'll bring us in heading south/southwest. We stay below a hundred feet, flying parallel to the line of Dubai's skyscrapers, and using the skyscrapers as cover from the S-400s on the opposite side. At the last minute we'll bank right, or west, for our approach to the racecourse.

You can tell most of the TF Valor teams are on the ground already. Firefights have broken out in a dozen different locations. Red and green tracer rounds mark exchanges of automatic fire. A burst goes high and stitches holes in the aft left part of our cabin. Everyone flinches but no one is hit. The holes generate a high-pitched whistle, adding to the racket from the earlier missile damage to our right wing. But the flight controls don't seem affected and the pilots don't even mention it.

"One minute out, brace for impact," the copilot calls. Thirty seconds later the pilot makes the hard right bank for our final approach.

There it is. We're lined up perfectly on the length of one straightaway. Just shy of the leading edge, the pilot feathers the engines. We slam hard and bounce up several feet. Then we slam down again, plowing earth. The Emiratis surface the track with oiled sand. Grimy clumps splatter across the windscreen. The 280 skids to a halt, in a grinding rotation halfway over on its left side, my side. Tearing composite screams loudly as the left wing and engine shear off.

Everyone unbuckles harnesses. Canted like this, we're all dropping down onto the left side door, which is now the floor. Puppy climbs up the seats and yanks the emergency handle on the right side door, over our heads. It jettisons.

"Come on!" he calls, straddling the doorway and pulling us up one at a time. I'm third out and stay low at the opening so as not to silhouette, then drop down beside the fuselage. You can hear a firefight about five hundred meters away, but it's hard to say where. Due south?

Ken Bowerman calls out, "Alpha section, get local security on the bird now! Bravo, need you to recce northeast across the road. Find a spot to hole up in that strip mall or one of the houses. Let's go." Ulysses, Puppy and I will run command and control, and also keep personal watch on Court. Ken will run the remaining nine operators plus himself as a close security team. He'll maneuver them to make sure we don't run our billionaire boss into a hornets' nest.

Ulysses gets our immediate group of four organized underneath the right-side wing. He also checks that everyone's uninjured from the landing and tells the two pilots and crew chief to fall in with Bowerman's security team.

"Contact!" An operator on the other side of the aircraft warns, as we hear semiautomatic small arms fire ping off the top of the fuselage. Our guy returns with slow, aimed fire. "They're not maneuvering on us," he adds. "It's one or two shooters up in the stands. Probably observers." The stands are on the other side of the oval, some two hundred fifty meters away. Our side of the track doesn't have stands, fortunately.

"Alpha, put suppressive fire on them now!" Ken orders. "Bravo section, you got a good route yet?" Bravo has already pushed out, and he calls them by line of sight radio. They confirm they've found a clear path to the strip mall. Alpha section pumps a slow but sustained stream of aimed fire into the stands.

"Ken, get us out of here *ASAP*." Ulysses orders. "Those shooters in the stands see a big fat target. For sure, they're calling for something heavier to hit this bird."

"Roger," Ken says. "Bravo's already securing the far side of the road we have to cross. You guys move next. Alpha will keep putting fire on the stands and then tuck in as rear security."

"Copy," Ulysses answers. "Let's go," he orders our group of four. We move out in a loose wedge, weapons at the ready. Ulysses is in the lead, I'm on the left and Puppy is on the right. Court, as we rehearsed him exhaustively back at Camp Diamond, is ten meters behind Ulysses.

Arriving at the multi-lane Hessa Street, we see one of the Bravo section operators signal us to cross over to him. We do a quick scan to ensure no hostiles in sight, then we sprint across. Two other Bravo operators guide us the next hundred meters into our hole up spot.

- 16 -

01 October 2029, H plus 0:40 – Hessa Street, Dubai

"I'll have a venti soy latte," says Ken.

"Double espresso," I add.

"Straight black coffee please, grande." Even Court gets in on it.

"Screw all you guys," Puppy shoots back. Bowerman's Bravo section has found an empty Starbucks as our hole up spot. A thick layer of dust cakes all the surfaces, and most of the tables and chairs are overturned. It's OK for now. The storefront faces back to Hessa Street, which we just crossed. Just enough streetlights remain functioning to give us some ambient light in here.

The storefront gives us good north/south visibility for any approaching threats along that axis. Ken's team has sector security in place. Immediately behind the strip mall is a large residential subdivision. You can hear a good firefight somewhere back in there. From the sounds of it, at least two of our teams are in the mix: Three Mark 48 machine guns pound sustained bursts, and we're carrying two per team. It sounds like at least ten Russians are fighting back, including one PKM machine gun barking its slower rate of automatic fire.

This is against a backdrop of several other fights within earshot.

They spread along the general axes where TF Valor teams infil'd, the length of Sheikh Zayed and Al Khail roads. Disturbingly, about five minutes ago we heard the loud report of an Armata tank cannon not more than a mile away. Petrikov has at least some of his armor in the city.

Ulysses is up on the roof, seeing what status relays he can pull off the comms net with our manpack radio set.

"This is what you get," Puppy scolds, from behind the serving counter. He raided the back storeroom and has put a bunch of Via instant coffee packets and some bottled water on the end of the counter marked "pickup" in both English and Arabic. Counting our forward refueling on Socotra Island, we've been stealing sleep in two- or three-hour chunks for the past two days. We first carry coffee packets and bottles to Ken's team on security outside, then we head back in, each take a bottle, and mix the coffee in cold.

Court cocks an eyebrow. "I figured you military types would fire up hot coffee while you have the chance."

Ulysses has just climbed down from the roof and walks in, overhearing Court's comment. He grabs a bottle and explains, "Too much signature. Check out all the dust in here. From the looks of it, this place sat abandoned since the Russians arrived. Last thing we need is to attract attention with the smell of hot brewed java."

Court nods approvingly. "You get any updates?" he asks, gesturing toward the radio.

"Well, none that I can decipher. Puppy, you got a second?"

"Yeah man, what'd you pull down?"

They go over to the seating area and set up a small Toughbook on a café table. Ulysses uploads his data haul onto digital map graphics. The map populates with several dozen team and vehicle icons, plus reported status updates: blue for ours and red for the Russians.

"Don't trust any of what you see," Ulysses advises. "There's still spectrum jamming on all the satcom channels. And we're too low in the urban canyon to get much real-time update off the laser relays. These are a bunch of random redirects that could range from ten minutes to more than an hour old."

Puppy's staring at all the icons, trying to paint an accurate picture in his head. I pull up a second table and spread out a paper military grid map that we can work from. It's best not to look at the faulty data any longer than you have to. The brain assimilates a screen shot as real.

Puppy moves over to the paper map, to point out key locations and brief his assessment. "Here are the big pieces. First, when Petrikov reacted to TF Mauler outside the city, he hedged bets and left at least three hundred dismounted special operators to defend the S-400s. Our TF Valor teams will have to fight their way through those operators." He traces a line through downtown toward Palm Jumeirah island.

"Second, it gets worse. He's pushing about twenty Armatas back into the city. We heard that first main gun a few minutes ago. So, our Valor teams will have to contend with armor too." He shows the general lines where Armatas are coming back inside the E-611 ring, looking to engage our teams.

This is bad news. Each Valor team carries a one-shot, man-portable Spike anti-tank missile. That's to have *something* for self-defense, in the event like this where we're separated from our Merkavas in TF Mauler. But a hard push by twenty Armatas will eventually tear us to shreds.

"Hate to be a downer," Puppy sums up, "but if our TF Valor teams do end up tangling with three hundred emplaced dismounts *plus* twenty Armatas, we're not likely to break through and take out those S-400s in time for TF Zeus, our paratroopers, to fly in from

Kuwait tomorrow and make their airborne drop. And if TF Zeus doesn't get in here, we really start getting in trouble. At the current level of fighting, we'll burn through our munitions in thirty-six hours max."

"Can TF Mauler push straight in and support us?" Court asks. Looking over at him, it's new to see his brows knit together and such concern on his face. He's not used to such loss of control.

"OUT NOW!! RALLY ON ME!"

A Bravo section operator has flung open the emergency exit door, leading to the alley behind the strip mall. In one swoop Puppy scoops up the map, Toughbook and the manpack radio, and sprints for the door. The rest of us follow a step behind.

We're no sooner out in the alley than Ken Bowerman, who's getting reports from his team over headset, yells, "Keep moving away from Hessa Street! Get into the housing area. We've got an Armata maneuvering on us!"

Ken's got three Bravo section operators in the alley with him. We get bearings and are about to push out when Ulysses and I look around and shout in unison, "Court!" He's not out here.

Ulysses and I run back inside to find Simons face down. He's tripped in the dark into a pile of unused chairs. He's on top struggling but not moving. We each kneel down and I shine a red lens, the beam bouncing around the room in my haste. A piece of his web gear has gotten stuck on a chair underneath him. He's struggling to climb off but the weight of the whole interlocked pile is holding him down.

"Hurry!" Bowerman yells from outside.

Ulysses flicks open his knife and slices the web gear loose. We each grab Court under an arm, yank him off the pile. We drag him full force out the door, where he regains his feet.

"MOVE!!" Bowerman yells, hoarse. He points toward the residential neighborhood. We fan out, sprinting at top speed. We're fifty meters away from the Starbucks, lungs burning with effort, when we hear the thunk-thunk-thunk of auto cannon rounds firing. A split second later, grenade-sized explosions erupt inside the coffee shop where we'd been. We keep running and help each other over a five-foot cement wall that fences off the housing area. As I'm lowering off the wall, looking back at the far corner of the strip mall, I see an operator from Ken's Alpha section fire a portable Spike missile. Backblast lights up his position. A few seconds later, a large explosion plumes about two kilometers north, somewhere on Hessa Street.

Ken gets a report on headset from his team. We keep moving quickly, knowing this area hasn't yet been secured. Ken points to the house that's our next hole up spot. We burst in. The house is dark. Ulysses and Puppy bring rifles up and clear the house. They flow through rooms using night vision goggles. I control Court by one arm and steer him into the dining room on our immediate left. I sit him down in a chair and briefly flash white light to check him for wounds.

"I'm fine!" he says, irritated. Then in a lower voice, "Sorry I screwed up."

"You're good, Boss." I reassure him while inspecting his kit, readjusting his assault vest. "We've got as much practice running around in the dark as you have coding software, that's all. You're getting a hell of an OJT right now."

He nods and exhales with ragged breath. He gets his composure again.

Ulysses and Puppy return. "House is clear. Let's set up." They reconfigure the Toughbook and manpack radio, spread out the hard copy map again too. It's pitch dark so I shine a red lens for us to work by.

Ken comes in and updates: "That was a T-15 Armata, the infantry variant with auto cannon. We're lucky. A main gun round from the tank version could have punched through the strip mall and blown up in the middle of us."

"You kill it?" Ulysses asks.

"Don't think so. Alpha section reports it was a good hit. But looks like its countermeasures cooked off the Spike warhead early. That's our only missile for the team. Both sections have a good perimeter established around this house. But as you can hear, it's getting busier. We need to be out of here in twenty minutes max. You tell me where to, but out of here."

Ken's comment dials us in to the other firefights going on. There's one not more than a half mile away, sounding bigger than it had before. It sounds like at least four of our teams converged there.

We're all standing or sitting around the dining table now, with the map spread out.

"OK," I say, looking at Puppy, "get us reset here. Our forces, their forces, and Court's question about can TF Mauler push in directly to reinforce us?"

Puppy nods. "Right. Here in the city, I think they are posturing about twenty Armatas and three hundred or more dismounts, to hold off our TF Valor push to take out the S-400s. For TF Valor itself, I think we've got teams amounting to just under a thousand operators. But we're spread out. And again, twenty Armatas will play hell with Valor so long as we lack armored support from TF Mauler."

He points to the E-611 ring road. "Now, as for TF Mauler pushing straight into the city, I doubt it. Mauler's probably down to one hundred twenty Merkavas. Petrikov probably still has forty Armatas out past the E-611 as a blocking force. If you had Mauler push through frontally, it would be bloody. You might get enough Merkavas through to help us, you might not."

It gets quiet as we all take it in.

"Is there a flank open?" Ulysses asks.

Puppy nods affirmative. "The way TF Mauler approached the city, it was more from the north. So, roger, when the Armatas arrayed in a blocking line, they weighted to the north, too. That Armata that just popped rounds at us, it's probably the southernmost armor that they've got right now."

"Yeah," I'm nodding. "It's risky, but probably the best move we've got."

"What's that?" Court asks.

I point to Mauler's position out past the E-611. "We split TF Mauler. Half the Merkavas stay there, to keep those Armatas pinned in place. The other half, sixty of them, pull off the line moving east, away from the city. They move back a good fifteen kilometers, out of sightline from the Armatas. Next, those Merkavas head south for twenty-five kilometers, then they turn west and push full force in a combat echelon out to the coast. If they can do that without the Russians getting wise, it boxes around the defense line that Petrikov has built. Those assaulting Merkavas will be out on the coast, south of the S-400s, and they can roll up that Russian flank. They'll push north along the coast and pick off the S-400s as they get in range. Petrikov's stuck at that point. We'll have him pincered on two sides with our armor, and we'll have him outnumbered almost three-to-one in the city. No matter what he does, enough of our folks will get through to kill those S-400 batteries."

"Mark, if it can work, that's a great plan," Ken speaks up. He's come back inside to join us. "Just one question, how are we going to get the word out to TF Mauler? The jamming is still killing our satcom radios, and we're way too low in the city to push laser comms by direct line of sight to Mauler."

"Hotel Victoria," Ulysses says without missing a beat. He points to a spot on the map due west of us, on Sheikh Zayed Road.

"What's that?" Ken asks.

"That's it, yeah," I say to Ulysses. Then I answer Ken. "We had a layover here, years ago, flying civilian air out of theater. Hotel Victoria is over twenty stories tall, with a rooftop pool and patio. It's just outside the main band of skyscrapers, so you can see for miles back into the desert. We get up there, we can push laser comms unobstructed to TF Mauler and get them moving."

"The other good thing," Puppy adds, "from that rooftop we'll have a good view onto the Palm Jumeirah. We'll be able to ID the S-400 batteries and we can vector our dismounted Valor teams by laser comms too, as they approach for the assault."

"OK," I say, "that's the plan." I turn to Ken. "We need you to get us to the Hotel Victoria."

"Right. I'll brief the team real quick. Same order of movement; Bravo section in the lead, you guys in the middle, Alpha section in the rear. It's a three kilometer move. Here's the plan when we get there. That sucker's gonna have multiple stairwells and hundreds of rooms. We can't clear the whole thing with one team. So, we'll run a floating clear all the way up one stairwell and get you guys on the roof and secured up there. Then I'm putting Bravo and Alpha sections on security in the top two floors, while you guys are parked on the roof. Any questions?"

No questions. We prep to move.

- 17 -

Events zoom in and out of focus as I lie on my back, staring up at the olive green Kevlar panels that line the ceiling of a V-280. Through the window I see we're flying over water with the sun on the horizon. Dusk, I think? Yes, dusk. That means we're flying south along the coast, headed back to Sohar, Oman.

I'm in a medevac bird. There's an IV drip feeding into my arm. Everything feels warm and comfortable.

I lie there for a bit, dozing lightly to the hum of the engines. Then, with urgency, my mind screams to try and remember.

It seems important to put the pieces together in a coherent way. If I can remember now, maybe that will help store the information for longer term recall. I struggle to pull up the sequence of events.

The last move through the city, to Hotel Victoria, went smooth. Working our way north through the residential area, we stayed tight along a row of houses. Ken's operators spotted a team of ten Russians at Sheikh Zayed Road. We skirted south before crossing and then continued on. We heard lots of sporadic gunfire but didn't make any other contact.

At Hotel Victoria, moving up the stairwell was all clear. Any

Russians in that area must have used a different high rise for their observation teams.

We set up on the roof. The laser comms shot made it through to TF Mauler on our first try. Mauler thinned out sixty Merkavas nice and slow, without kicking up a lot of dust or otherwise tipping their hand. They boxed around the open desert, then back out to the coast, just as planned.

The big fight for the S-400s kicked off around ten in the morning.

It worked. A bloody mess, but it worked. For a good two hours, there was the steady thrum of high-order tank round and missile explosions, more thunks of auto cannon, and small arms fire filling in the gaps. The Russians tried desperately to reposition their defenses. But it was too little, too late.

Afterward, you could see a hundred armored vehicles mangled or burning throughout the city, both ours and theirs. Flames shot high out of the odd hatch where someone had managed to bail out. In most cases that didn't happen. Overpressure generally killed all the occupants, with smoke and fire belching where the armor had ruptured.

Looking at Palm Jumeirah, you could see the S-400 batteries were utterly destroyed. Mauler's armor that had boxed out to the coast ranged a good two thirds of the island from their position just south. Main gun rounds and auto cannon tore through the missile launchers. In many cases hits on the launchers caused larger secondary explosions.

For a brief while it seemed like several S-400 launchers on the north end of Palm Jumeirah might escape into the city's urban canyon. Their crews feverishly broke down the launchers and prepped them to move by wheeled vehicle. Then came the *coup de grace*. Several of our TF Valor dismount teams in the north commandeered boats at a marina. They organized a swarm attack along that side of the island. Not a single S-400 system survived. Across Palm Jumeirah, the bodies of dozens of Russian missile crewmen lay visible.

We took big losses too, but we'd turned the corner. With the S-400s knocked out, there was a clear entry for TF Zeus, our paratroop reinforcements. At dusk, TF Zeus would launch from Kuwait, with the remaining F-35s as escort and close air support.

I lie there for a while, feeling foggy and unsettled. I try to pull up the other piece. The thing that's gnawing.

And then it snaps back, sharp and clear. I'm no longer staring at the ceiling of the 280. Now I'm back on the roof of the Hotel Victoria, earlier in the day.

We're on the Hotel Victoria rooftop, beside the pool. I look out to strings of thick black smoke rising across the city. Puppy has pulled together two outdoor tables, and he's working the comms. I stare at the water. It's still crystal clear, amazing. A swim, washing off the grime, would be heaven.

Looking down into the city, there are still small-arms engagements. But now only a handful of Armatas seem to be left in the fight. One is holed up to the northeast. Near as I can see through binoculars, it's rammed its way inside the Mall of the Emirates, trying to use the first floor concourse as an escape path. Outside, three of our Merkavas are circling the building perimeter, their turrets scanning. They're looking to catch the Armata when it pops out of the mall.

With the disruption the Russians have suffered, satcom jamming has abated. Puppy's able to get better status updates from Kuwait.

Ulysses connects his tablet to the radio set, too. He's collecting status checks from all of our ground elements.

It's time to ask. "How bad?"

He looks at me. "It's going to take a while to know for sure. The 280s were hauling casualties throughout the night. We'll have to get an update from our MASH in Sohar. A first guess, I'd say we took over four hundred killed, plus at least three hundred seriously wounded."

Court's been peering over the railing that faces Palm Jumeirah and the coastline. He swivels around and asks, "Isn't that reversed from normal? Shouldn't we expect more wounded than killed?"

Ulysses nods in agreement, then adds, "Yeah, that's the normal rule for dispersed, dismounted fighting. But we took a lot of hits during our infil phase. Almost a hundred dead were in the backs of V-280s that got shot down. And the Namer variants of the Merkavas that got hit, during their initial move across from Sohar, those each had a crew of three plus six operators in the back. Each one of those that ate a main gun round or a Kornet missile, the numbers add up pretty quick." He stops there.

Ulysses' jaw sets in that way of his, where he's done with any talking. Many of those KIA were former 8th Groupers. Friends.

I look over at Court, at his squint. He's listening to Ulysses' readout, with the same look I've seen a couple of times during breaks back at Camp Diamond, when one of the corporate bean counters brought over bad news about an investment or a subsidiary in trouble. The corporate officer would always bring a spreadsheet or two that summarized the financial hit. Court would grunt, and with a hint of bragging he'd say, "Well, you need deep pockets for the big losses, to get the even bigger wins."

Hearing the news right now from Ulysses, Court grunts in that same way. But he doesn't say anything. He just slowly turns back around to look out over the railing, out to his latest win.

We each get lost in tasks. Silence settles on the rooftop for several minutes, and battle sounds continue to drift up from the city.

"Jackpot!" Puppy announces. We all look at him.

He continues, "Our Kuwait ops center has been scanning Russian comms intercepts. The Russians sent a flight of two SU-80s, flying here to Dubai from Syria. They have two SU-57s forming a blocking position up over Bahrain, to keep our F-35s at bay."

"SU-80s, that's not a strike package, is it?" Court asks.

"Negative," "Puppy explains, "they're STOL transports, short takeoff and landing. The intercept says they're inbound for a pickup on the Emirates Hills golf course." We can actually see that golf course from here, off to the south. Puppy gives the wicked smile he saves for when he's about to administer a truly deserved ass beating.

I smile too. "Puppy, what's the ETA?"

"Probably thirty minutes."

"All right, we've got time." I'm laying out the plan quickly. "Ulysses, take five minutes to organize a package. Leave Bowerman's team here for security with Court. But within a two- or three-block radius down on the street, we ought to have a couple of our teams we can rally for support."

Ulysses is nodding. "Yeah, roger. Petrikov will be in a small element, trying to scoot out. We can do it."

"Wait a minute!" Court interrupts, scowling. "What are you talking about?"

"Sorry, boss," I reply, realizing that from Ulysses and Puppy's common ops history, the three of us have an implied conversation that Simons isn't tracking. "Here's what's going down. With that mix of Russian aircraft, it's got to be a high-value pickup. Meaning Petrikov's trapped in the city and can't get out by ground. They'll use their SU-57 fighters to block our F-35s. And they'll land an SU-80 right on the golf course for pickup. The other SU-80 is probably just backup. Petrikov will move in a small element to stay as low vis as possible. Our odds are 50/50 at best. But if we can organize teams now and get moving, we have a decent chance to get Petrikov before he escapes. Alive preferably, but we'll take him out of the fight either way."

"No," is Court's only response.

"Boss, no, I get it. You *need* to stay here. That's why Ken's team will stay up here for security. Trust me, if we had the F-35s overhead, we'd just vector them in and splash Petrikov on the exfil flight. But they'll never push through a dogfight with SU-57s in time. This is our only chance."

Court looks at me. "I get all that. I'm saying NO."

"No, what?"

"No, we're not going to go after Petrikov. He needs to fly out."

I'm incredulous. "What the hell are you talking about, needs to fly out? That's why we're here! This whole fool's errand started because of Petrikov. Because the US government was desperate for a way to defeat the Russians here. And now we've done it. And we've taken almost a thousand American casualties in one morning as the price of that."

I breathe for a few beats, careful to spell it out. "And the major Russian player, who's run their incursions for almost twenty years, is on the street down there. He's not much more than a mile away. And no, taking him out won't *solve* the problem. But it will help. Petrikov runs a tight little empire. They won't be able to replace him any time soon."

Court's been looking at me without a single twitch. "There are higher issues to consider."

"What higher issues?" I ask. "The United States of America chartered this mission. Petrikov is the enemy commander. *It's that simple.*"

"Mark, this conversation is over."

I look at him in silence.

Behind him, pillars of smoke still spiral upward.

I speak slowly and deliberately. "Mr. Simons, I hereby resign my position at Enterprise Performance. Effective immediately."

Lying on the stretcher, looking again at the ceiling of the medevac bird, more scenes drift into view.

I remember one time when I was six years old.

Our family went to visit friends who owned a farm in rural Maryland. It was about ninety minutes north of the city. Their property had beautiful rolling green hills, with three horses in the pasture and a red barn. The barn had hay bales stacked inside, to just a foot or so under the crossbeams.

The family friends had a son maybe a year older than me. The adults cut us loose to run and play. We ended up in that barn, looking up at the hay bales, and said why not? Let's climb up. I went first, all the way to the top. I turned around and kneeled over the edge. I held a hand out, to pull my fellow adventurer up the last few feet to the summit.

He grasped my hand, then his footing slipped and he jerked both of us off the bales. He was still facing the bales and quickly grabbed hold. But I flew from the top in a headfirst swan dive toward the concrete floor. To this day, I don't understand how the landing failed to break my neck. There's just a still photo image in memory: me floating, looking at that concrete. Nothing is moving. Somehow, I tilted and rolled at just the right angle. It didn't even knock the wind out of me.

In the calculus of little kids, the only thing we cared about was not getting in trouble. We swore secrecy. I can't remember the last time I thought of that day.

But it comes to mind now as I stare closer at the ceiling of the V-280.

And I remember, in screen grabs and short clips, the next

moments after Court tried to stop our move to capture or kill Petrikov.

I remember Puppy, Ulysses and me grabbing our assault rifles and rushing to the stairs. A mad dash down twenty stories.

I remember being out on the street, how bright the sunlight seemed after the darkness of the stairwell. The air was golden-orange and sparkling.

Puppy gets an SUV running.

We pile in, with Puppy driving max speed through the city. Ulysses is in the back seat. I'm sitting front passenger side with a map open on the center armrest. Ulysses leans forward. We call out turns to Puppy as he circles toward an ambush spot at the golf course entrance.

Were we alone? Did we find any other teams down on the street, to join the effort?

Puppy slams the SUV to a halt, right beside a row of courtyard-walled houses. Now we're on foot, running to our ambush setup.

I remember just the quickest flash of movement, the nose cone facing us at three quarter perspective. One tail fin was visible. A brilliant white light filled my world. It was pure, with no noise.

And then I'm floating, suspended, looking down at the ground. It felt timeless. It reminds me of that day in the barn.

The memories recede.

One final time, I'm inside the V-280 medevac, still on my back looking up. The IV drip works its magic in full. I feel totally relaxed, floating once more, and drift off to sleep.

- 18 -

The blinds are open, and I'm taking in the afternoon sunshine. From the fourth floor hospital bed, I look across the expanse of lawn on the medical center's campus. Sugar maples ring the lawn's edge. Their leaves show the full glory of fall. It's a nice respite from endless rounds of surgery and physical therapy.

Yesterday, the charge nurse gave a heads up that Courtney Simons would visit today. I have no idea what to expect. And frankly, I don't much care what he has to say. I wouldn't have handled the situation in Dubai any differently, if given another chance.

Petrikov got away. As near as I can figure, there must have been a surviving Armata providing long-range overwatch to his pickup zone on the Emirates Hills golf course. The Kornet missile hit us as we were moving into ambush position. With the three of us down, and with no other friendly teams nearby, the SU-80 made a clean landing and whisked Petrikov back to Syria.

Puppy will recover fully. He took shrapnel to the legs and torso, plus a concussion, but he's progressing well. The Non-Surgical ward plans to discharge him soon.

Ulysses is a different story. He's across the hospital campus, in the Long Term Care ward. I'm not ambulatory; can't go see him yet. Several hospital staff have relayed updates. And Puppy has visited several times.

None of the news is good. A small missile fragment penetrated Ulysses' skull. The external wound is barely visible, but the damage is severe. He's in a coma. The immediate concern is brain swelling and the cognitive implications. They don't foresee any quick improvement in his status. Possibly he'll never recover.

I took injuries less severe than Ulysses but worse than Puppy. My left leg sticks out beneath the covers, with an external spatial frame attached. It's basically like a big aluminum bird cage, bolted on from mid-thigh down to the ankle. The biggest risk to me on medevac was a pneumothorax, or collapsed lung. They stabilized that with a chest tube, and rumors about chest tubes are true. The pain is excruciating, and broke through the painkillers until they upped the dose. Overpressure from the missile blast ruptured my left eardrum. They think I'll get most or all of the hearing back on that side.

Footsteps echo on the linoleum. I look up as Simons walks in. It's the first time I've seen him since the Hotel Victoria rooftop, when we disobeyed orders and went after Petrikov.

"You were *stupid*, you know that?" He chews me out even before fully closing the door behind him. He looks around at the room. It's small, but at least it's private.

I don't take the bait. Let him call me whatever he wants.

He looks at the cage. "Are they going to save it?"

"The docs think so," I reply. "The next couple rounds of surgery will tell. A long road of rehab after that. I'm staying on them about functionality, though. Don't want to keep a useless appendage. If we can't get the knee and ankle working, I'll have them take it off and learn to use a prosthetic."

He studies the contraption for a few more seconds. "Well, like I said, you were stupid."

"I can't believe you took time out of your victory lap just to come rub my nose in it."

He grunts at that. And what a victory lap it is. I've had nothing to do but surf a tablet since arriving here. The news feeds all hail him as the "hero of Dubai." He's the man who reopened the flow of Persian Gulf oil, at a time when (so the stories say) the American government and other Western democracies all shrank from the task.

It's not surprising to see him get the singular credit. His publicists had their spin campaign prepared well before we hit H-Hour in theater. At the first breath of success, they pushed that messaging into high gear. And with Enterprise Performance software laced into all corners of the internet, EP algorithms made short work of getting his Dubai publicity onto the page views of nearly every American.

The Simons hero worship has now built to a level that's alarming. It wasn't *just him.* Quite the opposite. The Air Force assets, the F-35 fighters and C-130 transports for the paratroopers, they were his assets in name only. The ground combatants – TF Valor's special operators, TF Mauler's armored crewmen, and TF Zeus' paratroopers – they were all direct hires from the military. Even the Merkava tanks came courtesy of State Department negotiating and coordinating their off-grid transport to Oman. Enterprise Performance merely took custody. But it's clear that Court wants to make this all about him.

It's also disturbing the degree to which our casualties don't get mentioned. We lost more than five hundred KIA before the fight ended. Hundreds more took wounds or serious injury. Enterprise Performance message managers don't seem to want this known. They've spent years building the brand of Simons as the billionaire with the magic touch. I guess the stark reality of war doesn't jibe with the super-human image of success they seek to project.

Simons pitched to the US government that outsourcing the Emirates operation would provide a kind of political heat shield. If it failed, the administration would have some distance from blame.

I don't think that would have been the case. The EP information machine also had spin products ready in the event of mission failure. I wasn't privy to the details, but that "mission fail" messaging would almost certainly have deflected blame back onto the US government, for preventing Enterprise Performance from executing an otherwise stellar plan.

Now that it's succeeded, though, both political parties seem caught completely off guard. Simons is touring the country as the American victor returned. To all accounts, no one in national government leadership has any idea how to handle that.

Simons continues looking at me, controlled but incensed.

He finally says, "No, Mark, I didn't come here to rub your nose in the stupid way you and your friends got wounded. I came here to give you the best deal you're going to get."

I just look at him, still not in the mood to reply to the question he obviously wants me to ask. What deal? He's going to tell me anyway.

He points at my ortho cage. "Mark, what do you think was going on here?" Then he adds, "I mean *strategically, geopolitically,* what do you think was really going on?"

"Let's see. Strategically, we had our sights on the Russian architect of every major operation they've run for the past fifteen years. And we had a chance to take him out of play. And if you'd chopped over additional teams like I'd wanted, we'd have fielded a big enough ambush team that one Kornet missile couldn't have stopped us. And we'd have succeeded. But instead, it *was* just me and my two friends. And Petrikov got away, free to run future operations against us. And that's what I think. Strategically."

"You need to grow up."

"OK, I need to grow up. I go back to the same question. Are you really just here to call me stupid and immature? Or are you going to get to this deal you're offering?" Damn. I wasn't going to give him the pleasure of me asking about his deal. But now I just want him gone.

"I'll get to the deal," he says. "But first you need to stop and see the world as it is. Why do you think I undertook this mission? What gain is in it for Enterprise Performance and for me?"

I have no idea how he'll answer that question. I just stare.

"Mark, the international construct of the past seventy-five years is *ending*. The idea of Western democracy and a human-rights-based global commons – that was a grand experiment. It was noble. In its time, it was possibly even effective."

He looks out the window. "But those are worn out concepts."

Then he turns back from the window to me. "Look at what's coming. *Really look*. Take the United States. Three hundred and fifty million Americans. Globalization gutted us for forty years. We kept the lid on unrest by pointing to a low unemployment rate. But most of that was bait and switch, from old jobs that used to pay a living wage, to bottom-end jobs that barely scratch along. Then, in the 2020s, the seams *really* came loose. The Second Great Depression hit. First Wave automation took out forty million jobs. We lost all the truckers, postal workers, most heavy industry workers, all the fungible admin and data management positions."

"I know all that!" What, does he think I've been under a rock the past couple decades?

He continues, not even registering my protest. "But that's just the fallout so far. Why do you think they called it the *First* Wave? It's because a second wave is coming, and a third. Automation and AI will eliminate even the high-end jobs. I'm about to roll out machine learning algorithms that will render every, I mean *every*, accountant, banker, economist – you name it – unemployable. Most doctors will get sidelined, permanently."

I take this in, thinking of the throngs of people who are already scraping for handouts on the street. Is he for real? Those numbers would be horrifying.

Simons steps closer to the bed. He fixes his gaze, his eyes lacking any emotion. "The economy will restructure to an owner class, a very small caretaker class, and then everyone else. In the next four years, you're going to see another seventy-five million out of work. No, it will be more. Six out of every seven working age Americans will be desperate for employment before it's done."

He pauses a few seconds but continues before I can say anything. "Add to that an increased global competition for resources. We went to Dubai for oil. Soon we'll be fighting for water. Before too long, we'll come to accept there just isn't enough of *anything* to go around. Every country will wake up and realize their social contract is changing. Right now, the politicians all point at each other and say there are solutions that can save everyone. They claim it's just that the other side won't play nice. But here's the deal. The world we remember is gone. It's not coming back, none of it. We can't fit everyone in the boat. And trust me, Mark, you want to be in that boat."

I'm confused. Part of it's the painkillers. But I don't accept the darkness of Simons' world view. I ask, "If all that's the case, I still don't see why you helped Petrikov escape. Why help the Russians come out on top?"

"You're not listening!" he scolds. "*There's no such thing* as countries anymore. There's no such thing as Russians or Americans. There are only haves and have nots. There are masters and servants. No in-betweens! Petrikov is a master. *I'm* a master. You? You *could* be a master, if you didn't squander your talent and energy on some fool notion of duty to country. Mark, what you have to realize is, you and I have more in common with Petrikov than we do with some vagrant who's begging for scraps at the gates of Camp Diamond."

I protest in disbelief. "Those 'vagrants' outside of Camp Diamond are Americans."

Simons is calm now, his emotion played out. "Look, if we had killed Petrikov in combat, so be it. But once there was a chance to let him go, that was good business. He knows how the world works. We might need him later. I'm banking Petrikov is a man we can work with."

This is mind blowing. I try to clear my head. There are questions I should ask. "If you really believe all this, then why put everything on the line like you did? Why risk so much for an operation that, statistically, had such a high chance of failure?"

"Because," he said, "if I'm right, if there's no such thing as countries anymore and it's every person for themselves – well, then you'd better have your own army. The force we built for the Emirates was small potatoes. But it's a start."

Simons sees the look on my face. "You're probably wondering why I'm talking so freely? It's to try and help you understand, Mark. I do want to offer you a deal. You're useful. But I've gotten to know you and your friends. I suspect right now you're already thinking, is there someone you should warn? Someone you should give a heads up about me, that is. And here's the thing. *They've already heard it from me.* The people that matter, anyway. But they're not going to act. Too many of them have this foolish belief that America will pull through, because it always has in the past. Some are too scared to act. Others want to angle for their own good deal. Whatever their motivation, the outcome is the same. The Administration and both aisles of Congress will agree to outsource even more military capacity to Enterprise Performance. The public wants it. Social media is screaming for it. Winds are blowing in my direction."

His words hang in the air for almost a minute. It's a deafening silence.

Then he gets to his deal.

"Have you done any homework on how you're here, in Walter Reed? After you, Puppy and Ulysses were all involuntarily separated from active duty? Congress voted down pensions. They voted down health care benefits, too. All were deemed too expensive. Enterprise Performance sponsors your care here."

I don't say anything.

"Your little cabal's stunt about resigning from the company, that would not be a smart move. It would mean immediate discharge for all three of you. You'd all three owe the medical bills, enough to bankrupt each of you and put you plus your families in the ranks of the panhandlers."

The room feels hot. That happens when the leg wounds are throbbing. But I know this time it's not the leg.

"So, what are you saying?" I ask.

"Mark, I'm saying you need to stay in the boat. I'm the hero of Dubai, as it should be. I took all the risk and I was the only one who could pull it all together. But you three were known in enough circles as my senior military advisors for the operation. It's bad business if I toss you out to beg for scraps. Well, Ulysses, he wouldn't beg for anything. He'd just die."

Simons keeps talking. It's overwhelming, too much to process. I stare out at the sugar maples. When you know you're trapped, it's easy to disassociate. I look out the window and revel in the beauty of the red leaves. I imagine myself walking on the lawn and smelling fall's splendor.

Part II

- 19 -

Sunday, 2 September 2035 – Bethesda, Maryland

"Uncle Mark! Aunt Linny! Is today a water day?" Matthew calls out.

It's barely past dawn. I bury my head under the pillow, hoping for just a second more sleep before the bounce.

"Hiyaaah!" Matthew wails in his best martial arts imitation. He takes a running leap and sails over Linny's side of the bed, splashing with all fours on top of the covers, square on top of me.

"Uhhh!" I give out a fake groan of surrender. The ritual concludes with Matthew's giggle.

Emma, his sister, walks in calmly. She hugs her favorite stuffed Tigger, with her chin tucked down. Somewhere, Linny found the matching Tigger nightshirt that Emma's wearing. She walks to Linny's side of the bed, lifts the covers with a little hand and nestles in on that side. Her brother may wake up in full-energy mode. But Emma needs more time to greet a new day.

I shift Matthew around in the dog pile to where I can give Linny a kiss. We luxuriate in a hug for a minute.

Emma asks, "Uncle Mark, is today a water day?"

"I don't know, baby girl. If not, we've got all the water cans topped off. I'll rig up the gravity shower so you guys can clean up before we take you back."

"Do we ha-a-ave to go back?" she asks, throwing the turbo cuteness into her voice.

"You guys know the rules. Our visitor permits only allow two days per month. But we're working on it so you can come live here for good. I'll go check and see about the water."

I start out of bed, but Matthew's clamped both hands onto my left arm and is trying to twist me into an arm bar. I let him have a faux-struggle for a bit and then pry him loose while he's laughing. God, I think, give it a few years and I'm done. Once he gets to be his dad's size? That gets me choked up. Matthew and Emma Harris – Ulysses' young twins. It's infuriating to think what they deserve versus what I can actually make happen. I go back to thinking about water.

Down the stairs in our little Cape Cod, I walk gingerly over to the desk. All things equal, I'm lucky: blown out eardrum, sucking chest wound, pins and rods holding together the left tibia and fibula. It could have been worse. The first couple hours of each day are the hardest. The rehab was painful but slowly progressed to where I can function with most of the old capacity. Linny hates that in the past year I've even built up to running again. I keep the mileage reasonable. But it's important to stay in shape now more than ever. Going up the Pike, outside the walls, it's everyone for themselves.

It's a short walk across the first-floor living room to my desk. I take a seat, fire up the laptop, and sigh. It's a long wait for the messages to scroll through.

WARNING: Pursuant to the Server Nationalization Act of 2034, all actions on this account are monitored in accordance with national law. Any unauthorized use of this account will result in immediate arrest with users subject to incarceration and loss of Full Privileges.

I scroll through the rest of the warning text, clicking "accept" at all the right places. It's not done yet. The next screen auto populates a succession of articles.

Today's highlights from the Courtney Simons Administration:
- Latest news regarding the disbanded traitorous Congress: Click here to see former Rep. Johnson's video-recorded confession.
- President Simons to receive European Union representatives at White House meeting, to kick off major economic summit.
- Enterprise Performance domestic security highlight: Full Privilege zones are now established in three more American cities. Click here for more information.

Nothing new, it's all the usual pronouncements. I click "skip" as soon as the auto timer allows. It's not smart to do that every day. It hurts your user reliability rating. But I'm cranky and would like to know myself if we can take real showers today. Finally, the mandatories are done and I can surf. I pull up the state web browser to the Favorites tab and click through.

Welcome to the Full Privilege zone of Bethesda. Today is September 2nd, 2035. Today's water status is: Amber, fifteen gallons per household.

Sigh, figured as much. It's not surprising. We're three months into hundred degree days, and we just hit a record at one hundred and twelve last month. The city probably won't get back into green status for water until October. At least fifteen gallons is enough to give each of us a turn in the gravity shower. With what we have in storage, we can still spare a few gallons to take over to the orphanage when we drop off the kids. We complain about amber status here in the city, but the camp followers out there get nothing.

Linny makes her way downstairs. She leans over and gives me a hug, looking at the computer. "There's no way it's green?" she asks.

"Nope, amber."

We hear the bongo drums of four little feet running down the old wooden stairs. "Aunt Liiiinny! Do we get a real shower?" Emma calls out.

Linny kneels down, smiling, and gives her cheery reply. "No, but we'll use the gravity shower."

Matthew puts on a half pouty face. "But when we were at the store during our last visit, some boy there was saying they take real showers EVERY day."

"I'm sure he did." I turn and say with a chuckle. "And that means he lives at least in Chevy Chase, which is a High Privilege zone. They get more than us. But you know what? The Chevy Chase people look at Georgetown and think about all the things that Chevy Chase privileges don't allow. So, we'll stay thankful for what we have and enjoy our gravity showers." I try to keep a smile. You can't blame the fella for asking.

Welcome to the new strata. The Ultra High Privileged, or UHPs, live in Georgetown and the heart of the District. The High Privileged, or HPs, in Chevy Chase and the middle ring neighborhoods, don't have it nearly as good. Then there's the mere Full Privileged, FPs, like Linny and me. We're lucky just to have a spot inside the city walls. Past that, just outside the barricades, the camp followers band together as best they can.

As usual, Linny's got the better touch. She gets the kids excited for breakfast and soon they bound out of the room. She looks back at me with a smile and whispers, "Better to distract than defend." Her eyes crinkle in the way I fell in love with. I give her a smooch and head out to the garage for the water jugs.

- 20 -

Walking out to the garage, I look around and think about how lucky we are. Who cares about everyday showers and full time running water? We're inside the FP zone. With luck, we'll get adoption rights for Matthew and Emma, and bring them inside the walls full time. We've got longer term plans, too. Maybe try and transfer to a more northern city. Maybe aim for Canada after that. But first things first: getting privileged status for the kids.

Linny and I just have to be smart. We've got probably the smallest house left in the FP. The other old ones have been torn down. Families with the money or connections to stay inside a city want nothing but the best. They can't display proper status in a ninety-year-old Cape Cod with single-car detached garage.

But what connections I had have long since atrophied. No one's going to give me the kind of work to buy the big house. Linny could have scored a topflight job in the city, most likely, except for the black mark of being married to me. Oh, they'll give us just enough to keep from getting kicked out. Just enough to have kept me from making a ruckus when it mattered.

This is all a way of saying, I did take Simons up on the offer he made during his Walter Reed visit. I took his offer for employment. My wounds needed a couple years to cycle through the surgeries and rehab. There was no question of me returning to field work during that long recovery. Plus, Simons would never again trust me to be on the inside of an operation. Instead, he transferred me to a subsidiary providing municipal service management for the DC metro area. I ride a desk. I report to a boss who could care less what work I do in a given week. But my showing up there bolsters his status – the larger the headcount, the more important his little empire.

That's where I found myself as The Struggles rolled across the country.

Simons had figured out all the angles before even walking into my hospital room in 2029. He knew I'd keep my mouth shut about Petrikov. Puppy would, too. We understood the implicit message that our silence was the price for Ulysses continuing to get treatment.

Soon after the day Simons paid me a visit, Puppy and I reached out to Major General Saiz for counsel. Saiz agreed it was the right course. As he put it, "There's not a four-star general on active duty right now who can stop the winds that are blowing. The two of you, you're *definitely* not going to gain anything but more trouble if you make noise about Petrikov." My new status, desk bound in DC, also could have advantages according to Saiz. He said that with all the unpredictability the near future would hold, it would be nice to have some DC-based contacts who were out of the spotlight.

As events unfolded over the next several years, Courtney Simons showed he could disrupt the national security and political communities in the same way he had taken Silicon Valley by storm. He leveraged the accolades for pushing the Russians out of Dubai, and he continued to grow the Enterprise Performance military arm.

Enterprise Performance became the leading US mechanism for foreign policy and security matters. OPEC awarded EP a hefty contract to maintain a security presence in the Emirates. Simons parlayed this into other stabilization contracts. Enterprise

Performance deployed to Singapore in 2030, as a counterweight to Chinese expansion. In '31, Simons won a sole-source bid to provide a counter terrorism task force of seven thousand operators to contain unrest in France.

Puppy stayed employed in EP's growing military services arm. It was a weird situation for him. Internal to the company, he was demoted in status. But publicly, those were the days of highest regard for Enterprise Performance. Simons sold national leaders and the public alike on the patriotic call that Enterprise Performance was answering. Puppy cared little about the public accolades. It was simply the only job that Simons offered him. Otherwise he'd be on the streets, scrounging like all the rest.

Back in the US, second- and third-wave job losses hit, just as Simons predicted. The country came to call this period "The Struggles." If anything, Court's unemployment predictions were a little low. Job riots wracked the country. Food riots followed. As tax revenue dried up and services broke down, the water riots came, too.

For someone so derisive of politicians, it's amazing what a natural stump speaker Courtney Simons turned out to be. He ran as VP on the Atkinson ticket in '32. The way Simons wove the tale, the savior of Dubai was the *only* one who could fix the country's woes. Throngs of supporters asked him to run for nomination at the top of the ticket. But by then, there were some hints in the press of the Petrikov situation. He probably figured the prestige wasn't worth the extra attention that comes to a presidential candidate. Besides, he had designs on how to turn the vice presidency into the real catbird seat for his next level expansion.

Congress awarded Enterprise Performance the nationwide domestic security contract one week after Simons was sworn in as Vice President. The social upheaval was awful as EP's domestic task forces performed brutal work. At Simons' direction, they walled off major US cities, to preserve safety for the economic elite. This cut off more than eighty percent of the US populace and sentenced them to waste away outside the new security barriers. Rumors were that President Atkinson had deep disagreement with his VP over this policy. But the lines of authority were murky. Simons was number two in the administration, but not at Enterprise Performance.

Simons had retained his title as CEO at EP. He sold his "Shining Cities" program to lobbyists, pundits and lawmakers, who kept media feeds alive with supportive commentary. Those supporters knew a good thing when it appeared. They wanted to stay safe inside the walls. They wanted a seat in the boat.

I miss Puppy. And I wish Major General Saiz was still here as a source of counsel. They're both missing, long presumed dead.

When the Korean situation went down in late '33, the Administration and Congress passed resolution for Enterprise Performance to send a quick-response task force of thirty thousand combatants. Saiz had just retired from active duty. EP reached out for him to command the formation. Saiz took Puppy with him as a tactical advisor.

No one back in the US seems to know how it went so bad, so quickly. The Chinese intervention was not unexpected. But the swiftness of Chinese victory belied precedent. To date, a few thousand stragglers from the EP task force have made it back to the States. The news feeds never mention them. I continue to ask around. But none of the survivors have any info on General Saiz or Puppy.

The irony was, everyone blamed *President Atkinson* for the Korea failure. Courtney Simons never took the least bit of heat, even though it was his company and he was Atkinson's sitting VP. The whisper campaign, put out by EP lobbyists most likely, was that Atkinson had gone against Simons' advice on some key aspects of the deployment. This rumor mill claimed it was Atkinson's lack of full commitment that led to the failure. The same whispers also said Simons had better domestic solutions to offer the country, but that Atkinson was keeping him at arm's length.

It caused a real row in the moneyed class.

Then Atkinson's helicopter went down in early '34, as he was returning from a weekend trip to Camp David. Tragedy though it was, many thought it might actually be for the better. Atkinson's popularity was at a historic low by the time of his death.

In the country's eyes, the accident cleared the way for an invigorated *President Simons* to take the helm and perhaps make some real improvements.

Except the domestic threat alerts kept rising. With the cities walled off, neither party could agree on how to hold the midterm national elections. Disputes grew so heated that fistfights broke out on the floor of the House. Then came the first case of one Congressman shooting another since 1838.

In the summer of 2034, President Simons went live on all media feeds. He declared that he had evidence of traitorous elements in both the House and the Senate. To preserve national security, he stated he had no choice but to dissolve the Congress and invoke direct Executive law. Future elections would remain suspended until a new polling mechanism could be determined.

As an additional domestic security measure, Simons established the Server Nationalization Act of 2034. Enterprise Performance would manage and enforce the Act.

The country has seen seismic changes in the past five or six years that generated an almost compulsive need to talk about what was happening. The same way I remember hearing about survivors of the 1930s Depression. People want to talk about what it was like before. Or how it all happened. Or whether it can ever get better.

One group you won't hear giving it much concern are the current hired members of the Enterprise Performance domestic security force. They're just here to do a job. After all, it's not like this is home.

When Simons won his big domestic security contract, back when he was still VP, one of the provisions he insisted on was that he'd need to bring in disinterested parties. He needed security specialists who would show no hesitation or favoritism when putting down the violence of The Struggles and securing the major cities. He won contract terms allowing him to give preferential hiring to foreigners, on the grounds they would be neutral third parties.

Today, more than ninety percent of the Enterprise Performance domestic security force are hired Russian nationals, working here on one-year contracts. They police our cities. More importantly, they enforce Simons' will, and report only to him. The word is, Simons' hiring manager in Russia is none other than Dmitry Petrikov.

Snapping out of it, I look around and realize I'm still standing in the garage. I try to figure out how long I've been spaced out and ruminating. What did I come in here for?

Little Emma runs in all frustrated and says, "Uncle Mark! We need the water jugs. Aunt Linny's going to make *pancakes*!"

I look down at her and laugh. "Sorry, baby girl. Got lost for a second. I'm on the way!"

- 21 -

We finish up breakfast – pancakes with real blueberries. This prompts a mental note to check Linny's jewelry when we get back tonight. Doting on the kids is good, but blueberries are expensive in the city. I caught her pawning a pair of earrings some months ago. That was also to give the kids a luxury – some clothes they can wear to the parks downtown and not get made fun of as "FP kids" by the upper crust young 'uns. It's understandable, considering what they've been through. But we might need that jewelry for something big. It's not worth saying anything now. Better just to check later on.

"Uncle Mark, why can't we stay?" Matthew asks as we're carrying our plates to the sink.

"I'd love that," I say, smiling and giving his hair a light tousle, "but what are the rules?"

"I know, two nights a month," he says, a little deflated.

It would be great to keep them here longer. But there's not much we can do. If we exceeded their city pass by even an hour, an EP detention team would arrive to kick the kids out permanently. Probably us too.

And it's not like there's any chance of hiding them somewhere else in the city. When the walling-off started, those lucky enough to stay inside gladly checked "agree" on all the consent decrees. Every vehicle is geotagged and has biometric cameras inside to confirm occupants. More biometric cameras line the streets, every four hundred meters. The list goes on. Want to take your chances outside the barriers? No problem. Live in freedom and good luck. But in here, the price of security is lockdown. This means the kids go back out until the permanent approvals come through.

"Hey buddy," I say to Matthew, "we'll have you guys back here in two weeks for an overnight. But for now, it's back to Mister Dan."

Then Linny lays on the charm. "But we're taking you two back with a care package of treats. Enough to share with the other kids!" They're beaming at her, as am I just watching the scene. And I definitely need to check the jewelry. The kids bound upstairs to grab their things.

Linny leans in close and asks, "Am I coming with today? Or are you headed up the Pike?"

"You're good to come along. Just going to the orphanage and back. The kids will enjoy you riding with us." She knows I won't let her beyond the camp followers belt.

It's funny how easily modern America confused the ephemeral with something that would last forever. Our high water mark of postwar wealth lasted just about seventy-five years. Yet we ascribed a sense of permanence to it. Interstate highways. Strip malls with cold water and abundant food at every corner. Civility. We forgot that in 1932, most inter-city trips would have taken days across a rabbit warren of back roads. And in 1832, those same inter-city trips were basically expeditions, with a real possibility of encountering bandits or violence. The truth is, from the late twentieth century to early twenty-first century, America was living in a historic anomaly. We hardly even took the time to appreciate it.

One thing I have to hand to Courtney Simons: he recognized the timeless pattern of struggle that humans succumb to when a system breaks down and resources run thin. For example, Rockville Pike today organizes along a caste pattern that pre-Roman city states would have recognized.

The haves live inside the walls. In the DC area, the wall generally follows the old Capital Beltway. Outside that barrier, it's a free-fire zone for a full kilometer. Houses and anything else in the way were razed, the easier to shoot dead any trespassers. Just past the edge of the free-fire zone cling the camp followers. They're the ones not lucky enough to be within the walls, but with a sponsor who can siphon out enough money or barter to keep them in the kind of semi-safety that proximity to a city offers.

After the belts of camp followers come the markets. Traveling out the Pike, the main market is at the old Rockville Town Center. You can buy anything you want, so long as you have the cash to pay and are amenable to the risk of traveling there.

I go to the market once a month. Most city dwellers are afraid to go near there, for good reason. But, in season, you can get fresh fruit and vegetables, sometimes a good side of meat. I turn that for a tidy profit back in the city – cash on delivery at the loading dock entrance of Dean and Deluca in Georgetown. The proceeds go either to orphanage costs for the twins or to the necessary bribes at Walter Reed for Ulysses.

Finally, out beyond the markets, you hit the badlands. You're one hundred percent on your own there. In some rural areas there are settlements; farming communities or small towns that run their own security. I went up to Hagerstown two years ago. Scored a trade that helped grease palms for a good eight months. Linny was pissed, though. And she was right. It's too high risk. If I burned in, what happens next? She still gets legal work, but not enough to make up for the bartering. And when our payments at the hospital and the orphanage stop? There's some good people at both those places, but they're not running charities.

"All right, let's pile in!" Linny says. The kids hop into the back seat of our sedan, towing along their overnight bags. I pop the trunk and double check that the stash for Dan is all there in a box: a bottle of Jack, some DVDs that are now at a premium on the outside, and a printed instruction manual for their generator, which has been on the fritz lately. We'll also hand off two five-gallon jugs of potable water. Technically, Dan runs the orphanage on a cash basis. But we want Emma and Matthew to get well taken care of, so we help out where we can.

The windows stay down while we're still in the city. My shirt's soaked through. It's 10 a.m. and already over a hundred degrees. I keep the AC charged as best as possible, but it's never really enough.

There's no passage point through the barriers on Old Georgetown Road, so we drive across Cedar to get to Rockville Pike. The traffic's pretty light, Sunday morning and all. Still, there's enough traffic for us to stand out as an anomaly, with two adults in the front seat. The other cars in sight are autonomous, with a roomier passenger area in the back. Anymore, the only part of the city with a majority of human-driven cars are the UHP enclaves in Georgetown and Capitol Hill. There, they want a human driver as a status symbol.

We turn north on the Pike and immediately approach the outbound signs.

> *"Warning, you are departing the Privileged Zone. A free-fire zone exists for the next 1,000 meters. All persons departing the perimeter are responsible for their own safety. No persons will be readmitted without demonstrating proper identification and proof of Full Privilege or higher status."*

As we approach the exit, eight-wheeled armored personnel carriers line either side of the street. Their remote machine gun mounts are trained on the wall opening. A couple of guards stand outside each vehicle. They wear the typical Enterprise Performance security outfit: khaki cargo pants, blue long-sleeved shirt and a black ballistic vest, with an assault rifle slung across the chest.

They watch without much interest as we crawl by at the prescribed ten miles per hour. No one cares about the outbounds. That's on you. Every so often, a UHP will head out in a two- or three-SUV convoy. The UHPs head to the market at the old Rockville Town Center, where the cash they throw around can buy any and all kicks. For sure, the guards straighten up when those SUV convoys roll through. But a cheap-ass sedan like ours going out? That's low-rent FP all the way. It's nothing the guards will break a sweat over.

We exit the wall and drive through the free-fire zone. I scan across the cement foundations, where the old houses and buildings were scraped away. Samsung autonomous bots patrol the zone. They're man-sized, upright, and travel on treads. Their infrared sensors slave to a 7.62mm machine gun and four hundred rounds. One of them is about a hundred meters off to our right. Its gun swivels to track us along the designated daytime road through this sector. The bots automatically engage anything that enters the zone during curfew, or anything that goes off road during daylight. Even the deer have learned to stay out.

Next we pass by the old Georgetown Prep campus on our left. Linny looks that way and lets out a wistful sigh.

"Not worth the money," I shake my head, speaking quietly so the kids don't pick up on it. It's a tough call. The old Prep campus has been hardened pretty well. It doesn't have twenty-foot concrete T barriers with cameras and gun towers, like the city walls. But they've run triple strand concertina around the perimeter, with armed guards roving. Any of the UHPs or HPs who can't get a relative into the city, they generally set them up at the Prep. After all, there's a limit to how many even the upper crust can get inside.

Right turn into Strathmore, and I'm scanning more aggressively now. Garrett Park is still camp follower territory, but daylight ambushes have been known to happen. Another half mile, and we're left onto Einstein Street, into the neighborhood.

"There's Celeste!" Emma squeals.

For the orphanage they took over the fourth through eighth houses on the right side of the street. Outside the walls, there hasn't been grid electricity since the start of The Struggles. The mid-morning heat drives kids and custodians alike out of the houses. You've got to hand it to Dan's crew. They still run classes, trying to give the kids some semblance of an education. But today's Sunday, so the kids are running wild. The high-pitched shouts and laughter are all the barometer I need to gauge the level of care the kids receive.

This contrasts in a sad way to the rest of the houses on the block. Forlorn, castoff adults sit on stoops. They call out to each other, in the idle chatter of those who have nowhere to be. From one porch, a cheap battery operated CD player blares a Kurt Cobain song.

"Wait for us to stop," Linny chimes, with her I-love-you-but-listen voice as we pull up. The instant the car stops, they're off with their jumble of friends.

We park as Dan walks up. "Hey, Mark, hey, Linny." He hugs Linny and then he and I shake hands.

"Hey, Dan," Linny says with a smile. "Where's Sarah?"

"Out in back. She'll be happy to see you."

Linny gives me a nod and heads that way. Sarah is Dan's wife. She was a nurse back in the day. Dan was a Montgomery County police officer. Most orphanages have some combination of cops, firefighters, nurses, maybe an ex-teacher or two. It's good steady work. One thing people will pay for is the kids they want to try and save from the badlands.

"How was their visit in the big city?" Dan wasn't here when I picked up the kids yesterday. It's our first chance to catch up in a couple of weeks.

"Good. Short." Then I remember. "Got that generator manual for you. Looks like there's a pretty good trouble shooting section in the back."

"Brother, that's great. Our guys can normally get anything working, but that cheap Indian knockoff has been giving us fits."

I hand him the next four weeks' cash plus the other goodies from the trunk.

"How are things on the street?" I ask, looking around. The grass is all gone around the orphanage row of houses, just like the rest of the street. In the summer, it's hard-packed dirt. In the rainy months, it's mud. The orphanage houses themselves show their wear, with mismatched shingles and different color paint on some of the wall patches. But Dan keeps them maintained and clean.

Up and down the rest of the block, it's a different story. A boarded over window here. Part of a missing roof with blue plastic covering there. The adults on those stoops show the same neglect as the houses. No one was ready for how fast the jobs evaporated. Even after the First Wave eliminated blue collar jobs, people in this area thought they'd be safe. They had degrees suited for the knowledge economy. They'd built a professional niche. Then the Second and Third Waves exposed the folly of that logic. There just weren't enough jobs to go around.

Dan's looking around, too. "Around here?" he says, "It's the same as ever. It's fine. No one gives us any trouble." He hesitates a moment, then adds, "Hey, Mark. Um, just so you know. Matthew and Emma have been asking again."

"Who's talking to them?" I ask in a voice with more edge than intended.

"I don't know. You know how it is. Kids talk."

"What did you say?"

"Same as always. I say all I know is their dad was hurt in the war, nothing else. That's what their Mom had been telling them, when they still lived in West Virginia before The Struggles. But you've had them here what, almost two years now? They're getting older. And Ulysses was, *is*, a well-known name."

I don't reply, just stare down at the ground and listen.

"Hey," Dan continues. "I'm not telling you what to do at all. They saw their Mom die. And I understand why you don't want to tell them about their Dad unless you can get them permanent into the city. I'm just giving it to you straight. They're getting older, and I can't stop what the other kids might say."

"Thanks, Dan. I know you guys are doing your best. We'll just take it as it goes."

He nods, and we shake hands. Dan turns to go check on the generator.

- 22 -

Saturday, 8 September 2035 – Bethesda, Maryland

"ID card."

I'm at the checkpoint entrance for Walter Reed. The Enterprise Performance gate guard betrays no emotion behind his sunglasses. I hand him my card.

"Purpose of visit?"

"Going to visit a friend."

"What friend?" It's a natural question. By the look of both me and the sedan, he's got me pegged as former military, coming to visit a casualty from overseas. But Korea was our only overseas engagement in the past three years. And, well, our wounded never came home from Korea. The government has mostly kicked out the other military patients.

"I'm visiting a friend at Long Term Care," I explain.

"Your friend's name?"

"Ulysses Harris."

He searches information on his tablet for a moment, then says in a bored voice, "You may pass."

The guy's English is actually pretty good. Whenever going through ID card check here, or coming back through the walls from the Pike, I always wonder: Were the two of us on opposite sides of a firefight in Dubai?

Pulling onto the campus is a study in contrasts. Back in the day, Walter Reed served as the nation's premier military medical treatment facility. You mainly saw uniformed types walking around. The patients in civvies were typically retirees or family members. When you came to get treatment here, there was a sense of belonging.

It's different now. I look across the wide lawn adjacent Wood Road. The main building's art deco style serves as backdrop to a string of UHP chauffeur-driven SUVs parked to one side. The drivers stand in the shade of nearby trees, waiting for the return of the moneyed patients inside. HPs can also use the hospital, but they have to park in the high-rise garage.

And someone like me, with mere Full Privilege status? I'm supposed to count myself lucky even to come here for visits. The Administration kicked almost all military out of the Walter Reed care system, to make room for the higher privileged patients. Whenever Linny or I need medical care now, we pay cash at one of the house clinics set up outside the walls, in the camp followers. Technically, we can get treatment in the city, at DC General. But the baksheesh to get seen there is horrendous.

I pull off Wood Road and park in level two of the America Building's garage. As I walk back down the ramp, a couple of HPs walk by headed back to their car. They laugh in cheery conversation and sip drinks from The Daily Grind, the coffee stand in the main building.

Seeing that sends a little pang. It calls back to carefree days of grabbing a Starbucks just to kill time, or as mild distraction for the long stretch of a road trip. Now, we don't dare blow that kind of cash at the few Starbucks left in the city, in the UHP zone. The Daily Grind is cheaper though. Two or three times each winter, while here to visit, I'll splurge and get a latte to go. I bring a little cooler on the passenger seat of the car, and place the coffee drink inside – swaddled with towels to prevent spills. Then I drive directly the five minutes back home. Linny and I will sit on the bench in our little sunroom and share. We never talk. We just sit side by side with my arm around her. We smile, trade sips, and bask in the nostalgia of a small luxury from the old days.

I exit the parking garage and walk along Palmer Road as it curves downhill farther into campus. This takes me away from the main cluster of midrise buildings, toward more utilitarian, low slung, one- and two-story facilities. Long Term Care is at the very bottom of the hill. The walk takes four or five minutes. I use this time to put on an upbeat look.

Entering the building, I walk up to the one nurse at the front station. "Hi, I'm here to visit Ulysses. Any changes?"

She pulls up his status page, looks pensive, and says, "No, you can visit him though."

I swing around the corner into his room. "Hey brother! How's it going? I got another picture for the collection."

This room has been Ulysses' home for the past five and a half years. For two of those years, he had varying degrees of lucidity. Linny and I put reminders of his old life up on the wall, hoping that might help. Closest to his bedside is the sonogram of Matthew and Emma. They found it in the same left sleeve pocket on his combat shirt, when collecting his personal items during our medevac from Dubai. Over the years, we've added a couple dozen photos. These range from pics of our days on active duty at Camp Diamond, to more recent pics of the twins, ever since they showed up.

"This is from three weeks ago." I show him the most recent photo for the collection. "We took the kids down to the C&O canal. Matthew caught a frog and wanted to keep it as a pet. Emma said no, because people would think that *Matthew and the frog* were the twins. Don't worry, he still has your natural good looks. And Emma only gets more beautiful every day." His eyes are open but nothing I say appears to register. The bed is raised with him in a half-sitting position, his head on a pillow, and he appears to focus on a spot high on the wall at the far side of the room.

To our knowledge, Ulysses has no awareness that the kids are in our care. The shrapnel wound to his brain has been a nightmare of changing symptoms over the years. Sometime in '30, he came out of the coma. He was wheelchair bound. His speech was almost unintelligible, with asymmetric facial movements that had the look of a stroke. His recollections of who he was, where he was, varied. Some days, his memory mostly came back and you could have something like a real conversation. We were hopeful he could hold onto that or even improve.

We felt especially hopeful two years ago, when we received a message at our house about the twins. A stranger had shown up in the camp followers, claiming the two children with him were Matthew and Emma. By then we'd long since heard that Ulysses' ex-wife, Kathy, had died during The Struggles riots in West Virginia. The twins seemingly vanished, an all-too-common occurrence during the coast-to-coast upheaval.

Fortunately for the twins, Ulysses still had enough name recognition that a Samaritan of sorts had taken them in. The guy's main hope was that they'd be his ticket into a city. That hope was good for the twins, too, as it accounted for the proper treatment they'd received. It was crushing for the Samaritan when I delivered the news that even the kids weren't going to get to live inside the walls without months or years of waitlist. We had more money then, and I paid out as much as I could to the guy. Still, sometimes people pin everything on one last, frantic hope. We later heard the

Samaritan killed himself in a flop house at the Rockville market.

But we had the twins, and the next several days were a fever of activity. We arranged for care at Dan's orphanage. We did more cross checking, to fully confirm their identities. Between our research and the stories the kids were starting to talk about, it proved one hundred percent they were Matthew and Emma.

With our certainty in hand, I was ecstatic driving onto Walter Reed. We hadn't wanted to say anything to Ulysses until we were sure. I parked and flew down the hill to Long Term Care.

The ward nurse, Jill, said he had regressed just the night before. Ulysses no longer showed any sign of lucidity. So far as we know, he's never been aware that the twins are here.

The time since then has been tough. Some days, Ulysses seemed to reach a state of semi-consciousness. On those days, Jill and the ward team wheeled him into the dayroom, to try and give him a broader range of stimuli. Then eight weeks ago, he slipped into a full coma. He's on a feeding tube right now.

With the kids so close by, it's heartrending. All we can do is keep up the routine. Maybe when Matthew and Emma get Full Privileged status, and if I can arrange for them to visit, it will help. For now, I start the usual routine of reading out loud for a couple hours. Today we're covering Eisenhower's biography, Volume Two.

We're well into my reading when I hear, "Hi, Mark." It's Jill walking into the room. She has a good demeanor that's businesslike but conveys her concern for the patients.

"Hi, Jill, how are you?"

"Pretty good." She looks at the book. "Almost finished with Eisenhower? Ulysses, give Mark a request for the next one, if you can. If not, I know he'll pick out a good one for you."

I hand her the envelope of cash. "Here you are. Thanks for all you're doing." I bet she keeps none of it for herself. She hasn't raised rates since the day we first met. There are a lot of palms to grease, and Ulysses' care isn't cheap. She's always in scrubs and I've never even asked if she was military, or if she worked at Walter Reed before The Struggles. It's clear she doesn't approve that this campus has become the city's concierge medical hub for HP/UHP medical treatment.

"Thank you, sir," Jill says and quickly pockets the envelope. Looking more serious, she says, "I need to talk to you in the dayroom."

We head in there and find a quiet corner by one of the floor-to-ceiling windows. The view looks out to the bucolic woods on this part of campus.

"What's up?" I ask.

She hesitates, seems to be choosing her words, then says, "Dr. Nantz will be in here soon, making his rounds. You'll probably see him. But Mark, he won't want to get you riled up. So, he's not going to give you the full picture."

"Full picture about what?"

"Ulysses' brain functions are continuing to regress. In the next week or so, he will need a ventilator to breathe."

"OK." I get it. More money. "How much do you need? We've got emergency cash."

She stammers. "It's, it's not a cash issue at this point. It's a privileges issue."

"What do you mean, a privileges issue?" I'm keeping my voice low, but punching the words out in anger. "*He has privileges*, that's why he's here."

"Mark, look around this campus, will you? No one can be bothered with *Dubai* casualties anymore. The whole world has changed. *Millions* have died across the country. Ulysses moving to a feeding tube? That's an entirely different level of resources. It's got the hospital administrator having to answer, personally, why we are diverting care away from UHPs."

Jill pauses for a moment, collects herself. "He's been here over five years. Even if he doesn't need a ventilator, and he will, they're going to terminate care. The only one who can change this is President Simons. It was his directive that got Ulysses here in the first place." She asks me, "Would Simons help?"

I guffaw. "The last time I saw Simons was when he visited the hospital in 2029, a month after we were wounded. It's impossible for me to reach him."

I think for another bit, and then ask, "What about a transfer to DC General?"

She shakes her head. "They can't provide long term ventilator support. When Walter Reed became the UHP campus, DC General was forced to hand over most of their high-end care equipment."

"So, terminate care? What, you're just going to discharge him and send him out to die?" I ask, incredulous.

Jill, calm and steady, looks at me with sadness in her eyes. "No. No, they won't discharge him. There will just be one day that you'll show up to the main gate and your access will be canceled. And then you'll know . . ."

I nod and look out the window for a few seconds. Then I start back toward Ulysses' room.

"What are you going to do?" Jill asks, still standing by the window.

"Finish reading," I say as I walk, not looking back. "I owe him another thirty minutes."

- 23 -

As I make my way back up the hill, toward the garage, my legs almost buckle. Realistically, this conversation with Jill should not come as a surprise. It's just hard to process how close things came but still missed. The paperwork to grant the twins their city residence has been slowly working its way along. Even though Ulysses slipped back into a coma, I was hopeful there could be an improvement. At the least, Linny and I wanted to bring the kids in to meet their Dad, no matter what shape he was in. Now that seems to all be for naught.

It's time to snap away from that. There's another task coming up fast.

Ken Bowerman wants to meet. He said it was something urgent, and it must be for him to take the chance on seeing me in person. Of anyone who flew into Dubai with Courtney Simons on our command bird, hands down Ken came out of it the best. While Puppy, Ulysses and I were on the Hotel Victoria roof arguing with Simons about a Petrikov ambush, Ken was two floors down. When the three of us left to go chase Petrikov, and then got blown up, Ken took over as Court's primary advisor for the remainder of the Emirates operation.

The two of them clicked. It never went to Ken's head. He's not that kind of guy. But it did set him up well in the years after. When logging on, you see his name on the Administration news feeds occasionally. He's Assistant VP for Operations at Enterprise Performance. Technically he's not in government, except that an Assistant VP in Simon's company outranks pretty much any government official but Simons himself.

Ken didn't deploy for the Korea operation, by then being too important to the oversight of daily plans and operations for the entire company. Ken is single, High Privileges all the way. He's really what's referred to as HP *plus*. At just thirty-five years old, he's a poster child to get UHP status before long.

He'll up his UHP odds if he marries well, which is likely. Ken's living in the most exclusive singles apartment building in the HP, just off the Friendship Heights metro. It's stocked with well-connected men and women who are smart enough to know the right play. Alliance is the best path up to the next rung.

I don't begrudge Ken any of that. But it does surprise me that he'd take the risk to make contact. We've said hello in passing a couple times on the street, most recently about a year ago. But if anyone questioned those interactions, he could pull up the camera feeds and show it was just ten words, not even a conversation.

Still, if he says there's something that needs a meeting, then that's the way it is. Ken Bowerman's a straight shooter. He covered my back and the backs of other Americans any time he went out. More than that, actually. He's a true hero.

Ken won the Silver Star at age twenty-two, while serving as a paratrooper in the 11th Airborne Division. In 2022 buck Sergeant Bowerman led a fire team, part of an infantry platoon of forty on patrol in northern Afghanistan. He was ninth in seniority by rank. The platoon leader's award nomination, however, stated that Ken's actions were key to their survival that day.

Mission orders required their platoon to make a highly undesired foot movement through a narrow mountain pass in the Hindu Kush range. The formation moved single file, flanked on both sides by steep slopes that rose a couple hundred meters. Rocky outcroppings made it impossible in advance to confirm or deny the presence of enemy. The platoon moved quickly, with good tactical security, intending to minimize their exposure in the pass en route to the far side.

Upwards of three hundred Taliban attacked.

By 2022, the Taliban were third generation fighters who leveraged a home court advantage. They encircled the platoon with a complex ambush from upslope vantage points. Automatic weapons fire raked the American formation from end to end. Three paratroopers died instantly. The rest took what limited cover they could find at the bottom of the pass. Key leaders organized return fire as best they could, but the platoon was in peril.

The platoon forward air controller furiously worked his radio for close air support. Both sides, American and Taliban, knew this would decide the outcome. If the Air Force could get the angle for a bomb run or cannon strafing, they might break the back of the ambush. Failing that, given the imbalance of firepower raining down, it would end badly for the paratroopers. At best they might hold off a complete overrun before a quick reaction force could arrive. Every few minutes, another paratrooper went down wounded or killed.

Eager to press their advantage, the Taliban pushed in closer. They bounded down the slope in teams of two and three, with PKM machine guns firing from fifty meters upslope to keep the Americans fixed. The paratroopers fought hard and were hopeful when F-15s swooped overhead, only to hear the prospects dashed over the radio. At this altitude, the mountain pass was up in the cloud line. An overcast started swirling through – wispy stretches punctuated by thick dense gray for a couple minutes at a time. Given the enemy's proximity and the tightness of the terrain, the F-15 pilots worried any dropped bombs would kill more Americans than Taliban.

The enemy sensed this. Their rate of fire bloomed. The American quick reaction force was seventy-five minutes out, and paratroopers kept taking hits. At this rate, the platoon couldn't hold on for those seventy-five minutes.

Then Bowerman made his move.

Taking cover behind a beachball-sized rock, he had noticed a natural drainage channel just off to his right. It was about a meter deep and ran directly up the slope for a good hundred meters. With Ken was a wounded M-240 machine gunner. Ken grabbed the gun and extra hundred-round belts of ammunition. He dropped his body armor, water, assault rifle, everything he could ditch to cut weight.

When the next dense segment of cloud cover came in, he sprinted up the drainage channel. As the clouds thinned and visibility returned, he lay flat and waited for the next obscuration. The Taliban continued their murderous fire down on the platoon. But by then Ken was above the enemy lines. They weren't looking for an American upslope of them.

By now the Taliban lines had pressed to within thirty meters of the platoon. After two more bounds through the dense patches, Ken worked his way into a firing position.

He was smart. Instead of firing wildly, he picked out the PKM machine guns and started taking them out in six- to nine-round targeted bursts. After every third or fourth burst, Ken relocated between the boulders, making it appear to the Taliban as though more than one shooter was putting fire on them. He yelled out commands during the moves, as if he was maneuvering a combat unit.

Bowerman took out three PKMs with the first two belts. The Taliban still had a huge advantage in numbers. But confused and not knowing who had flanked them upslope, the enemy commander decided to quit while they were ahead. As quickly as the ambush force had appeared, they melted into the rock formations and fled the area. The fight ended.

Eight Americans died that day. Two lost limbs and another four suffered wounds that required medical discharge. Among that battalion in the 11th Airborne, the Bowerman Bolt became something of legend. Not just for what he'd done, but for the utter calm he displayed throughout the entire episode.

Going down to Long Term Care, I had taken the sidewalk on the main road, the same as most visitors would. But going back uphill, I veer onto one of the well-worn paths through the woods. The evergreens here limit visibility. About two hundred yards into the woods, I follow the path on a blind turn to the left, closing in on the spot where Ken and I are supposed to meet.

I discreetly scan for passersby. No one is around. The Walter Reed campus is as heavily videoed as anywhere else in the city. More so actually, given the privilege level of most patients these days. Fortunately, there are no cameras in the wooded areas.

It's a winding little section here, a good spot, the perfect place to meet.

I round the last curve in the path to our linkup, and it's everything I can do not to turn around and tear out of there. At the meeting spot is the normally calm, unflappable Ken Bowerman. The man who's faced it all. He's standing in the middle of the trail, swiveling his head rapidly, distress on his face like he's in a snake den.

- 24 -

"Jesus, Ken, you look like we should head to the pharmacy and get you some valium." It's a lame joke, just something to maybe break the tension.

He forces a slight laugh and says, "Hi, Mark. Thanks for showing up today. I'm sorry, man. I wouldn't have reached out, but at this point, you're the only one in the city I trust."

"Yeah, I figured it had to be hot." I feel myself slowing down inside. Whatever this is, it's important to digest and retain exactly what he says.

"What's this about, Ken?"

He gets straight to it, but I'm not ready for his reply.

"What do you know about the Reclamation?" he asks.

A jolt shoots up my spine. Now I'm the one fighting an urge to look and see who's watching. Ever since Simons dissolved the Congress, the Reclamation is something that lives out there in whispers. Rumors describe it as a movement that aims to take back our rights for representative government. But with the economic bomb that went off and the fight for survival at every strata of society, the Reclamation has never been anything more than just rumor.

"What do I know about the Reclamation?" I parrot back Ken's question. "Frankly, I haven't given it much thought. Beyond some muttering out at the markets, you just don't hear much about it. There's no talk about it in the city. And that makes sense. Every online server in the country has been nationalized. What little media we have left is government controlled. How would any of us know anything about it?"

"Ok, I got it," Bowerman says, a little irritated. "But what do you *think?*"

I'm quiet for several seconds. "Ken, what I think is, by dissolving the Congress, Simons pulled off the most successful coup in history. I don't buy for a second that there were illegal plots brewing in the House and Senate. And it's sickening to see Russian thugs patrolling American cities, sickening to hear what they did during The Struggles."

I'm quiet a little longer, then continue, "But you know, Simons spun his narrative and the country basically gave him the keys. To that telling, *he* built the plan that saved Persian Gulf oil in Dubai. He put down the problems in Singapore and in France. Who's going to stand up to him now? People in the cities are just happy to have a finger hold on food and shelter. And the survivors in the countryside? They're consumed with other problems, just scrounging to survive.

"As for the Reclamation, to get people to go against Simons' vice grip?" I say. "Well, the first thing you'd need is some irrefutable proof he's broken laws, big laws. Do I personally think the guy has? Yes. But thinking and proving are two different animals."

"What if I have proof, and what if I know where to get the kind of proof you're talking about?" Ken's looking at me closely as he says this, gauging my reaction.

"Proof provided by who?"

"The Reclamation."

"They showed you something? How can you know it was real?"

"No, I mean, I found it on my own, the first piece. Then they arranged a meeting with someone I could trust, for the second piece. And Mark, some of this affects you personally, in the past I mean." He's so worked up, he's trying to get it all out at once.

"Ken, alright, slow down. I'm going to listen to everything you have to say. But you're spitting out highlight bullets, and I need the full story."

He takes a deep breath, purses his lips, then says, "Right, sorry. Here's the first piece. What do you know about the missile that hit you guys in Dubai?"

I grow progressively more numb as Ken walks me through his discovery.

"When the three of you took off to ambush Petrikov, you called me to come up on the roof and maintain security for Simons."

"Yeah, I remember."

"I was two floors down, on the other side of the building. We'd had some weird movements in one of the stairwells. I didn't get up there right away. It was more important to ensure we had the access points sealed off. By the time I got up to the roof, Simons was over standing next to the manpack radio you guys had left on one of the tables, by the pool. I had the impression he'd been using it, and I wanted to know if he'd gotten any situation reports. But he said he hadn't been on the net. It was an odd moment. Like, he had been bent toward the radio as if he had just been using it. Then Puppy called in that you three got blown up, and of course all hell broke loose. I was immersed coordinating the medevac. The next several days blurred by, consolidating our gains and cleaning out the last resistance from the Russians."

Ken then describes how, about a month ago, he was approached by someone claiming to be from the Reclamation. Like me just now, he expressed skepticism about the movement itself and that anyone might have meaningful evidence of any Simons transgressions. The contact person arranged for Bowerman to prove things to himself, and in the process Ken would help the Reclamation gather evidence.

In his role as a corporate VP, Ken had access to firewalled portions of the Enterprise Performance archives. The rep from the Reclamation advised Ken to pull up archived radio transmissions from that morning in Dubai, the morning that Ulysses, Puppy and I were wounded.

"Mark, I pulled up the mission timeline, digital maps, all of it. Then I played the audio cuts that the Reclamation guy said I should listen to."

"And?"

"And that was no Russian Kornet missile that hit you guys," Ken said. "At the same time as you three parked the SUV and were moving on foot to ambush Petrikov, somebody got on the laser comms net and called an emergency suppression mission using *your* personal call sign. The requested point of impact location was right on top of your SUV. It wasn't a Russian Kornet missile that hit you. It was a Spike missile from our own force."

"Where? From who? They would have figured it out!"

Ken's shaking his head no. "There was so much chaos going on, that's the last thing anyone would waste time on. There was another round of F-35s tangling with the SU-57s. The paratrooper reinforcements jumped in from Kuwait, which generated a whole other boat load of confusion until we got them organized. The strike onto your position was one of several dozen emergency suppression missions that morning. When you listen to the actual audio cut, it's your call sign, but it's *his* voice calling in that strike. The missile that hit you was probably one of the long range Spikes that the Merkavas used. They wouldn't even have been in visual range, just launching indirect suppression on a requested grid location."

"He tried to kill us?" I ask, still taking it in.

"It looks that way. It looks like that's the point where he started thinking he had more potential need for Petrikov than he did for any of us. I wasn't sure what to make of that audio. But I knew what to make of it after the second meeting with the Reclamation."

Ken goes on to describe his second meeting. The Reclamation contact at the first meeting was someone he'd never seen before. But at the second meeting, it was someone he had known and come to trust while doing business in the city. Ken didn't want to tell me exactly who, other than it was a woman who had been a staffer on the Hill, before the Congress was outlawed.

"She was a close advisor to the House Majority Whip, Congressman Neff," he explained.

"Neff?" I asked. "He went down in the Marine One crash with the President, didn't he?"

Bowerman nods and adds, "Yeah, plus two other Congressmen and two Senators who were on that flight. You ever think anything suspicious about that crash?"

"*Now?* During this conversation? One hundred percent. At the time, honestly, I can't remember. The whole world was going nuts. And helicopters do fall out of the sky."

Ken continues. "They get me in that second meeting with the Reclamation, with one of Neff's advisors. She shows me a memorandum that Neff wrote and gave to her in advance of him going to Camp David to meet with the President. He gave it to her *in case he didn't come back,* he was that worried about it." His voice trails off.

"You read the memorandum?" I ask.

"I did. Don't have a copy on me. But I read it. It said that he and the others had been summoned to Camp David by President Atkinson . . . for a close-hold discussion. The President would not specify further. But in Neff's memorandum, he writes that he suspected it pertained to an attempt to impeach then-Vice President Simons."

We both stay silent for a minute. I remember reading in history books about the emergence of the Stalinist era in Russia, and Hitler's path to dominance in Germany. In those histories, for the everyday person living their life and trying to just take care of their family, it was hard to pinpoint the exact moment when they realized that pure evil had taken over their country.

I think about America of the recent past. I knew there were real problems earlier. There were things I found abhorrent. But this conversation, today, this is my moment of realizing pure evil.

"What next, Ken?"

"I was supposed to go get the smoking gun. Supposedly President Atkinson had the whole Camp David session video recorded and cached, up north of here."

"Then you're going to get it? The cache?"

"I was, and then I was supposed to deliver it to a third meet, in the Rockville market. In a few days. But two days ago, I got an emergency message from the Reclamation. They're concerned we've been blown. I'm actually headed from here directly outside the walls. To link up with the first Reclamation rep and with that Hill staffer. They've ordered all three of us into their evasion network."

"Ken, you came here to tell me this?"

"No, Mark, I came here to ask for help. On behalf of the Reclamation. I need you to get that cache."

- 25 -

Sunday, 9 September 2035, 0215 hours – Bearing on 39.627 deg North, 077.465 deg West

Twelve hours ago, I was looking at Ken Bowerman and wondering why he was so spooked. Now, I'm the one about to jump out of my skin. It's so dark, I can't see my own hands trying to pick through the rolling hills of scrub trees and oak in northern Maryland. At least the darkness provides cloaking from the naked eye. On the other hand, if anyone has infrared or night vision on me, it's all over.

What a difference the years make. Since coming out of rehab from the Dubai wounds, I've been an urban dweller. Yes, going outside the walls means going into the wilds of the camp follower belts or the markets. But that's been all concrete jungle. Which means I'm rusty in the woods. At the moment it feels like I'm stumbling over every root and rock out here. Funny how that reminds me of the time Ulysses and I had to free Simons from the pile of chairs in the blacked-out Starbucks, before an Armata shot it up with auto cannon.

Hurried as this excursion is, Linny and I agreed it was the only thing to do. Bowerman did in fact depart the walls to begin evasion, immediately after our meeting. I kept everything normal. I went back to the house as usual, and then promptly told Linny *everything* from the meeting with Ken. Driving home that day, I briefly considered if there was a way of sheltering her from association with this mess. But the reality is, if anyone connected me to the Reclamation, they'd roll her up just as fast as me. I owed her having a say in the decisions.

We agreed that I had to go investigate the cache. Ken was convinced that things are moving quickly within the Reclamation. According to him, they've lost the window for anyone else to get the cache and transport it to handoff at the Rockville market. If the cache is as important as Ken thinks it is, Linny and I could never live with not at least trying to retrieve it. We also agreed that I had to go make the recovery before the workweek started. Come Monday, I'll still have to show at my municipal services job. The city algorithms presume more irregular activity by residents on the weekends. With me heading out during the weekend, it's less likely to trigger an automatic "knock and question" warrant to the house. And if this really is a mother lode of information, then I have to get it to a meeting in the market in just a little over seventy-two hours.

The plan itself was pretty simple. First, I drove out to the orphanage. My car is there overnight while I'm out here. Linny stayed back at the house, ready to give an answer if anyone checks up on my whereabouts. We have a decent story. When the twins first arrived from West Virginia during The Struggles, they were having nightmares. So occasionally we'd go out to the orphanage and stay overnight. That's where Linny will say I am at the moment. When I dropped off my car with Dan – bless his soul – he gave me a beater to use with no questions asked. I fronted him some cash for it. But he knows I'm up to something off grid. Even though our family sedan is junky and embarrassing by city standards, it's as wired with trackers as anything else inside the walls. The beater car lets me make an anonymous drive into the badlands.

The cache lies west of Catoctin Hollow Road and a couple miles south of Camp David. Besides stumbling on roots and rocks during my foot traverse through the woods, bites from late-summer mosquitos remind me how much I've become a city dweller. I swat the skeeters as quietly as possible, and curse myself for not bringing Deet.

For the rest of the necessary kit, it was a quick foray in our garage. There wasn't much I needed from my old military gear; just a lensatic compass and a camouflage poncho. Night vision goggles would have been ideal, but those are organizational equipment you leave behind when discharged from the military. Linny and I had a topo map that covered the Camp David area, from our days camping at South Mountain State Park. I grabbed the map and mentally plotted the lat/long that Ken had provided, careful not to put any markings on there should I get rolled up. After driving to the Camp David area, I parked at what used to be the William Houck Campground.

All things considered, the approach walk to the cache has gone smoother than expected. From the pace count, it should be another four hundred meters to the boulder.

One thing that plays to my advantage here: after the Marine One crash and President Atkinson's death, Camp David was abandoned. Atkinson had kept the presidential retreat as a symbol of national normalcy, despite the budget challenges. But as the country soon found out, Courtney Simons holds no such sentimentality. Unless Enterprise Performance left functioning cameras out here, the whole area should be clear.

Checking the greenish tritium reading on the lensatic compass, I'm still on azimuth. The pace count says it's down to the last two hundred meters. I still can't see crap, and decide to do a listening halt. I kneel down by the trunk of a large oak tree for ten minutes. The cicadas chirp. An owl hoots about fifty meters off to the right.

Otherwise, it's all quiet. The skeeters keep biting.

I start the final approach to the cache. My heart's pounding so loud it's all I can hear. If anyone's waiting, they'll pounce as soon as I pull the thing from the ground.

I come to the end of the pace count and briefly panic. There's no boulder like Ken described. Is this a setup? But it's so dark out, the thing could be right ahead. I was probably a little short on the pace. That's not uncommon, especially being out of practice at night land nav. Another twenty-five steps on azimuth, and I literally bump into a huge rock.

Even this dark, it's easy to follow the slanted overhang that Ken described. I trace down to the actual burial point. From the backpack, I pull out Linny's gardening spade. It's easy digging. The briefcase-sized, waterproof plastic Pelican case is out of the ground in less than five minutes.

I briefly consider relocating before investigating the contents, but there's no point. If anyone has me under observation, they'll move in at will. I tuck underneath an overhang on one side of the rock, and drape the poncho over me to block out ambient light. Using a red lens flashlight to work by, I open the case.

The case contains a ruggedized tablet and four thumb drives marked "Original" and "Copy 1" through "Copy 3." Pushing the power button, the tablet fires up and shows a fifty-five percent charge. I insert the original thumb drive. There's only one file, a video, which I open and play. A young sailor in navy field fatigues faces the camera. That's right, Camp David was garrisoned by a Navy unit.

"Test test test, this is Boatswain's Mate Second Class Ryan, audio-visual check for Presidential conference at Camp David, Maryland, dated 12 February 2034." The sailor looks off camera, *"Sir, we're all set."*

President Atkinson's voice says, *"Thank you, Alan."*

The camera now pans to the President, seated at the end of a conference table. Three senior officials sit to either side. Everyone is dressed in Camp David work attire: a combination of fleece and button-downs. The mood is decidedly grim.

The President commences. *"This is President David Atkinson, hosting an emergency conference at Camp David, on February 12, 2034. I am hereby advising all members present that this conversation is being recorded in its entirety. This tape will be made available to any and all necessary parties of the Congress, the Department of Justice, and any other pertinent federal agencies."*

The President then nods to and introduces the other participants.

"On my left, from my party, is Senate Majority Leader Oliver Washington and House Minority Leader Natalie Robinson. Also on my left is FBI Director Rodrigo Lopez. On my right, from the opposition party, is Senate Minority Leader Amy Chong and House Majority Whip Jim Stevens. Also seated to my right is NSA Director Patrick Scott. For reasons I will clarify later, I have intentionally not invited the Speaker of the House to this meeting."

There were name plates in front of each individual. The key pieces of the next seventy-five minutes leave me feeling gut punched and woozy. It's all I can do to sort out who's saying what at critical moments:

The President: *". . . I am proposing that following this meeting, we fly directly to the Capitol to present the facts we will review presently, in an emergency joint session of Congress . . . NSA Director Scott will now present critical findings, which he has only just confirmed and made available to me in the past twenty-four hours . . ."*

NSA Director Scott, ashen faced: *". . . this provides irrefutable evidence that Vice President Simons, knowingly and deliberately, plotted with the Chinese for the envelopment and destruction of his own Enterprise Performance combat formation that our country dispatched to the Korean peninsula."*

The table erupts in shock with angered comments, barbed questions and accusations. The President regains order.

Senate Majority Leader Washington: *". . . the point is, why! Why would he do this? It doesn't make any . . ."*

FBI Director Lopez: *"We have conducted extensive consultation between the NSA Director, the DNI Director, Director CIA, and myself. After reviewing the intercepts, our assessment is that Vice President Simons had two goals in betraying to the Chinese information that would allow for destruction of the Enterprise Performance combat force in Korea. First, it provides a major national security blow, with which he could attack the credibility of President Atkinson. It is no secret the Vice President has worked to actively undermine the President in order to strengthen his own political standing. Second, and this leads to a further point domestically, but the second point is that we believe the Vice President wanted to remove a critical mass of seasoned American combat soldiers from being a factor here in the homeland. Over the past year, he has hired and deployed record numbers of former US military onto Enterprise Performance overseas missions. The Korea task force had many of the most seasoned and experienced military professionals left from our uniformed force. In light of domestic developments . . .*

The House Majority Whip cuts in, *"Stop! What are these domestic developments?"*

The FBI Director looks at the President.

The President hesitates. Then he states slowly and clearly, *"Across the country, we no longer have reliable control of US military major weapons systems and arms inventory, on any American active duty military base, reserve base, or national guard base."*

Stunned faces. Arguments, but colder now. The House Majority Whip again: *". . . and if we don't, then who does have control of these arms inventories?"*

The President answers, *"Enterprise Performance security teams control our bases and arms inventory. As part of the domestic stabilization contract we awarded them."*

Silence in the room.

The FBI Director adds, *"We now believe there are more than two hundred thousand Russian nationals filling these Enterprise Performance security positions throughout the country . . ."*

Arguments flow back and forth. Someone reminds everyone why, or rather, how Simons made the case that, during The Struggles, foreign nationals would lend a degree of reliability and neutrality to domestic security measures. There was belated admonishment among the group that they had allowed Simons' reputation and track record to have too much sway in crafting these contracts.

The Senate Majority Leader: *". . . okay, okay, but look. Even if it is two hundred thousand Russians, they're spread throughout the entire country. I'm an Army veteran. We can call a mobilization and have enough strength to overpower them at any given base. Start with a major base like Camp Diamond, get control, arm with those weapons, and then get stronger as we take more bases."*

More thoughts, arguments.

Then the NSA Director: *"Ladies and Gentlemen, wait! There's the other piece of this, in addition to the Russian contractors who control our military bases."*

They look at him. He continues, *"The bottom line is, we no longer reliably control the major communications systems in this country. This includes our national command and control networks."*

The Senate Majority Leader, angry: *"Who does?"*

The NSA Director answers: *"Enterprise Performance."*

Several more minutes of explanation by the NSA Director: The cost saving measures to privatize. The efficiencies gained by outsourcing government data and automation services. The national security controls that stipulated no company could own more than forty-nine percent of government communications and data contracts, which of course was the forty-nine percent contract owned by Enterprise Performance. But then, the more recent discoveries by the NSA that EP had, surreptitiously, installed backdoors and taken de-facto control of most of the other contracted servers. In essence, Enterprise Performance now owned the internet. And with it, the company owned the backbone to all current means of American mass media and government communications.

Further, the NSA Director explained, it wasn't beyond the realm of possibility that Enterprise Performance was able to monitor NSA's investigation of Simons and EP, in real-time. He says, *"We've tried to keep critical components of this investigation off the servers we contract to Simons. But EP servers are so pervasive to everything NSA does, it's hard to know for sure."*

Off camera you hear vomiting. Boatswain's Mate Second Class Ryan, the sailor who'd introduced the session, *"I'm sorry, Sir!"* Then more vomiting. Two more Navy men rush into the room with paper towels and move behind the camera.

The President, looking weary: *"That's OK, Alan. We all feel that way."*

It gets quiet again.

Then the Senate Minority Leader, who has not spoken much: *"What now, Mr. President?"*

The President: *"Now, I am proposing that we all board Marine One, and fly directly to the grounds of the Capitol."*

The House Majority Whip, of the opposition party: *"Mr. President, I understand from your prior inferences, prior to today, that you intend to impeach the Vice President. But Sir, how do you plan to regain your credibility to govern?"*

The President: *"Jim, I can never regain the credibility to govern. I am going to submit to the Congress my commitment in writing to resign, concurrent with the successful impeachment and conviction of Vice President Simons."*

Silence around the table. A few tears. Then the President: *"That will hand order of succession from my party to the Speaker of the House, who's from the opposition party. That is the only way for our country to possibly move forward."*

The Senate Majority Leader: *"Mr. President, that doesn't address any of the other challenges we have – gaining access to and control of our military bases, regaining control of our communications infrastructure."*

The President: *"Oliver, I understand. But we have to start with this. We have to start with the rule of law. Upon our landing at the Capitol, we will summon an immediate meeting of both houses of Congress. We will also summon the military Joint Chiefs."*

Solemn nods and discussion wind down the remainder of the tape.

I sit there under the boulder overhang, wedged against the rock, and feel a lot in common with that young sailor on tape, the one who had the bout of nausea.

The Presidential helicopter went down halfway to DC. No one survived.

- 26 -

"Why? Why would he do all of that?" Linny asks, her voice plaintive with disgust and shock. We sit on the bench in our sunroom.

"Yeah, that's what the Senate Majority Leader, Senator Washington, kept asking in the video."

"And what did people say when he asked?"

I start to reply, drained. It's been a crazy few days. Coming back from the Camp David area, I pulled into the Frederick market stalls. It was best to check the vibe before barreling straight down I-270 back to DC. Sure enough, folks in Frederick market said bandits were shaking down cars on the interstate. Normally I'd be OK with giving out some cash and a few throwaway items. But I had the Pelican case with the thumb drive videos and couldn't risk those being discovered. I backtracked north up Highway 15 to Thurmont, took farm roads over to Mount Airy, then picked my way back towards the city. Next I found a good hiding spot just off the Pike, and cached the Pelican case again. There was no way I'd risk bringing that inside the walls.

At the orphanage, I swapped from the beater car back to my car. It was late Monday afternoon by the time I got back to the house. I crawled upstairs, lay down for the first sleep since Saturday morning, and passed out for twelve hours straight.

This morning I reported to my municipal job and took an ass chewing for missing work yesterday. I pray they bought my explanation about going to Frederick to get a good trade item, and then the bandits made it hard to get back. That story seemed to work, for now. The supervisor reamed me out and said I can pack up and trade outside the walls full time if that's my preference. He's probably already put in to refurbish my job.

"Refurbish" is the term for when you arrive to work one day and find someone else at your desk. At that point, you're reported to the city as unemployed. Without either a job or eight figures in the bank, you have forty-eight hours to depart the city. People fear refurbishment worse than death.

Right now, though, it's hard to pinpoint the biggest threat facing Linny and me. The situation called for our bottle of wine. We'd been saving it for over a year, a Malbec for a special occasion. This wasn't what we'd had in mind. We've already gone through our first round of tears at realizing the goodbyes coming up.

As to an answer to Linny's question: Why did Courtney Simons do all of this?

"Well," I say, "If you ask me, it all goes back to that time in the hospital room."

"When he visited you at Walter Reed? After Dubai?"

"Right," I say, nodding. "I mean, there the man was standing in the room. He knew he'd called in the missile that hit me, he knew he'd ruined Ulysses' life, yet he was chewing my ass about how *I* didn't get it. It gives me shivers. I knew at the time he meant everything in his rant; about countries not mattering any more, about the haves banding together against the have nots. In his world view, it's every man for himself, period."

I pause, unable to go on for a second.

"What I didn't realize was that he was espousing more than just trying to ride a wave that was rolling in. He was going to try to actively undermine the country for his own favor. No matter what the consequences to anyone else."

Linny asks, "So he makes an alliance with the Chinese against our own people in Korea? And he makes an alliance with the Russians to take over his own country?"

That's the same kind of question I'd asked about him helping Petrikov escape Dubai. It's the same as everyone on the Camp David video was wrestling to comprehend. I answer, "Well, yes and no. I mean, in his mind, nation states are extinct. In his words, there are too many people to fit in the boat anymore. Now it's purely transactional. The top zero-point-one percent help each other, to keep a sanctuary away from the hordes. Bringing Russians in to help him take power? Well, for him that was just the best way to get business done. And our Korea force? He needed them gone. So he had to sell them out, too."

"Do you think he shot down the helicopter? With President Atkinson and the Congressional leadership?"

I think on that for a second. "After watching the video, absolutely. At the time of the crash, there were vague references to it being possible terrorist activity. But that was at the height of violence during The Struggles. Cities were trying to secure their walls. No one cared to get to the bottom of the crash. It was the same with the losses in Korea. Thousands of deaths overseas paled in comparison to the hundreds of thousands dying here."

"Yes," Linny said, remembering the news feeds and chaos of those times. "And Atkinson was hugely unpopular. There was so much myth of Simons as the problem solver. His talking heads and online scribes were all pushing that he was the last, best answer."

I agree, "Yeah. We just all moved on with life. It didn't even *have* to get swept under the rug. The helicopter crash. Korea. They were each replaced by the next big crisis."

We get past trying to deconstruct Simons' descent into evil.

We go back to sorting out the goodbyes.

Ulysses will die.

There's no way around it. Linny had to walk me off the ledge on that one. I kept trying to spin some way, somehow, that we might transport him. But even if we were staying in the city, there's no hope for him. Jill, the charge nurse, has made that clear. And now that we're going to have to run? It's done.

I cry again, thinking about it.

The worst part is, we can't go say goodbye to him. With all my algorithm anomalies of the past few days, Linny and I are surely percolating up toward the "find and detain" threshold. By tomorrow morning sometime, when Bowerman's been gone three weekdays, they're gonna feed every data signature he's ever generated, lifetime, into its own server. And then it's probably just hours until they match his anomalies with mine of the past few days.

No, we've got exactly one shot for us to escape before the net closes in. We drive out the walls at open of curfew tomorrow morning. No extra baggage, no nothing. As if we're just doing a quick run to the orphanage.

And we never come back.

"And Dan can get us to Canada?" Linny asks.

That's the other part that has us sick. Canada itself, that's great. We don't get any news from up there, not since Simons nationalized the media feeds. But word travels. Supposedly, it's still possible to get *out*. As far as the Simons administration cares, every expatriation is one less mouth begging for food. Linny will have to avoid an official border crossing point, as there will be a warrant for us by then. But it will be possible to arrange crossing at a remote site for her and the twins.

The gut wrenching part is splitting up. I'm terrified at the thought of Linny and the twins heading north without me. Best case, that's about five hundred miles of badlands.

I flesh out the plan for her. "I had a chance to talk to Dan briefly at the orphanage, when I was swapping cars after Camp David. You know how savvy he is. He already knew something was going down. Dan maintains contacts with ex cops who run transport networks going north. Working with ex cops is the best way to get through the badlands. The cops know their local area. They hand off travelers between their old jurisdictions, all the way to the border. You have to pay a transfer fee each time, but our cash should cover it. And we can get you extra security, too. Dan said two of his folks have been wanting to go, but they didn't have the money. Now they can go free of charge, with you. We'll pay their way."

Meanwhile, Linny's concerned about where I'm headed.

"And how can you trust – whoever it is – that you'll meet at the Rockville market tomorrow night?"

She's got a good point. It's the biggest unknown. Still, "There's no choice but to trust them. Whoever it was, whoever had been working with Ken, they knew about the Camp David video. They tipped off Ken to leave. And, for now at least, you and I haven't been detained. It means something is working. So, it's just a chance I'm going to have to take."

"Any idea where you'll go?" Linny asks.

"None whatsoever."

Once we get to the orphanage tomorrow morning, Linny and the twins are going to take off as soon as Dan rallies his escorts. I want them a couple hundred miles north before I go anywhere near that site in the market. I'm going to the meeting that Ken tipped me to; the one where I'll hand over the thumb drives with the Camp David video. I'll only have one condition at the handover.

I'm joining the Reclamation.

Something is going down. And after all I've learned in the past few days, I'm not sitting it out.

There's something too deliberate about the sequencing. They only approached Ken recently. They obviously knew about the Camp David video for a while, but now is when they're running the risk of trying to retrieve it. They're building for something, accomplishing tasks on a timeline.

And the reality is, I have a responsibility to join. I need to make right the fact that I helped Simons build his military component at Enterprise Performance. It would be easy to downplay that. After all, it was General Saiz and even the Joint Chiefs who asked me, Ulysses and Puppy to throw in for the Emirates mission. And yes, someone else would have joined up if we hadn't. But some things in life are personal. It *was* the three of us that joined up. *We* helped launch Dubai.

Now, one of those friends, Puppy, is missing. And I'm going to let Ulysses die.

I'm going to put my wife and Ulysses' two orphans on the run up to Canada.

If there's someone out there, in the Reclamation, trying to fight what started years ago, then I'm in. I just pray that's what this is really all about, that there really is a plan to take down Simons.

I'll find out tomorrow night, at that meeting in the Rockville market.

- 27 -

Driving north from the orphanage in Garrett Park, I find it hard to describe exactly where the camp follower belt ends and the big market begins. You see a gradual thinning of shell-shocked civilians and semi-sponsored encampments. Somewhere past Randolph Road and Rollins Avenue, the bones of old strip malls have reinvented. About every fourth storefront along that part of the Pike has hand-scrawled signs and the haphazard activity of cash and barter commerce. They're mini-markets, I guess you'd call them.

As the car noses past the former Richard Montgomery High School, on the left, there's no doubt that I've entered *The Market*, as it's known up here. It shows the skeleton of times gone by. Like other hubs from the early twenty-first century, Rockville Town Center fashioned a midrise, mixed-use destination experience. A Gold's gym and street-level retail anchored for residential and office space on the upper floors.

I generally park at one of the surface lots by the old police station. The police are long gone, but the parking lot sits adjacent to Courthouse Square Park. The immediate surrounding buildings are mainly one and two stories tall. This gives a chance to take in the vibe, before entering the urban canyon.

In macro, the market keeps itself in check. There's too much money to be made. People won't bother a local jefe or a visiting UHP. But no one will care if a random like me gets greased. Death could come from a trade deal gone bad, or from the crazies. Crazies are the ones who've lost their minds. They shelter on the sixth or seventh floors of the old midrise buildings. Once prime real estate for their views, the upper floors have gone vacant and untended. With the elevators dead, no one wants to climb that many flights. This lets the crazies run amok up there.

Back in April, I almost got brained. While walking back to the car, a pack of crazies on one rooftop tossed a load of bricks down on the street. They do this for kicks. The bricks missed me by inches, and the crash scared me half out of my skin. The worst part was, I'd scored a big canvas bag of apples and carrots in a trade. I dropped the bag in the middle of the street during my panicked rush to an alcove. And they knew I'd go back for that kind of loot.

It turned out mostly good. The crazies had shot their bolt with the bricks, so I didn't die grabbing the fruit and veggie bag. But a golf ball-sized rock hit me square in the back. It made life hell for about a month.

I pull into the police parking lot. Two men my age take payment to watch cars. Five young dudes serve as their lieutenants. The lieutenants wield bats for security.

I lock the car and approach the older guys. "Any problems or anything I should know, before walking downtown?"

The older of the two replies, "Not tonight, nothing beyond the usual. Be careful next Friday, though. Bunch of UHPs coming up to watch a tough man fight on the school football field. I've seen you here before. You know how those nights end."

These fights are legend in the city. A posse of UHPs will pool cash for a series of dudes to bash each other's faces in. Rumors are, one time they threw in machetes and offered a death bonus. Afterward the UHPs walk over to the market, surrounded by security details, and hit the fleshpots.

I study the parking lot managers; the older man has on a faded blue button-down shirt and old khakis. He's missing a front tooth, but otherwise he seems pretty well taken care of. You have to be careful, asking people about their pre-Struggles life. But I'm curious. "What'd you guys do before?"

They both chuckle. "We were locals," says the older one wearing the button-down. "I taught high school history right over there, at Richard Montgomery." You can tell a lot by their tone, when they describe the old times – whether they'll be OK, whether they can adapt. He sounds OK.

Then his wingman looks off in the distance, blank. He has on old dress slacks and a white T-shirt. The shirt's untucked and has food stains on the tail where he's used it as a napkin. He doesn't talk for a bit, and I realize it might have been a mistake to bring up past lives.

The wingman finally speaks. "I had a family. I owned a small law firm, here by the courthouse. We had a good practice in contract dispute, civil litigation." The wingman stops talking, still looking off in the distance. He looks back to me and asks, "How about you?"

"I was in the Army."

"Hah!" He barks, a little too loud to sound balanced. Then he smirks, "Thanks for keeping us safe!"

"It was my pleasure."

Walking across the courthouse park, I'm thinking about how nuts it is to be here. The sendoff at the orphanage went as well as could be expected. Linny had her game face on. She kept the twins occupied and cheery as they packed a vehicle and departed, in company with Dan's two folks. But no one was fooling the twins. Like all kids their age who lived through The Struggles, they have a well-tuned radar. It was a hard goodbye at the end.

I really hope the next four blocks don't prove I made a stupid call by going to this meeting.

Walking east along Montgomery Avenue, I make a final touch check for the thumb drive that contains the Camp David video recording. It's hand-sewn into my left pants seam, by the ankle. The spares are in the Pelican case, still hidden back down the Pike. Next, I reach back and confirm the short-barreled .357 revolver sits at just the right spot in the small of my back, beneath an untucked shirt. Dan offered a larger automatic pistol, but I wanted concealability. If something goes south, I can pop off a couple of rounds and haul ass. If that's not enough, I'm toast anyway.

At the next block, I turn left onto Maryland Ave. This block has a midrise on the right side of the street. The left side has an open surface lot, mostly empty. I make note of that lot as my last good egress option.

Crossing Middle Lane now, it's full commitment into the canyon. I pick up the pace just a nudge, careful not to trigger any predator reactions. Opportunistic eyes are watching, just waiting to pounce on the distracted, the scared, or the weak.

Halfway up this block, a pedestrian plaza cuts to the left until it dead ends at Gibbs Street. I take that route for better concealment. The plaza has accumulated all forms of detritus: overturned tables and chairs that used to be an outdoor dining area, leftover plywood and trinkets from vendor stalls that have since been abandoned. At night, it would generate a horror of noise to skirt through here. But in late afternoon, this beats walking exposed up the full length of Gibbs Street.

Near the end of the plaza, the storefront for the abandoned pub faces me from one o'clock, just across the street. The windows are dark. I see two individuals inside, but can't make out any real detail.

Taking a breath, ready to draw the gun, I walk in.

The two men flank me from either side of the entrance. They're fit, early thirties. They look like former military, each with an assault rifle slung at the low ready. The one on the right motions me toward the back room.

No easy way out now. I walk into the back room. It's pitch black, with dark wood paneling absorbing what little light comes in from the street. I bring my right hand around back, to the butt of the revolver, force myself to keep slow, controlled breathing. I mentally map the placement of the two guards who are still in the outer room. Two rounds into each of them right at the belly button, and I just might make it through the pedestrian plaza and out of the market.

From the corner, a flashlight in an unseen hand spotlights me. I'm momentarily blinded.

Out of the shadows steps Major General Diego Saiz. I just about have a heart attack.

"Hello, Mark," he says.

Trademark Saiz. I figured him for dead, and he's as low key as if we were back in good times at Camp Diamond, passing each other in his headquarters' lobby.

"Sir, I'm really glad I didn't shoot you just now."

"Me too. Thank you for the risk you've taken. We have already exfiltrated Ken Bowerman from the DC area. He doesn't yet know it was me coming to this meeting. But through the contacts who spoke with Ken, we knew he'd handed the request to you; for retrieving the video and transport here. I had no doubt, if it was possible, you'd be here."

"Sir?"

"Yes?"

"I'm happy to see you. Overjoyed in fact. But you'll excuse me for having some big questions. About how you got out of Korea, and how and why you took the risk of coming here?"

Saiz nods and replies, "Yes. Well, let's start with Korea. I'll tell you, in summary, what I know. Hopefully the information you brought will corroborate or expand on some of this."

"OK," I say.

"Mark, as you know, I assumed command of an Enterprise Performance combat force of over 30,000 personnel, in late 2033. It included the top former military professionals that the country could provide. By order of President Atkinson, and with a confirmation vote in Congress, we deployed to Korea on 4 January 2034. We commenced combat operations on the 5th, trying to hold the line against a combined North Korean/Chinese military push to unify the peninsula. By January 7th, we had ceased to function as an effective fighting formation."

"What happened?"

"It was hard to say at first. We were compromised in a major way. The Chinese lay in wait. They anticipated any tactical adjustment we made, even as I increasingly improvised commands. I thought our communications were being intercepted."

Saiz pauses for a moment.

"Late on January 7th, I issued the evasion order. We were combat ineffective. There was nothing else to try but disperse and exfil as many of our task force members as possible. And this was where, over the next forty-eight hours, I learned that something truly horrifying was happening. As you know, the evasion plan is pre-built, specifically to hedge against a communications compromise. I sent the activation code word to our formations, nothing else. There should have been no way to compromise our evasion routes."

"And your task force was still rolled up?" I ask.

"Yes. Our elements made their way to pre-designated rendezvous points, at locations only coordinated during compartmented planning back in the States. And yet, four of every five task force members in the evasion network were getting caught and detained at the final approach to their rendezvous. Twenty thousand in total. The few thousand that did make it back to the States, they were the ones taken in by local South Koreans, before they had gone on to the established rendezvous points. Thank God for South Korean help to our people."

"What happened to the twenty thousand that were detained?"

"They were transported to the Chinese mainland," Saiz explains. "We have had some intel, of moderate reliability, on their disposition." I want to ask more about this, but don't. Saiz will have reasons for what he does or doesn't share about them.

"Sir, you assessed twenty thousand captured. A few thousand made it back to the States. That leaves another seven thousand from the original EP combat force that went to Korea. Where are they?"

"*They* include me," Saiz says. He looks pained, and I understand.

"As commander, my place in the evasion sequence was to take the last safe passage out of country. Unfortunately, from our hide position, this meant that I was gradually receiving reports of the catastrophe unfolding. Thanks to longstanding professional relationships, I knew how to reach the British and Canadian Defense Attaches in country. Working backchannel, their governments sent confirmation that the evasion network had been fully compromised. They advised us to cease our remaining personnel movements. Over the next two weeks, they moved heaven and earth and worked to evacuate the rest of us. But at that point, I could save only seven thousand."

I nod and don't say anything at first. It's a struggle for words. "Sir, those last seven thousand would have been rolled up too, except for your leadership."

Saiz ignores this. He says, "Mark, the video you brought. Does it corroborate any of what I've just told you?"

"Yes, sir. Not in the same detail. But the NSA Director presented national findings that Courtney Simons actively colluded with the Chinese. Simons fed them advance notice on each of your moves in country."

Saiz nods. "Mark, you asked why and how I'm here. We should discuss that. Ken told you he was contacted by the Reclamation?"

"Yes, sir."

"And what do you know of it?"

"Not much. It's a rumored grassroots resistance movement, formed after Simons threw the constitution and democratic rule out the window."

"The resistance part is correct," Saiz says. "The grass roots part is not. You are looking at the current senior commander for the military wing of the Reclamation. The Reclamation formed within days of Simons dissolving the Congress. The founding members had intel that it was Enterprise Performance that shot down Marine One with President Atkinson and Congressional leaders on board. There was nothing the Reclamation could do at the time. Simons' coup was total. His company controlled virtually all national security communications by then, and his Russian mercenaries effectively locked down our country's military arsenal."

"Sir?" I ask. "You say the Reclamation formed within days of the shoot down. But it would have taken you a while. I mean, you must have spent weeks or months working through the allied evasion network?"

"That's right, Mark. The Reclamation founders are a bipartisan collection of the Congress, the survivors anyway. Simons imprisoned all the members he could get his hands on."

"Yes, sir. The news feeds occasionally play taped confessions of the Congressional members he imprisoned."

Saiz continues. "A certain number of the members who escaped simply wanted to save their own hide. We don't know where they are. But, thankfully for our country, there was a critical mass from the House and Senate who immediately started to take action. The Speaker of the House is the Reclamation's political leader, with bipartisan membership of twenty-seven Senators and one hundred and seventy-three members of the House. The British, Canadians and Australians are actively cooperating with the Reclamation. They recognize our movement as the legitimate US government in exile."

"Where are they?" I ask. "The Reclamation's governing body, I mean?"

"Most are in Canada at the moment. That's where my task force is located as well. The Brits arranged transit for us from Korea to Alberta Province. They've been assisting with refit as well. The rumors you've heard, of the Reclamation being grass roots, that was intentional disinformation. We didn't want to tip our hand just yet, that the Reclamation has real backing and real momentum. We wanted people to be aware of it, but not enough to get Simons overly alerted."

"And yet, you're here now. Pulling out people like Ken Bowerman. Risking transport of this video. You're making a move, aren't you?"

"Yes. We timed it as close as we could, and as late as possible in the planning process to mobilize our full numbers and final activity. We had plans to reach out to you as well, but Ken got to you on his own even sooner. Our operation commences in just over two weeks."

"Your operation to do what?"

"Our operation to remove Simons from office, re-install the House and Senate, and restore democratic rule. The Congress in Exile has already held impeachment hearings on Simons. In short order, they will give notice and offer him the opportunity to step down from power. If he refuses, we will remove him by force."

Saiz is a brilliant leader, but the math for a military operation isn't adding up. "Sir, you're going to take back the entire country with such a small, cobbled together force?"

"No, we could never do that. Fortunately for us, Simons isn't interested in holding the entire country. He's too busy walling off the cities, thinking he can let the rest of the country wither away. And the people outside the walls know they've been abandoned. If we can take a critical mass of cities and galvanize support of the population at large, we stand a good chance. We plan to move directly on the ten largest cities simultaneously. I will personally lead the operation to capture DC. That's why I'm here, for reconnaissance and preparation."

Taking this in, it doesn't seem to fall into place yet. Especially if the plan is to galvanize popular support. I ask, "How are you going to get word out to the populace at large? Enterprise Performance has a lockdown on everything. Even FM and AM broadcasting – it all passes through the server cloud at some point."

Saiz nods. "That's the most difficult part of the operation. You're right. It's the one thing forcing our hands to act now, before we raise a larger force. As you know, EP's main server farm is in San Jose, at their original campus. You probably also know that shortly after Dubai, Simons built a second server center in West Virginia on Camp Diamond. That server farm is at the old Special Forces compound N3 that he leased – Cardiac Gap. It now provides his backup for national communications."

"I'd heard about that," I reply. "Haven't seen it though. The last time I saw the compound was on our prep for the Dubai operation. It was still just the old cabins and utility buildings."

"Yes, the old buildings are all gone now. To your point, Mark, about being able to communicate nationally to the American population: concurrent with fighting to regain control of the largest cities, we also will run strikes to destroy both of those server farms. As I mentioned, time is precious. Enterprise Performance has a third server site due to go online next month, and a fourth site two months after that. We haven't been able to determine either of those new locations. Once those servers go online, Simons will have too much redundancy for us to reliably take control of national communications. We're lucky about one thing. Enterprise Performance had planned to have the extra servers running by now. Fortunately for us, the herculean task of walling off the cities consumed more time than they planned."

"Sir, ten cities and two server farms? That's twelve targets simultaneously. You're going to be *past* stretched thin."

"Yes, that doesn't begin to describe it. The San Jose site will require several hundred special operators. I can't spare them, but San Jose is in the middle of a major population center. I won't play lightly with the civilian lives that will be at stake. We'll need to invest in a manpower-heavy assault that can also act discriminately."

Saiz pauses, looks away for a moment, then back at me. "But Mark, for the Cardiac Gap servers, we have the option for an economy of force strike. I have part of the team assembled, working on key components of the plan. With you back on scene, I'd like to ask if you would lead it."

"Sir, I'd already made up my mind to join the Reclamation. As long as it turned out to be real. So, yes, if my efforts can help, I'll gladly lead one of your strike teams."

"Well, don't say you'll gladly do it until you hear more details. But first, let me introduce you to one of your teammates."

It can be embarrassing when two grown men hug in public. Especially when the big guy, who just stepped from behind the flashlight, has your feet lifted about two inches off the ground.

But I could care less. Puppy Jackson, my good friend, is alive after all.

Shortly after this, Saiz' security element repositions us a few blocks away, to a different safe room. We were in the old pub long enough. Secured in a new location, I learn more about the trials of their exfil from Korea. Saiz and Puppy were the last two from their task force to step onto a British exfil boat.

They ask about Linny and also about Ulysses. I tell them about losing our friend, and about some of Linny and my days inside the city walls. I share the good news of how the twins were shepherded to DC. It chokes me up when Saiz says he can have someone reach out to Dan and coordinate a reception for Linny and the twins in Canada.

Accepting the help for Linny and the twins is especially hard, knowing Saiz' own situation. While they were in Korea, and later making their circuitous way to Canada, the worst of The Struggles raged in the States. Saiz' wife, Jasmin, and their twenty-year-old son, Victor, decamped from West Virginia to California. They attempted to join family members on the West Coast. The two were never heard from again.

Toward the end of the conversation, I ask, "So, how big of a team is this—the one we'll take to strike the servers on the N3 compound?"

Puppy starts to speak, but Saiz leans in and says, "Mark, before you hear the details, just know it's not too late to opt out. You deserve to make an informed decision. This is a unique target, and it calls for a unique strike profile. The first thing to understand about Cardiac Gap is – it's not a US target. It's Russian."

"Yes, sir, I'm aware of the Russian contractors Enterprise Performance has installed, to control their critical locations."

Saiz shakes his head. "Not Russian contractors. The N3 compound is now *Russian government controlled.* We've verified this via NATO allies. We have satellite photos of *uniformed* Russian soldiers manning that compound."

"Why?" I ask.

Puppy speaks up. "We think it was part of a deal that Simons cut with Petrikov. From the sounds of it, their original plan was that the N3 compound would be *Petrikov's* out-of-country safe facility, in the event he ever had to flee Russia in a hurry. He's stepped on the toes of a lot of rivals over the years. Simons agreed to give Petrikov's own soldiers control of the compound. We think Simons has a similar arrangement in Russia, a bail-out site for himself over there."

"Then how did the servers get there, into N3?" I ask.

"According to intercepts the Reclamation has received, it appears that the task of securing and walling the cities greatly overwhelmed Enterprise Performance. They had originally planned to put the servers at a different site, the one that is due to go online next month. But that plan fell so far behind, EP informed the Russians they needed facility space on the N3 compound until their other two sites are emplaced."

"And this has relevance to the strike," Saiz says. "The servers themselves are managed remotely, from EP's San Jose campus. Enterprise Performance technicians perform maintenance on the N3 server facility during the day. But at night, the compound is manned exclusively by a Russian uniformed security detachment."

Saiz pauses briefly, then adds, "This means, for N3 and N3 only, Reclamation leadership has authorized much broader rules of engagement than anywhere else during our nationwide operation."

"All right, sir," I say, my interest really piqued now. "So, the size of our team?"

Puppy answers my question. "Counting you as team commander, we'll be taking in twelve of us."

Wow. Saiz had said it was an economy of force mission – get the most effect with the smallest size unit. But this is pretty extreme. "That small? Is it a small server system? Just a few rooms or so?"

"No," Puppy says. "Actually, they're housed in multi-story buildings that cover most of a city block."

"OK. So with only twelve of us, we must be calling in munitions? Non-line-of-sight missiles, or an air strike?"

"Negative again," Puppy says. "Enterprise Performance has air defense wired, for the entire Camp Diamond area, including remote-guided munitions. And they have multi-spectrum jamming. We'll cover that in more detail during our mission review."

I give Puppy the what-the-heck look. "OK, twelve operators, no missiles, no air strike, and a city block to destroy. What's the plan?"

Saiz looks at me. "Mark, after lengthy review of the security patterns around Camp Diamond, we have the ability to infiltrate a small team, by military freefall, into the vicinity of the compound. With the assistance of NATO allies, we have access to a special munition that will destroy the facility."

No one says another word.

Special munition. Man portable, can go in by parachute. Back in the days of the Cold War, a small number of Special Forces teams were trained to employ high-risk, high-payoff devices that went by the acronym SADM. They were never employed.

SADM stands for Special Atomic Demolition Munition. It's pronounced, "say-dem."

Our team is going to nuke Cardiac Gap.

- 28 -

Sipping coffee and standing outside the main conference building, I look out at the rolling hills and the trees showing a first hint of fall color. It's easy to see the draw of this place. Back in the old days, the Vistica-Myrer Corporate Retreat Center had a great gig going. Its cluster of buildings and cabins exude rustic Ralph Lauren, with rough log siding and hunter green, slate shingle roofs. Tucked into rolling hills near Fort Wayne, the retreat center offered easy access from six of the Midwest's most populous cities. It would have offered a welcome respite from the normal routine; a chance for office teams to bond while whiteboarding vision statements and eating good food. It suits us well, too. While this place gives good access to our next transit point, it's far enough into the badlands to provide the privacy we need.

The corporate retreat motif strikes a contrast to how our team has spent the past six days. Saiz assigned operatives with a panel truck to transport Puppy and me up here late the night of the 12th, the same evening we met in the Rockville market. The rest of the team assembled by the 13th. Ken Bowerman is here. Besides Puppy, he's the only other team member I've met before. Puppy hand-picked the others, and they're top notch.

Puppy and Ken wrung us dry during our initial train up. Each training day started at 1500 hours with kit shakeout and weapons range fire in a repurposed pasture. After nightfall, they ran us through all manner of tactical drills until sunrise. Unspoken but obvious to me, this was also my trial period. The team knew of my injuries and long rehab following Dubai. Fortunately, I passed muster during the dusk-to-dawn beat ups. We have individual rooms for our sleeping quarters, so they don't see me in pain afterward as I struggle to sleep through the day. I figure that's on personal time and none of their business.

We had varying degrees of operational rust at first. But by last night's tactical drills, muscle memory had returned across the team. By feel alone in pitch black, everyone can find any item in an assault pack or troubleshoot any weapon. We can move silently through the nighttime woods. We can adjust tactical formation without missing a beat, and we can react seamlessly to account for any casualties we might take during the strike. It speaks to the depth of past training, how well we've snapped in. It's a far cry from my slow plodding in the woods near Camp David last week.

Considering the logistics strain that the Reclamation faces, our outfitting has been admirable. There's no extravagance, but we have everything we need. The loggies even found uniforms in our old camouflage pattern.

With the foundational work moving along, it's time to start mission rehearsals. This afternoon is our first operational concept brief. We'll continue to crash during the day and execute mission specific dry runs the next few nights.

"Mark, we're ready in the conference room." That's Jason Barr. Red haired and lanky, he's in his late thirties. Back in the old life, he was an Air Force Pararescue man. He's our team deputy for the mission, mainly handling logistics and coordination for our infil. He's freed up Puppy and the section leaders to focus on their primary tasks for the strike.

"Thanks, Jason." I head in. All twelve of us assemble in the mid-sized conference room. Puppy has placed an ops sketch and maps up on the white board at the front of the room. Everyone has stepped around the conference table and moved to these graphics. They form a semicircle; half the team's standing and half are seated in chairs they've dragged up.

I step to the front of the group and lead off. "OK, so far, we've been working on gearing up and basic tactics. I know you've each studied your part of the mission. This morning, Jason will cover the intel brief and situation on the objective. Jessica, Ken and I will review ops. Then Puppy will take us over to the barn, to show us his science project."

Jason steps up. "Let's start with the physical layout of the target. After that, we'll proceed to guards on site and local reaction forces."

He points to a blow-up map of the ops site, along with two 8x10 photos from our NATO-supplied imagery

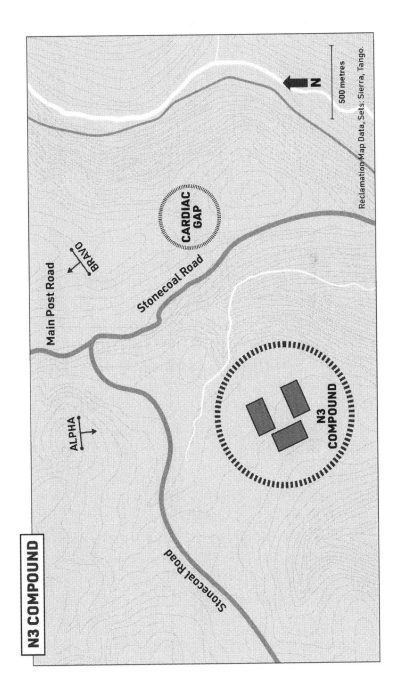

"This is the current incarnation of the N3 compound. For those who don't know, it was one of the original Special Forces compounds on Camp Diamond. As the photos show, the old buildings were demolished. It's now a U-shaped configuration of three large buildings. Each building is five stories tall. Any quick reaction forces necessary to reinforce the compound will arrive via Main Post Road, coming from the north. Main Post Road dead ends at Stonecoal Road, which bends in a horseshoe around the northern half of the compound."

Jason checks a three-by-five card for his notes. "In terms of enemy forces on site, the guard contingent is a reinforced company from Russian Special Operations Command. We have an assessed head count of one hundred fifty. As you've heard, these are *not* contracted personnel, like the rest of the Enterprise Performance forces across the country. These are active duty Russian special operators. They'll be wearing their latest digital flora pattern camouflage."

"What's their armament?" one of the team operators asks.

"That's actually some good news," Jason replies. "Even though their head count is high, this element is armed only for local defense of the compound. They'll have PKM machine guns and assault rifles. Nothing heavier. Enterprise Performance provides heavier armament for the outer defense layer of Camp Diamond. This gives us a window of opportunity for a close-in strike on N3, before a larger EP reaction force can arrive from main post."

He gestures to indicate the overall Camp Diamond defenses. "Enterprise Performance has brought in a number of S-400 missiles for air defense. Also for air defense, they have Russian-contracted pilots who fly what used to be US Air Force F-22s. Those are based down at Langley Air Force Base, in Virginia. They keep at least two F-22s on strip alert. Those planes are mainly to protect DC, but they're close enough to have a fast response time to Camp Diamond."

Jason points to Main Post Road, at the top of the sketch. "In terms of ground reinforcement, that would come from the quick-reaction force on main post. They keep a total of eight Strykers ready. For those who haven't worked around them, the Stryker is an eight-wheeled, armored personnel carrier. Each Stryker comes armed with a heavy machine gun or automatic grenade launcher. Also, our intel says that each Stryker will carry six contracted Russian special operators who can deploy from the back for dismounted assaults. Following our strike, we can expect they'll respond with at least four of the Strykers, possibly all eight." At eighteen tons and twenty feet long, the Stryker is impervious to rifle or machine gun fire, requiring a true anti-armor weapon to disable or kill it. The bottom line is, we really need to hit the compound and get out before those Strykers roll in. That mobile reaction force, plus the Russian special operators on site, could eventually tear us up, bad.

Jason directs our attention back to the N3 compound. "One last thing to point out. Climate change actually did us a favor. The servers we're aiming to take out – normal practice used to be to put them down in the basement or lower levels of a building. They're easier to service that way. If they were at basement level, the servers could possibly survive our weapon's blast. But Camp Diamond is as prone to surge flooding as every other base in the country. As a result, EP placed the server rooms on floors three through five of each building. The Russians use floors one and two for their barracks and office space. This means the servers will catch the full force of the blast."

"Thanks, Jason," I say. "OK, let's review our task organization and concept of operations. In addition to Jason as deputy command, we've broken into two maneuver sections. Jessica will lead Alpha section, consisting of herself plus four other operators." Jessica Steele is in her late twenties. She was a brand new operator in 8th Group when it disbanded. Along with Puppy, she's one of only a handful who served on the Dubai task force, later served on the Korea task force, and then successfully evaded to Canada.

I spell out the rest of the task organization. "Ken will lead our Bravo section with him plus three operators." This notice is a formality. Jessica and Ken have already started working with their sections.

Finally, I nod to Puppy. "The big guy here jumps in the SADM. At the end of the day, the eleven of us exist to ensure Puppy gets on target and can take the shot. Jason, over to you for the review of our infil plan."

"Roger that," Jason replies. "Mark and I have spoken to each of you individually, to make sure everyone understands this will be a direct parachute assault onto the target. The EP defense scheme for Camp Diamond rules out any type of long-range, precision-guided weapons that we'd normally use for a target like this. The F-22 fighters and S-400 missiles would take down any attacking aircraft or missiles we could muster.

"After analysis, though, we found a stealth means to insert a team by freefall parachute. Our plan leverages the way EP runs their aerial resupply network. With the problems in the badlands, Enterprise Performance incurs a high cost running ground resupply between the major cities. Whenever possible, they will fly items and people by cargo aircraft."

Jason points to a US map then continues. "They run a regular flight from Norfolk to Chicago. It brings in high-value imports from the Norfolk shipping port to the UHPs and HPs who live inside the Chicago walls. Going back, that bird doesn't carry much. There's a lot of unused room inside the cargo hold, which makes it the perfect infil platform for us. The flight route, with only a slight deviation, takes us over a release point for a freefall parachute insertion to the Cardiac Gap area."

One of the operators raises his hand and asks, "So, who's flying that bird for us? Not the Enterprise Performance pilots?"

"Great question,"Jason replies. "We have a team that's had access to the airport for a month now. On the night of infil, they'll surreptitiously take control of the crew. Former Air Force pilots will fly the plane. It gets tricky for them on the far end of their mission. After dropping us over Camp Diamond, on final approach to Norfolk, they'll declare an emergency and ditch in the Atlantic at a prearranged geo coordinate. A Reclamation boat will be on standby to pick them up."

"All right, here's the base plan for execution," I say as the team gets more focused on the map. "As a primary plan, the only one who fires anything is Puppy. Instead of having to hand deliver the SADM onto the target, he and his brain trust have modified it to launch the warhead from a fifteen-hundred-meter standoff distance. We'll freefall from thirty thousand feet along that air corridor, out the back of that resupply bird. We'll open chutes at seven thousand feet AGL."

Pointing to the map, I outline the team's dispositions. "Ideally, we'd land farther away, in an offset, and then take a few hours to walk into the target area. The problem is there are too many unknowns about the Camp Diamond patrols to try any of the suitable offset landing zones. The lesser of evils is to land where we can immediately trigger the strike."

Another thing we looked at was rigging the SADM on a steerable cargo parachute, to fly it directly onto the target and detonate. The technology is there. But our intel on Cardiac Gap says they have full-spectrum jamming that would defeat GPS-guided or radio-guided steering mechanisms. And we don't know what electronics or signals detectors they might have. So, everything stays old school. We'll jump the weapon to the target ourselves. No one transmits on a radio unless we get spotted or until after we detonate the SADM, whichever comes first.

I continue with the infil description. "By the terrain analysis, we have two good areas to land. One is the hilltop where Alpha sets in, north of the compound. They'll parachute directly onto there and establish a support by fire position. The rest of us land in the actual saddle on the Cardiac Gap ridgeline. It's a tight fit, but the Gap itself is the only open landing area on the compound's east side. The rest of that ridgeline has coverage with thirty- to fifty-foot trees. Something in our favor for a close landing: the steepness of the ridges will prevent the Russians guarding N3 from having much opportunity to see us under canopy. We'll be coming in from the east, and the Cardiac Gap ridgeline will block their view. Only during the final fifteen or twenty seconds of our approach would they have a chance to spot us, as we come in to land."

We take a second to digest that. I continue, "On command, once we've set our positions, Puppy fires the SADM onto the compound. He'll target the center of the U-shape courtyard. Then we get out of there ASAP. The blast circumference for the nuke is six hundred meters. It will basically vaporize everything in that circle. The fireball tapers off quickly, by eight hundred meters. As for us, sitting 1500 meters from center target, we'll walk out of there with a five to six-fold greater lifetime cancer risk."

I get a knot in my throat thinking about the commitment on this team. Previously, Jason and I met individually with each operator. We wanted to make sure they were personally opting in to each of the risk areas on this mission. We'll have to personally deliver the SADM in by parachute. We'll have to parachute directly onto the target, versus an offset which is far safer. And to top it off, after a successful strike, we walk out with the lifetime cancer odds stacked against us. But not one person flinches. No one even hints at backing out.

Jason covers exfil. "OK, presuming the primary plan succeeds, we're in pretty good shape for exfil. Once the SADM detonates, the Russians on N3 are gone as a fighting force. Our greatest threat at that point will be the main post reaction force. Jessica's Alpha section will ditch their heavy weapons and cross over to join us on Cardiac Gap. We'll move east fifteen kilometers and establish a hide site. Given the nationwide attacks that will kick off shortly after our strike, the odds of Camp Diamond security bothering to pursue us should be low. Enterprise Performance will have bigger problems than chasing us down. The following evening, we'll continue movement to the east, off of Camp Diamond itself. A ground contact team will conceal us in local trucks and transport us to join Reclamation units outside of DC."

"Thanks, Jason," I say. "OK, that's the primary plan. Jessica will review the alternate plan, in the event of compromise during infil."

Jessica commences. "Alpha goes in with four 240G machine guns and a thousand rounds per gun. Our mission is to prevent the Russians maneuvering tactically from the N3 compound against Puppy's firing position up on Cardiac Gap. If you look at the terrain, the Russians can't move directly from the compound to his firing position. There's a huge ravine in between. Instead, they'll have to exit the north side of the compound, circle around Stonecoal Road, then approach the Gap from the north/northwest. We'll position ourselves just about 800 meters from the northern edge of the compound. That still puts us at 1500 meters from ground zero. If the Russians respond with a sizeable force, we can't stop them. But we can slow them down for a good long while. Plus, with all the noise our guns make, they might mistake us for the main strike element and not even head for the Gap."

"Good, spot on," I say. "Ken, how about Bravo section?"

"Sure thing, Mark. We have two tasks. First, if the Enterprise Performance quick reaction force approaches from main post to the north, we need to engage and delay them. To accomplish this, Bravo will bundle jump two Javelin anti-tank missiles, which can each destroy one of their Stryker vehicles. As they approach from the north, there are a couple of good spots where the road narrows. If we do it right and hit them at one of those choke points, we'll bottle up the rest of the Strykers trying to maneuver on us. We'll also bundle jump two Stinger anti-aircraft missiles, in case they have any helicopter support we don't know about. Frankly, I wish we had four of each missile type. But with all other operations ramping up, two and two was all we could get."

"No problem, Ken. Nothing here is optimal," I reply. "What else for Bravo?"

"Our second task is flank security for Puppy and Jason, while they prepare to fire the SADM from Cardiac Gap onto the compound. Jessica mentioned the ravine between the Gap and the compound. That same ravine protects the Gap from the south. And the eastern approach is extremely steep too."

As he says this, it momentarily reminds me of our night in the Qualification course years ago, when we struggled up that icy eastern slope to the hunting cabin.

Ken continues, "This means the main threat for a dismounted assault onto the SADM position will be climbing the ridge from the area where Stonecoal and Main Post roads intersect, and trying to flank from the north. If the Russians assault up that part of the ridge on foot, we'll be in position to engage."

Ken concludes his part of the mission brief. We exit the conference room and walk to the barn, a hundred yards from the main building. A security squad protects the barn, and they check each of our IDs before allowing us to enter. Once inside, Puppy steps forward and removes the tarp covering the SADM. The rest of us gather around.

I'm taken aback at how diminutive the entire package looks, compared to the destruction it will produce. The launcher sits on a tripod that brings it only as high as my waist. The launcher tube, repurposed from a 122-millimeter recoilless rifle, is five feet long and flares at its widest to a foot in diameter. On the front end of the launcher sits the warhead, oblong and shaped like an oversized football with fins. Puppy will bundle jump the entire device disassembled and stowed in a large metal cylinder. Once landed, Jason will assist him with setup and configuration for firing.

"Here we are," Puppy says, "courtesy of one of the more outlandish ideas from the Cold War. Out of habit, we're all referring to this as a SADM. Technically that's correct. It's a W54 nuclear demolition warhead that one of our NATO partners has provided us. We destroyed our American stockpile during arms reduction programs in the 1990s. But one of our allies wanted to hedge bets and kept a few of these, off the books. For our mission requirements, we've rebuilt this to mimic what the Army called the 'Davy Crockett' during the Cold War."

You can see a few quizzical looks. Puppy explains further.

"In the early 1950s, the Army predicted that small tactical nukes would be widespread on the battlefield. Among other crazy devices, they built a nuclear bazooka named the Davy Crockett. The SADM and the Davy Crockett each used the same warhead. The SADM was designed as a hand-carried munition, to be emplaced like a demolition charge with a time fuse. But it turned out to be fairly simple to convert it for remote firing. We just had to make some modifications to launch it like the Davy Crockett."

"Modifications such as?" Jessica Steele asks, with a faint hint of skepticism.

"Well," Puppy answers, "we configured an impact fuse so we could fire it as a standoff weapon. We basically just wired the new fuse on top of the design's original timing mechanism. We also had to reverse engineer the warhead onto the same type of recoilless rifle launcher that the Davy Crockett used. Then, we had to confirm ballistic accuracy of our design. Courtesy of the Canadians, we had access to as many rocket-propelled rounds as we wanted. I built three dozen test rounds with dummy warheads. We practiced in the Canadian Rockies. There's a ridge overlooking the Icefields Parkway that exactly matches Cardiac Gap in distance and elevation: five hundred twenty meters above the valley floor, with a fifteen hundred meter lateral offset. By the end, I could hit within five meters of the bullseye without even sighting it in. We orient 262 degrees magnetic, elevation 33 degrees, and it's dialed. Of course, I'll sight it in to confirm during our mission. But it's nice to know how well the launcher works."

"Will you operate it alone?" one of the Bravo operators asks.

"It's only a one-man rig to jump in the bundle and set up. On the ground, Jason will assist me, and he can fire it as accurately as I can. For contingency purposes, we'll also cross-train Mark and everyone in Bravo section. There will be no shortage of people to pull the trigger when the time comes."

We grow silent and admire Puppy's handiwork. Back in 8th Special Forces Group, Puppy had universal respect as one of the top weapons sergeants around. Routinely on deployment, we'd run across an antiquated piece of hardware, and with no manual to use he'd get it functioning. Still, he's topped himself here.

I look at my watch. Puppy timed his brief to end right on cue. It's time to let the gang know what's coming next. "Listen up. Don't get spooked. In just under a minute you'll hear a helicopter making a low-level approach, to stay underneath EP's radar network. It's a UH-60 from the Reclamation, old Army inventory. Someone wants to speak to us."

We wait in silence. The bird flies in so low that we go from the first hint of noise to the roar of final approach in less than twenty seconds. It flares to a landing in the open grounds outside, less than fifty meters away. We can feel as much as hear the rotor blades' downdraft beat against the barn. Then the aircraft settles and the blades spin down to idle.

One of the guards outside opens the barn door. In walks the Speaker of the House, Valerie Daniels. She's the senior legislator leading the American Congress in Exile, and she's the political leader for the Reclamation. A Major in American Army uniform accompanies her. I've never met him before.

I approach Speaker Daniels. "Ma'am, I'm Mark Elliott from the old Army. The team is assembled."

She holds my gaze and offers a firm handshake. Then she looks around to study the group.

"Does your team have everything it needs for next week's operation?"

"Yes, ma'am. We are continuing rehearsals and refinements over the next several days. But we have everything we need and we will be prepared."

She steps closer to the SADM, standing among us now. The Speaker scans the length of the launcher, then she looks to Puppy. "You must be Hugh Jackson?"

"Yes, ma'am."

"Major General Saiz has briefed me in great detail, regarding the work you and your development team have completed on this weapon. Is it ready?"

"Yes, ma'am, it is. We've tested every component extensively. We'll accomplish the mission."

Speaker Daniels nods, then she relaxes just slightly and circulates among the team members. She takes over twenty minutes to learn each of our names, asking questions about each person's family following The Struggles, and listening for as long as each person wants to talk. Her security team outside must be doing cheetah flips. This is exposed, open farmland in daylight. I know they never wanted her on the ground this long with a UH-60 sitting as an obvious target. But she's clearly not going to be rushed.

Jason Barr is the last person she meets. After their chat, she moves closer to the barn entrance, facing us as a group.

"General Saiz strongly protested this visit. He felt the risks for my travel were too great. I appreciate that concern. But the surviving members of Congress had a greater concern. This is a struggle to restore democracy. The circumstances are extreme, and the manner of reconstituting our national military is necessarily very compartmented and decentralized. But we in the elected leadership felt it imperative to meet with every task force in the Reclamation before combat operations begin. You deserve to hear, firsthand, from duly elected officials."

Everyone on the team straightens up. This hits home.

"Right now, a surviving Congressperson or Senator is visiting each of the task forces preparing to retake cities. We are also meeting with the task force that will destroy the San Jose servers, plus your team, which will destroy the Camp Diamond servers. As the senior surviving American elected official, I felt it my duty to personally visit your team."

She pauses for a moment, as if collecting thoughts, then she continues.

"I won't go into each detail regarding our constitutional reviews. You have more important concerns, and I've already busted the time allotment for this visit. Suffice to say, the surviving Congressional members have unanimously impeached and convicted Courtney Simons. We have communicated this to his office from our exile location in Canada. You won't be surprised to hear, he does not abide by the decision and he refuses to step down. This necessitates our forceful retaking of control of the cities he's walled off, and re-installation of democratic rule in America."

"Will you be the President, then?" Jessica Steele asks.

"I don't know, and I'm honestly not concerned about whether or not it should be me. As you know, I'm from the opposition party. Senator Tanaka is the senior surviving member from the late President Atkinson's party. Following our national operation to retake the cities, we will work to establish communications with surviving members of the state governments. We will hold a unified national convention, and concurrently nominate candidates for Acting President from each party. From these nominees, we will hold a convention vote to determine the Acting President. That is how our government will heal. That's how our nation will start to heal. The most important thing to me is that we've got to get resources out from behind the city walls, and do everything we can to try and help *all* surviving Americans. No more Ultra High Privilege zones living like kings. No more camp followers begging for scraps, or people living in fear out in the badlands."

I look around at the team. I'm sure that, like me, several others have lumps in their throats. Everyone has their own story of friends and loved ones left to fend for themselves out in the badlands, or who perished altogether during The Struggles.

The Speaker lowers the tone in her voice. She was already serious. This is more severe. "Now, let's talk about your strike. You are about to launch the first nuclear weapon attack since World War Two. This is a measure taken only as last resort. You are employing this weapon against Russian uniformed soldiers, on ground that Courtney Simons has illegally ceded to the Russian government. This weapon will destroy a communications node that would otherwise enable

Courtney Simons to continue his dictatorship, through the control of information and communications systems in the country. Given these facts, the Congress in Exile voted unanimously for this weapon employment. This authorization applies to your mission and your mission only. I am here to answer any questions or concerns that you have about this operation."

She pauses, gives us time.

No one has any questions.

She nods. Then she gives her parting words. "Godspeed on your mission. Over the next several days, may we all live up to what our country and our citizens deserve from us."

With that, she turns to leave. The sentries open the doors and then close them behind her. Outside, we hear the UH-60 engines rev quickly from idle to full power. The engines thunder again as we feel buffets from the aircraft hovering above us. Just as quickly, the noise fades and disappears in the distance.

- 29 -

Monday, 24 September 2035, 1600 hours – Former FedEx Shipping Center, Chicago O'Hare

You've got to hand it to Saiz and the Reclamation. When I was living in DC after the walls went up, people rightfully felt they couldn't sneeze without Enterprise Performance saying *gesundheit*. But here we are, inside a partitioned portion of the old FedEx shipping center at O'Hare, and the room is decked out with our kit, weapons, and parachutes just like one of the old team rooms at Camp Diamond.

We traveled part of the way here concealed in trucks driven by the same team that guarded us at the retreat center. Reclamation contacts met us outside Merrillville, trans-loaded us and gear into their vehicles, and then snuck us into this place.

The air crew walk in, three of them. They're wearing Nomex flight suits adorned with all the correct EP patches and markings. The command pilot speaks up. "Well, we've dropped a lot of combat loads in our day, but the word is, this will be one for the books. For security purposes, we don't want to know anything else. Not your names, not your ground tactical plan, nothing. You can just call us Pilot One, Pilot Two, and Chief over there for our crew chief." Pilot Two and the Chief nod as Pilot One points them out.

"Roger that," I reply. I point out Jason and our element leads, introducing each of us by duty position only as well: Zero One and Zero Two for myself and Jason, Alpha One through Five for Jessica's element, Bravo One through Four for Ken and crew, and Charlie One for Puppy.

"We have some good news," Pilot One explains. "On today's run from Norfolk, EP flew an old Air Force C-17. That's what we'll be using to drive you over Camp Diamond. It should be returning empty, so you'll have plenty of room to rig once we're inside the bird and before takeoff."

You have to admire these guys. Best case, they're going to land a perfectly good C-17 in the Atlantic Ocean. Then they'll hope someone is there to pick them up.

We review the jump procedures and time hacks. From takeoff, it's roughly forty-five minutes until our release point over Camp Diamond. Things will move quickly.

Jason asks, "What's the status of the flight crew that came in on that aircraft?"

Pilot One chuckles. "As of now, they're blissfully unaware of what's going on. They're pre-flighting the aircraft and going about their evening."

He sees our puzzled looks, and explains further, "Don't worry, we've got them under tight surveillance. We have a pretty good sense of the pre-flight coordination calls and approvals they have to file, but it's cleanest if we let them do as much as possible. At some point in our flight ATC – air traffic control – might suspect that something is amiss. We want that to happen at the end of the flight, after we've dumped you over Camp Diamond. Once we're on approach to Norfolk, we'll simply drop off the radar and prepare for the ditch."

"Any change in air defense posture?" I ask.

Pilot Two answers, "No, but just to review, the closest response will be out of Norfolk: Former US Air Force F-22s, now flown by Russian contracted pilots for Enterprise Performance. So long as our authentication calls pass muster on the route, they'll be none the wiser."

We discuss a few final points. Then the air crew depart and leave us to continue prepping gear.

A few hours later, we're still waiting for the word to board. Everyone's time-killing rituals have played out. Jessica Steele has worked her way twice along the narrow table holding our freefall parachutes. Ken Bowerman has finished inspecting Bravo section's heavy weapons bundles, which lie on a tarp in the far corner of the room.

And I've finished fake-staring at the map, thinking back on the past several years, about my final active duty mission in Senegal and the bad turns we've taken as a country since then. The same conclusion holds true. It's pointless to dissect how we got here.

The only recourse now is to focus on the task at hand. If we don't take out these servers then the larger effort, to retake DC and our major cities, will be futile. This strike must succeed.

- 30 -

Tuesday, 25 September 2035, 0030 hours – C-17 Infil Aircraft, Pre-Takeoff

The engines fire up. Everyone's rigged and seated on red webbing bench seats that fold down from the interior fuselage, along the left side of the C-17 cargo area. We've been inside the bird for a little over thirty minutes, enough time to don parachutes and conduct the jumpmaster personnel inspections. Chief doesn't volunteer what happened to the original aircrew, and we don't ask. With our headsets plugged into the aircraft intercom, Chief passes updates.

"So far so good on ATC net," he says, referring to the air traffic control net that EP runs for approved flights between cities. "We're cleared for takeoff in a few minutes. No one seems to suspect us."

We're settled along the bench seat, with Jason closest to the rear ramp as our jumpmaster, then Puppy and the two Bravo section bundle jumpers, then me and the rest of the team. Chief advises Jason, "Weather over target is not too bad. But there are intermittent clouds at 8,000 feet. We'll plan on a CARP."

That stands for Computer Air Release Point. In case of unreliable visibility to the ground, the plane's onboard nav system determines the air release point for jumpers. All things equal, this cloud cover can help us. It will cut down on visibility from the ground.

Chief scrolls through more data on a handheld device and adds, "winds are sustained, ten miles per hour west to east." This is great news. Our ram-air parachutes function like glider wings. They have a forward drive of about twenty miles per hour. We were already planning to drop east of the target area and then fly a landing approach from east to west. The ten-miles-per-hour headwind will let us flare to a clean landing facing the wind.

"Any final questions?" Chief asks of Jason, then of the group. We all shake our heads, negative.

Jason speaks up, "All right, start pre-breathing now." We strap on oxygen masks, which are tied to the aircraft O2 generator for now. This will flush the nitrogen out of our bloodstream, to avoid the bends during the rapid descent of freefall. We don helmets and turn on our headsets as well.

The bird taxis over to the runway. Engines whine, and we take off.

After the adrenaline of loading, chute rigging and takeoff, most us follow the norm for an infil. We nod off to the hum and vibrations of the aircraft.

"Twenty-five minutes from target," Chief says over intercom, bringing us out of our doze.

We all stir, checking watches and altimeters. Tracking at 30,000 feet.

"Roger," Jason replies to Chief. So far so good.

Ten minutes later we're still seated and waiting. I watch Chief, standing up. He cocks his head to the right and holds his hand to the right headphone. He's straining to take in everything, as if he doesn't like what he's hearing on the ATC net. We're not getting that feed. I read his eyes through the goggles he's wearing. Whatever it is, it's not getting better.

"Norfolk's asking for an authentication check," he says, bringing us up to speed. "It turns out the one we gave expired an hour ago, at midnight. Pilot's bluffing them for now."

All we can do is watch Chief and take his reports.

It gets worse. He's nodding his head and talking urgently with the flight crew on their internal channel.

Chief updates us. "Norfolk is scrambling two F-22s. Not looking good, folks. We're gonna stay on flight plan. As soon as you guys are off the ramp, we'll close it – hopefully before the intercept flight has us in visual range. Then they can escort us wherever they damn well please."

Time drags. Chief looks more concerned by the minute.

"Ten minutes!" he finally barks. He's been crazy to give the call that initiates our jump sequence. We switch our O2 feeds to the jump bottles on our freefall rigs. This done, we stand up. The ramp opens. Cold air roars through the cargo area and beats against our uniforms. Jason's on the ramp, scanning in the event a cloud hole gives him a visual of the target. He prepares to issue our jump commands.

"F-22s are coming in on afterburner," Chief calls out.

This means they've gone supersonic. They're treating this as a confirmed threat. We can't do anything but wait and hope we get to the release point before the F-22s show up.

"Five minutes," Chief updates.

Wait . . .

"Four minutes."

Wait . . .

"Three minutes."

Wait . . .

Chief is standing next to Jason, close to the edge of the ramp and off to the left as we face out. The rest of us are huddled in the center of the ramp, ready to push off en masse. Chief grabs Jason by the arm and says urgently, "F-22s have received permission to engage. Our pilot's going to stay on path to target. Be ready to put your people out early."

"Roger," Jason replies and nods.

More waiting . . .

"Two minutes," Chief updates.

Our air crew, we don't even know who these guys are. They're three Americans risking it all for this mission. For a mission they believe in.

"Ninety seconds."

"Missile tone!" Chief shouts through our headsets. One of the F-22's air-to-air warheads is locked on us, but not yet fired.

"One min – MISSILE LAUNCH! GET OUT!" are Chief's final words.

"Follow me!" Jason commands. He dives off the ramp, and we immediately follow, head first. We're in a big mass initially and then spread out as we hit the on-rushing air.

Exiting a high-performance aircraft in freefall is called "coming off the hill." The relative airspeed of horizontal travel initially tips you with head toward earth and feet skyward, like diving in a pool. After several seconds, you flatten out with belly toward the ground.

Normally, the first action after coming off the hill is to check altitude, clear your airspace from other jumpers, and get oriented to the drop zone.

But every one of us takes a moment to look up at the brilliant orange fireball that was the C-17.

Thanks, Chief. God bless.

Now, we've got to find our way to the ground.

Passing through ten thousand feet, we've managed to group fairly well. Once under canopy, Jessica will lead her Alpha section for a landing on their hilltop position. The rest of us will aim for Cardiac Gap. We're still above the cloud deck, and the ground's not yet visible.

The problem now is distance. Exiting a minute early takes all the fudge room out of our landing pattern. You normally allow some extra altitude for horizontal transit to the drop zone, then bleed it off with an oblique landing pattern until touchdown. No such luxury tonight. Once under canopy, we'll have to fly direct to target and hope we can make it.

We fall through the clouds at eight thousand feet, rushing to our pull altitude. I've decided to pull my ripcord a couple hundred feet above the rest of the team. I want to be able to see their disposition and who lands where. Also, that will give me time to ID Puppy carrying his bundle – it's hard under freefall at night. If for any reason he doesn't make it to the Gap, we'll need Bravo section to help him carry the bundle quickly to the firing position.

Opening shock hits, flipping me immediately from horizontal to vertical with feet toward earth, sinking me hard into the harness. We're flying under canopy now. I flip down the night vision goggles mounted on my helmet and take in the scene. The whole N3 compound is alive with movement. Off to the north, it looks like Camp Diamond's main post is alerted, too. That's not surprising. Even with the cloud cover overhead, no one could miss a C-17 blowing up in a massive fireball. Surely those F-22s called an alert to all stations during their intercept. So the post had warning even before the shootdown.

N3 is going nuts. The current shift of fifty Russian operators is at full alert, manning positions and starting to sweep their immediate perimeter in twos and threes. The other hundred special operators, who were off duty, are already rousting out of their barracks. They're hurrying into the courtyard while adjusting kit and loading assault rifles. The sight gives a knot in my gut, but with the clouds masking our silhouette, no one from the ground has spotted us yet.

I get team accountability next. Swiveling my head around to scan with the goggles, we have all twelve chutes opened.

Alpha section forms up behind Jessica's chute, which is marked with her chemlite code. They're on glide path for Alpha's landing zone. Good.

For the rest of us, aiming for Cardiac Gap, it's a different story. We're lined up directionally, on the correct azimuth for our landing zone. But that early release means our current glide path will land us just short. I recognize Puppy carrying his bundle, and he's the only one who looks good to make it all the way to the Gap for landing. That figures. He can milk a ram-air chute like nobody's business. The rest of us will hit the tree-covered near slope, about a hundred feet below the Gap and on the east side of the ridgeline. All thing's equal, that's OK. Those trees are only about twenty-five feet tall. We'll bust through the branches most of the way to the ground. The main thing is Puppy will land his bundle free and clear.

Scanning the compound and the roads, I wonder if they see us? Not yet.

Probably another minute glide time to land.

Damn, there's a vehicle coming from the north along Main Post road. They're running spot checks as part of the base alert. A driver's side spotlight stabs along the high ground on either side of the vehicle.

Jessica's Alpha section flies over Main Post Road, on final approach to their landing zone.

Just then the spotlight swings up and centers directly on one of Alpha's chutes.

There's dead silence for about five seconds.

And then all hell breaks loose.

Tracers fly from the N3 compound toward Alpha section during their last seconds of glide to the ground. That's an eternity of canopy time under direct fire. Is one of them hit? More?

That vehicle spotlight pivots around like crazy now. Just in time, the spotlight hits the tops of two of our chutes that are aiming for the Gap, before we drop below the ridgeline and hit the eastern slope. Now, they know we're up on the Gap, too. Guns in the compound reposition to put fire on both Alpha's position and ours.

Last thing I see before hitting the trees on the eastern slope: Puppy's going in for a perfect landing dead center in Cardiac Gap.

Mmmph . . .

I bust through three or four branches, briefly knocking the wind out of my lungs. I crash to a stop with both feet on the ground. Looking to the right, there's Ken and the rest of Bravo section. Good, they've busted through the branches to the ground also. One or both of their bundles snagged in the trees. It's hard to tell. Off to the left, Jason's already out of his parachute rig. He's scrambling uphill toward the Gap, to help Puppy set up the SADM.

Russian shouting and cursing carries from the N3 compound.

I unhook from the chute harness and rush from the eastern slope directly up to the spine of the ridge, which places me just north of the Gap and thirty feet above it. I scan the scene, and we've got a mess on our hands. Puppy and Jason are in the small depression of the Gap, setting up the launcher. Bullets snap and tracers fly just a foot over them. Rounds punch through the trees above my head. Small branches fall to the ground.

Across Main Post Road, Alpha section opens up with their 240G machine guns. They're putting heavy fire onto the north side of the compound.

The Russians are firing back, with sustained suppressive fire on Alpha team. They've mobilized quicker than expected. The F-22s must have sent warnings well before the shoot down. At least fifty Russians run out the north side of the compound and begin to tactically maneuver on Alpha section.

I look north toward main post. Vehicle lights appear intermittently through the trees, traveling toward us on the approach roads. That must be the Stryker armored personnel carriers with the quick-reaction force. We need to act fast. We especially need Bravo's bundle with the Javelin anti-tank missiles. I can hear them still wrestling it from the trees, just back down the slope.

From the compound, Russian PKM machine guns continue their heavy echoes of fire. Thick bands of tracers reach out to Alpha's position.

Not all of us will get out of here. There's too much coming at us too fast. But we've got to hold on long enough that Puppy can take the shot.

I call to Jessica on our comms net. "Alpha! You see them moving on your flanks?"

She immediately replies, "Roger! We're taking heavy fire. I've got two guns left for providing suppression on N3. About twenty flankers moving on our west side now. I'm grabbing a 240 and moving to cover that approach."

I call back, "Roger. There's nothing more you can do from there. You've already created a good diversion. Get off that hilltop and join us over here if you can." The Russians moved too fast on Alpha's position. EP's Air Traffic Control net must have alerted Camp Diamond even before the F-22's took off. Those Russian flankers will swarm Alpha before they can bug out. Good luck, Jessica.

Now six Strykers approach from the north along Main Post Road, much closer than before. Definitely Strykers, with their eight-wheel chassis and remote-fire machine guns swiveling on top.

"We got the Javelin bundle free! Moving now," Ken reports.

"Roger," I call back to vector Ken on the new threat. "Bravo, you've got six Strykers closing fast from the north. Need your Javelins on them ASAP!"

"Will do."

Over at Alpha's position the Russians start a final assault, at least thirty of them closing in. A sole surviving Alpha gunner puts down good fire. It's all over for that fight, but their lone survivor is fighting to the end. Our assault rifles won't range that hilltop. We can only watch as that Alpha operator sprays one last, long burst of machine gun fire. The gun goes silent. All firing stops at Alpha's position.

Ken Bowerman's up on the ridgeline now, to my right, or north. He's laid in his section across a seventy-five meter span, oriented toward where Main Post Road approaches our part of the ridge. They're prepping for the Stryker advance, and for whoever else circles around from N3 to assault up that approach on the ridgeline.

To my left, down in the Gap, I can no longer see Puppy and Jason. They've positioned the launcher in a spot that's out of direct view.

"SADM team, need any help?" I ask Puppy over the net.

"All good. Couple more minutes."

"Backblast!" Ken gives the heads up on the net. They fire their two Javelins. Flame pops out the backs of the launchers. The missiles bob and weave toward targets. The two lead Strykers explode.

We need this to buy us time. The two destroyed Strykers are burning brightly. Will it slow down the rest of that convoy?

It doesn't for long enough. From one side of the flames, a figure in a tactical crouch steps around the two vehicles and through the woods. Behind him, the four remaining Strykers follow at a walking pace. The Russians in that convoy have found a track wide enough to bypass the destroyed vehicles and then get back on the road.

"Bravo, you're it now," I call Ken over the net. I sum up the fight that's coming our way. "You've got four surviving Strykers that will bring in their dismounts. About thirty enemy survived the assault onto Alpha's position and are moving on us too. Another forty or fifty just exited N3 compound, circling toward us via Stonecoal Road. All total, we'll have a hundred-plus dismounts assaulting up here. Good news is, we're up too high for the Strykers' heavy machine guns to engage us. Their remote-controlled mounts can't elevate this high."

"Roger, copy all," Ken replies, business-like. He's setting his guys in for the close fight.

The first Russian operators start moving upslope toward us. Bravo engages with assault rifles.

"Puppy, what's the status?" I call over the net. I'm moving north, closer to Ken's Bravo element now. We need every possible shooter to slow the Russian assault.

"We're moving it into position now," Puppy replies.

With Jessica's position destroyed, the PKM machine guns in the compound are hammering six- to nine-round bursts up and down our ridgeline and into the Gap. They're trying to sweep ahead of their operators who are climbing the ridge. From my vantage point, I can see Russians climbing and searching for flanking moves on Bravo.

"Stay low, suppressive fire about to sweep us!" I call on the net. Guys are busy, they might not notice the PKMs shifting their fire our way. Then it hits. Tracer fire arcs two or three feet overhead. We hear the sonic snaps of bullets, knocking down more leaves and small branches, smacking into trunks. Four long bursts of tracer reach out and impact on Puppy and Jason's position. Were they hit?

"What's the status down there?" I call.

It's silent on the radio for an uncomfortable interval. Then Puppy's on the net, winded. "Jason's KIA. They hit the launcher. I pulled it back behind cover. It's inop, but I'm trouble shooting."

"Flankers on both sides!" Bowerman calls on the net. His team's in a semi-circle, still spread across seventy-five meters. Ken's oriented them squarely on the Russian advance. But Bravo can't cover enough ground. Assault rifles argue back and forth along Ken's line. The Russians use the engagement to feel out Bravo's position. They'll gradually start to edge around and get behind us, toward Puppy.

I call down to the SADM again. "Puppy, can you fix the launcher? They're maneuvering hard up here. Not much time."

Silence. He must be checking. Then his reply, "I'm working something now. Give me a solid two minutes, and I'll have the warhead launched."

"Man down!" Bowerman calls. I'm about ten meters behind his line. Initially I shifted up here to cover any frontal assaults, but now I'm scanning our left and right. They'll hit hardest from the side or behind. At least fifty enemy have made it up here, close enough to discern the fractal pattern of their Russian-issue uniforms. They're firing hard into Bravo's positions to keep them pinned.

They make a first try to swing around our left flank. I shoot two before they realize I'm here. They both crumple hard. Now three more fire on me, pinning me behind a rock. The intensity drops just enough for me to sight and put several rounds into their position.

"Bravo, status?" I ask Ken over the net. Everyone's taking heavy fire now. I'm down so low in the prone, I can't see crap, even with Ken and team so close.

Ken calls back. "It's just me and Bravo four," he says referring to the only other operator still alive in his section.

"Roger," I acknowledge. I call Puppy. "Brother, you need to get that SADM in action _now_! They're gonna blow past us and onto you any second."

Two flankers have snuck by me on the right, rushing up fast at four o'clock. I wheel over on my back as they loom over, and pump the rest of a magazine into them. They flail and drop less than ten feet away. Jam in a fresh mag, back in the prone, and keep scanning for targets.

"Launching now!" Puppy calls.

I look downslope toward Puppy's position. From where I'm wedged and fighting on the ridge, the whole Gap is blocked from my line of sight. But that recoilless rifle puts out a hellacious back blast. It will light up all of the Gap.

When the hell is he going to fire? I keep looking anxiously.

"NOOOOH!" I scream, seeing Puppy's perfectly inflated parachute come into view, gliding toward the compound. He's re-rigged and used the westerly wind to give him a running start. The SADM bundle hangs from his waist. "Puppy!!" I yell into the comms net. No answer. He tracks directly for the server buildings.

A fresh hail of bullets kicks up all around me. I flop back over to the north, looking along the ridge. Bowerman's firing madly, now the only one left in his section it sounds like. Off to the half right, two more Russians sprint from the shadows. I fire six or eight shots. One of them doubles over and drops. The other dives behind a tree; can't tell if I got him.

Now three more coming from the far left, just below the slope. I adjust to a low kneeling position, to get a better sight picture on them.

The first bullet hits my pelvis on the right side and flings me like a rag doll.

Epilogue: Leadership Brief
21 October 2035 – Louisville, Kentucky

Transcript notes: Major General Diego Saiz briefing to a Joint Session of the 123rd American Congress (Reconstituted), Acting President Daniels Presides, Location – Provisional National Capital, Louisville, Kentucky.

Sergeant at Arms Note: By vote of a majority of the Unified National Convention, whose members comprised all surviving members of the House and Senate, as well as representatives from each of the reconstituted Free State governments; Speaker of the House Valerie Daniels has been elected Acting President and shall exercise that office, with full executive authorities granted under the Constitution, for four years or until such time as the American people can hold a secure national election, whichever may occur soonest.

<u>Transcript:</u>

President Daniels: Major General Saiz, I know you have many pressing matters to attend to. Thank you for taking time away from battlefield leadership to address this Congress.

Major General Saiz: Madame President, thank you for the audience, *and thank you for the opportunity to brief this forum.*

PD: General, please start with an overall status report. I know the situation has been quite fluid.

S: Yes, ma'am. As you know, we failed in our attempt to retake Washington, DC. For the first eight days, it appeared we had the upper hand. However, we underestimated the degree to which the Russians would shift to overt support of Courtney Simons and Enterprise Performance. Between Russian Air Force strikes on our formations, and military aid flights from Russia, it was more than we could match. We had to abandon that DC effort for now. The news is better in other areas. Thanks to the help of American popular uprising against Enterprise Performance security forces, we've now retaken nine of the fifteen largest US cities. Dallas, Chicago and Los Angeles are still contested but trending well. Boston, New York, and Atlanta remain beyond our reach for the foreseeable future.

PD: So it would seem they are attempting to prioritize holdings on the East Coast?

S: That's what we think. Yes, ma'am. This makes sense militarily and logistically. From these cities, Simons and Enterprise Performance can maximize direct aid and support from the Russians.

PD: Do you have any updates regarding the status of Simons' high-value prisoners?

S: What we assess is not good. We know that before our strike Simons had more than fifteen hundred in custody. This included members of Congress, cabinet officials from the Atkinson administration, senior military officers, and senior executive service government officials. From the military side alone, Simons detained every four-star general on active duty when he assumed power. After the touch-and-go fight for DC, we received conflicting intel about the prisoners. Either he flew them to a Russian-controlled detention facility outside the US, or he had them executed, or both. We just don't know. One positive note, ma'am: we have made contact with Lieutenant General Alfred Holt, the most recent commander of the Army's 27th Airborne Corps. He should link up with our forces by tomorrow night. He'll assume overall command of the war effort, and he will provide the next briefing to this Congress.

PD: How about the situation throughout the rest of the country? What's your overall assessment?

S: Considering that Simons still holds DC, we are gaining better traction than we expected. Most of this is thanks to the success of the strikes on the server facilities in San Jose and at Camp Diamond. Simons does possess some residual server capacity that he installed in the DC area. But he can no longer dominate internet and communications systems nationwide.

PD: And General, if you could, the impact this has on the rest of the country?

S: Uh, yes, ma'am, my apology. This means we've had better effect than we had hoped, for regaining strategic communications. It's what has allowed the reconstituted state governments to communicate with this Congress, as we work towards rebuilding national governance. We are also greatly aided by the Canadians, British, and other NATO allies. But I would have to defer to Acting Secretary of State Grant for any further details on the assistance from those countries.

PD: Thank you. General, I know you have to leave soon. I want to say first, please extend our congratulations to the surviving members from your West Coast assault force, who destroyed the San Jose servers. Being a large ground operation, and inside an urban area such as it was, that action has understandably received much more attention and reporting by the international press corps.

S: That's correct regarding the attention to San Jose. Thank you, Madame President, I will pass along your compliments to the survivors of that force.

PD: General Saiz, now that we are post-operations at Camp

Diamond, I'd like to hear what information you have been able to learn on scene.

S: Yes, ma'am. In accordance with Congressional authority following Courtney Simons' impeachment, and based on the in-extremis nature of that target, the fact that it was on land illegally ceded to a hostile government, and based on the forces available, we acted under this government's authority for tactical nuclear weapon employment. We had a successful detonation at the target site, the N3 compound server facility. The SADM blast is very small, and only destroyed the N3 compound itself. The day following the detonation, Enterprise Performance abandoned the rest of Camp Diamond by air evacuation. They used those forces to augment their defense of DC. Once the servers were destroyed, it appears that Camp Diamond itself held no strategic value for Simons.

PD: And the status of your team, the one that detonated that nuclear device?

S: Ma'am, we have confirmed that eleven of the twelve died in the fight. A search and rescue team reached the site within forty-eight hours of the operation. We found the body of Lieutenant Colonel Mark Elliott, who was in command. We also found the bodies of ten other team members. Master Sergeant Hugh Jackson is the only team member whose status remains unknown. Since that recovery operation, we have flown two overflights of the area, specifically looking for any emergency signals from Master Sergeant Jackson. Both overflights had negative contact. Unfortunately, we do not have any reason to think he survived.

PD: Thank you for your update, General Saiz. Is there anything else you would like to add?

S: Madame President, only to express my gratitude for all American men and women who are working to rebuild our democracy. And, in whatever faith or belief system we each practice, may we all bless the United States of America.

- 32 -

Epilogue: Sunset

21 October 2035 – Lagrange Quarry, outskirts of Louisville, Kentucky

"Stay out of the water, sweetie!" Linny calls to Matthew, as he bounces from the car and runs down to the lake.

"OK!" he yells without slowing down or looking back.

Linny locks the car. Emma walks hand in hand with Linny as they follow Matthew's path to the water line. The afternoon sun just touches the tops of trees on the far shore. Its rays blend with fall leaves of red and yellow.

Despite the hardships of their travels over the past several weeks, Linny is pleased to see that Matthew and Emma don't display any obvious trauma. As for the long term, what The Struggles – and now the war against Simons – might do to the twins, only time will tell.

"Is this where we'll say goodbye to Uncle Mark and my dad?" Emma asks, still holding hands as they approach the shore.

"Yes that's right, Emma," Linny smiles, but sadness shows in her eyes.

For the past few days, she's been explaining the concept of a memorial service to the twins. Their upbringing during The

Struggles left little time for such practice. In their lives, a loved one's death became subsumed in bigger issues like flight to safety and survival. When the stranger brought the twins to her and Mark, the kids were so reserved that Linny had no sense of how they had processed the loss of their mother. She and Mark focused on giving them love and helping them feel safe at the orphanage.

But now – with Mark's loss and the twins learning more from her about their father, Ulysses – Linny has found comfort in explaining what it means to remember and honor the ones we love. She had hoped that Diego Saiz might bring Mark's ashes, which they would spread by the lake this evening.

Saiz visited yesterday. He was in Louisville overnight, before today's earlier briefing to the reconstituted Congress and President Daniels. But Saiz explained that an abundance of caution against contamination prevented handing over Mark's urn. The recovery team had respectfully disposed of the eleven remains at a controlled location in Canada.

It was Matthew who offered a substitute ritual. He remembered a class that Mr. Dan taught at the orphanage, about the ancient Egyptians. He asked Linny if tonight they could build a small pyramid for Uncle Mark and his Dad.

"Of course," she'd said.

Tears overtake Linny every day. Mark had been in her life since she was twenty. A world without him feels so empty. But she's resolved not to turn inward or bleak. She'll live with the pain, and channel her memories into raising Matthew and Emma.

Linny has taken a job in the Office of Acting President Daniels, working on the upcoming national elections. She finds solace by working on the democratic restoration for which Mark and so many colleagues gave their lives these past few weeks. When the hurt from grieving becomes too much, she has no shortage of mind-bending constitutional questions in which to lose herself.

President Daniels' chief of staff, Linny's immediate boss, didn't like the idea of her heading out here alone with the twins, past the city outskirts. But Linny insisted. These days, Louisville is crawling with the hopeful, all working to rebuild a society. It's a great thing to be a part of. But it's nowhere to have a reflective moment. Linny heard whispers, and knows the chief of staff sent a couple of armed security officers trailing her to the lake. That's fine, so long as they stay out of sight.

Linny and Emma stop about forty feet from the waterline. They sit on the sandy beach, arms wrapped around each other. Linny looks to Matthew, who's bending down at the water. "Matthew, come over and join us."

He turns around to face them. His hands cup a pile of grey oblong stones, smooth with round edges. "Will these work?" he asks.

"Oh, those will be perfect," Linny replies, able to smile with her eyes this time.

Matthew trots up the shore and stops several feet away from his sister and Linny. He squats down in the way only children can and carefully, gently, arranges the memorial cairn. Then he joins them and nestles against Linny's free side.

"Does that look good?" he asks.

"Sweetie, that looks wonderful." Linny admires his work and gives him a squeeze.

She knows the rhythm of their questions. Many will be the same they've asked before, and she has answered. It's their way of processing.

"Did we fly here on the same kind of plane that Uncle Mark flew that night?" Matthew asks.

"No, we flew here from Canada on a C-130. Uncle Mark's team was on a bigger plane for their mission. But remember how I told you about the time your dad saved Uncle Mark and Uncle Puppy, and a bunch of other people, too? They all flew on a C-130 then, to a country named Senegal. That's when they were in the old Army, before The Struggles."

Emma wants to know, "Did our dad go on the mission where Uncle Mark died?"

"No, sweetie. Your dad got hurt a long time ago. He was really sick, and he was in the hospital. General Saiz has since learned that your dad passed away in that hospital."

"Because they didn't want to take care of him anymore?"

Linny's voice catches, but she holds it together. "That's right, Emma."

The little girl says, "Well, when I get older, I'm going to try and take care of people. All people." Linny pulls her close and kisses her on top of her head.

"Will your office be able to help people?" Matthew asks.

"I hope so. The Acting President is working incredibly hard. A lot of people are working with the States to hold new elections, so we can rebuild our democracy."

"Will it work?" he asks.

"I hope so."

Then Matthew wants to know, "And then we'll *all* get privileges again? Not just important people?"

"That's correct, Matthew, except they're called rights, not privileges. In a democracy, all citizens have rights, all citizens are supposed to be important. And also, those democracies recognize things called human rights. So we even try to help the citizens of other countries. We can't help everybody, and we can't help as much as we would want. But we do what we can. It makes for a better world."

"And that's why Uncle Mark and Uncle Puppy had to go fight the Russians?" he asks.

"Yes, to restore our rights as citizens. And that's why our new military is still fighting Enterprise Performance and the Russians working with them."

"Did we ever meet Uncle Puppy?" Emma wonders.

"No, unfortunately you never had a chance to meet him."

"Did he die with Uncle Mark?" she asks.

"For now, they're calling him missing. But I have to be honest, he was on a very dangerous mission. So, he probably did die."

"But what do *you* believe?" Matthew persists.

Linny thinks for a moment. "Well, I'll tell you what Mark – your Uncle Mark – would likely say. He'd say that until finding evidence to the contrary, he would choose to believe that Uncle Puppy was still out there in the woods somewhere, with his rifle and his compass, making his way back to a friendly place."

The twins grow silent, their questions finished for now. They stay nestled on either side of Linny. The sun is below the horizon. The last pink in the sky fades. Linny smells the crisp air and feels the evening chill. Briefly, it takes her back to college and the time she went on a walking date with Mark through the grounds of the Hillwood estate, the first time they had dared to plan a life together.

None of them speak for the next twenty minutes. They sit in shared observance of Matthew's pyramid. Dusk gives way to night. Linny studies the pyramid's grey stones in detail, how they slowly disappear, as if melting back into the earth.

A word from Bill

Thank you for your purchase. I hope you enjoyed Cardiac Gap. For a new author like me, every reader review makes a big impact on book visibility and future sales. Even just a sentence or two helps spread the word. I appreciate any time you might spare for that.

A great thing about writing in the 21st century is the opportunity to directly offer expanded material that readers might enjoy. I'll aim to post articles on my author website four times a year. The first article covers a 175-mile "book-launch bike ride" to Independence Hall in Philadelphia. Other articles will cover books that informed the writing of Cardiac Gap, fictional mission orders to accompany the story, and notes on future writing projects. You can subscribe and find this expanded material at billraskin.com.

If you want to directly share any thoughts on the book, please reach out. My author email is bill@billraskin.com.

For speaking engagements, including options for video conference participation, please inquire to events@billraskin.com.

About the Author

Bill Raskin served as a career Army Special Forces officer, retiring as a Lieutenant Colonel with 20 years on active duty. This included diverse overseas deployments, multiple combat tours in Iraq and Afghanistan, and service in classified programs and assignments. He led and commanded special operators at every level from small teams to command of a Special Forces battalion and battalion level task force. He continues to consult to the national security community, and holds an MA in Security Studies and a BA in History from Georgetown University. A native of Dallas, Texas; Bill now lives in Bethesda, Maryland with his loving wife, a wonderful teen, and an awesome dog. Together they pursue many adventures. Cardiac Gap is his first novel.

Acknowledgements

January, 2019

It took a reinforced platoon of help for this first-time novelist to write and produce Cardiac Gap. I can't begin to give enough thanks.

The draft-phase beta readers – Ted, Suzanne, Tony, Pete, Mike, Adam, John, and Bruce – lent tremendous time, care, and insight. They each helped make this a better story.

The late-stage editors – Dana Delamar, Kristine Cayne, and Brooks Becker – made key improvements with their copy edit and proofreading. They took time not just to edit but to educate. Others in the production team were equally a joy to work with. Rachel Lawston's cover blew me away, as did her expert navigation through the book graphics. Fritz Partlow also lent expertise in graphic design, giving patient tutorials. Marina and Jason at Polgarus Studio are total pros who taught how to package a final product.

The real hero of Cardiac Gap is not a character in the book but the writing coach who made it possible. Kathryn Johnson provided instruction at first, and developmental/line editing as we progressed. Picture any boxing movie, where the rookie fighter hangs on every word of the wise trainer. That's how much I depended on her guidance and education. She is a master of her craft and a gifted teacher.

Family and true friends are the ones who show up during the time of most need. In this case, they showed up as advance readers for the final manuscript. They brought to justice the kind of insurgent typos that escape even the best editors. I am thankful for a tribe of friends who have shared both good times and bad. I'm also thankful for my sister and our extended family who have given the most unconditional love.

At the top of this heap are Linda and E. E is the world's greatest teen, full stop. He's building a wonderful life for himself, and I'm lucky to share in the adventure. Linda has been the love of my life since the day we met. She hands-down read more drafts of the story than anyone. She spent untold hours beyond that just plain listening, encouraging, and offering feedback. These conversations and her belief were a bridge that carried me across the past year. I am the luckiest man there is to be able to share a life with her.

Finally, to all Americans who continue to put themselves on the line in service to our country and our society, whether abroad or at home, thank you for your belief and for all that you do. For those who paid with their lives, may we offer our unending gratitude and continue to honor their memory.

Made in the
USA
Monee, IL